In the Shadow of Alden Light

In the Shadow of Alden Light

A LIGHTHOUSE MURDER MYSTERY

Celeste M. Flores

RESOURCE *Publications* · Eugene, Oregon

IN THE SHADOW OF ALDEN LIGHT
A Lighthouse Murder Mystery

Resource Publications
An Imprint of Wipf and Stock Publishers
199 W. 8th Ave., Suite 3
Eugene, OR 97401

www.wipfandstock.com

PAPERBACK ISBN: 979-8-3852-4347-1
HARDCOVER ISBN: 979-8-3852-4348-8
EBOOK ISBN: 979-8-3852-4349-5

For my family, who taught me about love, honesty, and courage.

"All who have passed are not lost if we seek them with open minds and hearts."

CAROL DARBY—CHAPTER 9

Contents

Foreword

THIS WORK OF FICTION began as a way for me to stay in touch with my east coast roots when I was desperately homesick. It was fun and included all the things I loved about New England: the ocean, lighthouses, quaint towns, and ghosts. I didn't have much on paper when my father became terminally ill, and the project was set aside. With all her children grown and living in other areas, my mother became my father's primary caretaker. It was a role she accepted without complaint and fulfilled with much love. When he entered eternal life, she was at a loss, and the disrupted sleep that comes from being a caretaker persisted. So, I began writing again, sending her a few pages at a time in the tradition of Charles Dickens. She would read them at night when she couldn't sleep and would share what she thought with me the next day. She kept reading and I kept writing. The initial story was completed in one year and then took this final shape with the feedback of some excellent writer friends.

There is indeed a lighthouse in Pocasset, Massachusetts that the public can rent, along with its own private beach. The ocean, surrounding area, and the lighthouse are as beautiful as I describe. If you want to experience a truly impressive bluff, I recommend Mohegan Bluffs on Block Island. The view from Southeast Lighthouse will have you catching your breath and watching the horizon for breaching whales. Unless otherwise indicated, all the names, characters, businesses, places, events, and incidents in this book are either the product of my imagination or used in a fictitious manner.

Acknowledgements

I WOULD LIKE TO express my deepest gratitude to my family; especially Juan Carlos, Nicolás, and Alex, whose love and support made this work possible. I extend my heartfelt thanks to Lindy Coggeshall and Stephen Danowski, who proved to be excellent readers for this book and were not daunted by working remotely or in creepy gothic churches. Finally, I would like to thank my readers for choosing to spend their time with my story. I hope you enjoy reading it as much as I did writing it.

Prologue

She crouched in the cache under the wide floorboards and listened intently as the front door creaked open. The gray mist enveloping the bluff allowed scant moonlight to filter into the cottage, adding little to the glow of the oil lamp and embers of the fireplace. She sent a grateful prayer heavenwards when she remained hidden in darkness despite the small cracks between the boards.

Booted feet strode the length of the small central room before a token search of the second floor. It had happened before like this: the pacing, the muttering, and the fine sand that worked its way between the floorboards to dance across her cheek. Tonight, she had almost failed to make it into the cache on time. Peacefully stitching by the fire, she had not heard him until he was almost upon the cottage. She was becoming too slow, too complacent, and he was too determined for her to be careless. As before, impatience hung in the air tonight, but there was also a hint of expectation that made it difficult for her to breathe. She knew all too well who he was and had been playing this dangerous game of evasion for three weeks now.

She heard Nehemiah Alden nudge her sewing basket aside and fold his angular frame into the chair by the fire. "I know you are here. I have been watching for you, and I can be patient. Oh, yes," he said. "I can be very patient . . . when I choose to be. I also listen and am quite persuasive, you know."

Tears squeezed out between her tightly closed lids. She knew when he sounded the most reasonable, he was the most dangerous. She pressed her hands against her ears to keep his voice out, the piece of needlework she still clasped in one hand too thin to mute his words.

"*They'll not return, Cousin.*" *He sounded sure and satisfied.* "*It has been too long. The dream you weave is misguided and ungodly. Your father would never approve a marriage that would take you away from him and to marry you to a sea captain would ensure that. Think of your proper station, your responsibilities!*"

She began to tremble because she knew he was right. It had been too long. Even a sea voyage with unfavorable weather would have returned her father weeks ago. The fear and uncertainty of months secluded in this house on the bluff weighed on her, and the cache that had always been a haven felt like a tomb. She closed her eyes and clasped her hands, praying for intervention.

She sensed and heard movement as Nehemiah heaved himself from the chair to roam around the parlor. The shells she had collected on the beach below and placed on the mantle were lifted with a deliberate scrape and dropped onto the floor one by one. Tears filled her eyes. There was so little beauty in this harsh land, and he was deliberately destroying what she had collected to bring her joy. She regretted their loss, but most of all, it was the wearing of his patience that frightened her. What would he do when he finally discovered her hiding place?

"*I learned the secret of the cache at The White Horse tonight,*" *Nehemiah said.* "*You would be amazed what silver, or, in the case of a reluctant tavern keeper, a sharp blow or two will produce. Your villagers are very protective of you, my dear. Who would have believed that as isolated as you are, you would be able to inspire such loyalty?*" *There was a brief silence, then she heard him drop to his knees, his voice now strong through the boards.* "*Remove yourself from the cache or I will remove you myself. You would be wise to accept my offer and my protection.*"

She remained still, fearing even to breathe, and let the silence be her answer.

A bellow tore the air and the floor vibrated as he pounded the oak boards with his fist. "*Enough! Ungrateful wretch!*"

As he made his way closer to the hiding place, pounding each board in turn, she made herself as small as possible in the farthest corner and pressed her face against the cold, rough stones. Oh, how she wished she could melt into them, seep between the cracks, and disappear. She realized with a leap of fear that she still held her needlework. It would never do to be caught with it. She shoved the cloth between the crevice of two large foundation stones, scoring her knuckles.

When the boards to her back lifted and the warmth from the remaining fire seeped into the hole, she knew he had found the cache. The steps of the ladder creaked under his weight, and she could feel him probing the darkness for her.

"It will be far worse if you defy me," he whispered, shuffling closer and closer to where she pressed herself to the stones.

He cannot see in this blackness. Just like me, he can only sense. Be still. Be silent. She believed for a moment he might pass her by, but then his fingers scrabbled against her back, trying to grip her clothing. When he was unable to do so, he seized her by the hair, dragged her over to the ladder and out of the cache.

"Release me!" She clutched at his arm to ease the pain.

"I will treat you as the wicked child you are until you have learned to mind!" Nehemiah held her at arm's length and gave her a violent shake. His eyes widened in disbelief and then narrowed. "No, it's not possible . . . ."

1

The Point

Sophie stood in the doorway of Falmouth College's faculty office and felt sweat slide down her back and collect at the waistband of her slacks. She winced. She knew there just had to be dark stains on the pale blue fabric. Most of her colleagues hadn't fared any better with the ninety plus degrees on the Cape and the lack of air conditioning in Mason Hall. Everyone she had run into so far had looked as limp as dishrags.

She shifted the stack of syllabi in her arms and looked around the cramped office space. The professor she was replacing had told her the meeting space was on a first-come first-served basis, but it didn't look like the conference table had been cleared in years. It was littered with sliding piles of lecture notes, corrected papers, and ancient memos. "Cheer up," she muttered. "You could still be in Dayton."

Her job in Ohio had paid better, had air conditioning, and had as much security an adjunct English professor could expect, but it wasn't home. So, she had packed her car to the brim, leaving just enough space for her dog, Aesop. Together they had headed for the beckoning seacoast of New England. It was something she had done against the wishes of her older sister, Jacqueline. Her sister was convinced that Sophie's English degree would deposit her at the doors of the unemployment office. "Stick with the sure thing," Jacqueline had ordered. As the weeks passed, the advice had sounded better with every rejection Sophie had received. It was sheer luck she had fallen into a position for a professor on medical leave.

Bob Dylan's haunting "Oh, Sister" sounded out of her cell phone, and she grimaced. She had chosen the song for Jacqueline when one night a painfully long conversation showed her how foolish it was to answer without bracing.

Jacqueline launched into her rant before Sophie could even say hello. "The Cape is too expensive, Sophie. And nobody in their right mind is going to allow that dog in a nice apartment."

"Come on, Jac," she sighed, "You're exaggerating." She was glad this wasn't a talk she was having in person. "Talks" held in her sister's carefully staged loft, where you didn't dare touch anything or breathe wrong, always made her feel as though she'd been called into the Dean's office. She tried to sound reassuring, "There are reasonable places on the Cape. I just . . . ."

"For the wealthy, everything is reasonable," Jacqueline snapped. "I spend enough time appraising their property to know. But you are not wealthy, and you have absolutely no common sense. I can't understand why you would leave a perfectly acceptable job to go starve. You'll end up living on skid row and be dead by November."

"Jac, I . . . " she tried to explain, but her sister plowed on.

"You flit from place to place, one job to another, on a whim. When something grabs your attention, you're gone. Nobody can do that, Sophie. I can't do that. It would be different if you were in a stable relationship, then at least you wouldn't be alone. You're attractive but can't be bothered most of the time. You don't invest in your . . . ."

Sophie rolled her eyes. It wasn't anything she hadn't heard before. She let the words roll off of her as she carefully knelt on the carpet, wrinkling her nose as the stale smell of pencil shavings and spilled coffee surrounded her. As sisters, they looked too much alike for Jacqueline to say she wasn't attractive. Except what she would have called a slim build, pin-straight brown hair, and brown eyes, Jacqueline called "slender," "disciplined," and "cognac-colored." Why couldn't her sister see things, and people, for that matter, as they were? "Mm-hmm," she murmured as Jacqueline continued to complain about her lack of interest in all things cosmetic. She did care how she looked but drew the line at tinted moisturizer and mascara. There was no point in caking makeup on so thick that it hurt to move her face. Not that Jacqueline ever looked like her makeup was troweled on. She always looked like she'd stepped out of a glossy magazine, the kind Sophie usually snorted over in the doctor's office and felt set an unreasonable standard to meet, day after day.

As she leaned forward to separate the syllabi by class, arranging the stacks to avoid the coffee stains and a partially dissolved cough drop, the key in her pocket dug into her hip. She shifted to move the pointy end and couldn't help giving the pocket a satisfied pat. That key opened the door to her future home, and it reminded her of how lucky she'd been. Something, she thought wryly, she could tell Jacqueline about if she would just stop talking. Another adjunct at Falmouth had told her of a caretaker position at a nearby lighthouse and had urged her to apply. She'd hurried over to Blue Water Construction and been delighted to learn the job included not only lodging but a small stipend as well. Housing and a bit of extra money to offset the mound of debt she'd racked up moving back east, she couldn't have asked for a better arrangement. They had even agreed to take her dog.

"Are you listening to me?" Jacqueline sounded suspicious.

"Of course, I am." She sat back on her heels and tucked the phone under her chin as she collected her papers. "I was just waiting for you to wind down so I could tell you the great news."

"Wind down? That's not funny, Sophie." Now she sounded really annoyed. "There's just the two of us, and I feel responsible for you."

She pictured Jacqueline stalking around the loft in heels so high they would have made Sophie's toes scream for mercy.

"It's no picnic, paying off what we owe and managing investments. I've been watching out for you ever since Mom and Dad died, not that you appreciate it."

She should have expected it. Jacqueline always fought the dirtiest when she was angry, but she flinched anyways at the mention of their parents. "Sell the house, Jac. It'll make it easier on everyone. I could use the money to get settled, and you could stop giving yourself an ulcer."

"It's our *family home*." Her voice was cold.

"It was, Jac, when Mom and Dad were alive. But now it's a burden you worry about the tenants setting on fire." She paused. "Maybe you could swing it, if you had a run of outstanding estate appraisals and sales, like the one with all that Danish furniture and silver awhile back. But you can't keep your loft and the house when you're living from sales that feature Tupperware and furniture the owners have assembled themselves," she said in exasperation. She heard the sharp inhale of breath that told her that her words had hit home. She hastily softened her tone. "I'm worried, Jac. You're running yourself into the ground for nothing. You're not responsible anymore."

"Come home, Sophie."

"I can't." She rubbed her forehead against the dull throb that had started. "I have a contract here. Two contracts, actually." She rushed on before Jacqueline could find some other weapon to use against her. "I found a caretaker position with a construction company. They need someone to live in the lighthouse they're renovating into a Bed and Breakfast."

"Sophie," Jacqueline sighed, "have you seen it yet?"

"No, but I'm going right after I finish up at school." She hated that she sounded defensive. "It'll be fine. Philip Bishop and Blue Water Construction have a great reputation. I'll even be able to send you some money for the house." She hurried on before her sister could interrupt. "I'd better go. Aesop's waiting outside, and there isn't much shade."

"Get rid of the dog and come home."

And there it was again. Another reason added to why she couldn't go home. "I can't. Thanks for calling," she added softly. "I'll let you know how I'm making out when I get settled in the lighthouse." She hung up before her sister could answer.

Sophie carefully guided her car crammed with all her belongings along the winding coastal road. Never mind what Jacqueline thought. How hard could it be to babysit an empty lighthouse? Free lodging and a stipend? Most people would jump at the chance. A gull swooped past in the late summer sun. It raced her along the stretch of dunes and glimpses of Silver Beach that marked the way north from Falmouth to Pocasset. She inhaled the scent of sweet grass drifting in through her open window and knew she was exactly where she was meant to be. Aesop's low grumble in the passenger's seat pulled her attention to where the large white dog with brown ears was wedged between her bedding and a box of books.

"Look, it's not my fault." She ran her hand down his back while keeping a sharp eye on the road. "You weren't supposed to get any bigger than twenty-five pounds." Now fully grown, Aesop no longer looked like the sickly puppy she'd rescued from a shelter in Ohio. She had adopted him as soon as she'd landed the job, and they had been inseparable ever since. But she'd discovered over the last three years that few landlords wanted a forty-eight-pound dog in residence. It made landing this lighthouse gig even more of a jackpot, regardless of what her sister said.

Her optimism lasted until they turned down the dirt lane leading to Alden Neck and the lighthouse. As she negotiated the pitted road, she switched off between wrestling the wheel and keeping Aesop from tumbling onto the floor. He whined pitifully, and she couldn't have agreed more. She hadn't expected this kind of neglect. If the road was this bad, what would the lighthouse look like? Finally guiding the car around one last curve, she lurched to a halt in front of two sagging chain-link gates hanging drunkenly from their end posts. The thick shrubs on either side of the gates made it impossible to pass.

She felt the familiar clutch in her stomach that always followed her sister announcing that Sophie had screwed up again. Another botched attempt at independence. Another opportunity for Jacqueline to tell her I-told-you-so and demand that she come home, adding more fuel to the disaster of their relationship. Jacqueline would be dead set against her staying here. There wasn't another house in sight. In fact, the last house she remembered seeing had been a run-down cottage a couple of miles back. It was doubtful that anyone lived there, and if they did, they weren't going to be open to strangers. Sophie had gotten used to living in Ohio where your neighbor's porch light pierced the darkness and welcomed passers-by like a beacon. Even though she had never dropped in on them, at least it had felt like someone had been there. What would she do if she needed help here? While she reigned in her imagination and focused on her very real housing crisis, Aesop leapt out the open window and charged up the lane.

"Aesop!" She flung open the car door and hurried after him. "Aesop, come back here!" He paused at the crest of the hill to glance back, then charged on, tail straight as a flag. It would be impossible to cut him off through the thick woods, so she edged past the rusty post and stuck to the lane.

As she jogged uphill, she saw that the shrubs stopped suddenly at a tumbled stone wall, then opened onto a gravelly stretch of land that climbed toward an immense sky. Only the graying paint of the lighthouse interrupted the vault of blue before her. From a distance, the structure was encouraging: the shutters hung fairly straight, the porch appeared sound, and all the shades were drawn down the windows exactly halfway. The only exception was a completely round hole the size of a baseball in a rear-facing window. It must have been kids or teenagers. Who else would have the energy to haul themselves up here to break a window? She paused to catch her breath, then bent at the waist and braced her hands against her knees. She squinted against the sun as she straightened and gave the bluff a quick scan. Aesop was nowhere to be seen. She impatiently scraped up the damp hair that had escaped her once smooth knot and tucked it back in place.

A fresh breeze brought some relief when it pushed the damp sweetness of the briars behind her. Everything smells so alive here. She took a deep breath and savored the salty air. Ever since her first visit as a child, the ocean had drawn her, and she felt as if she'd been trying to get back to it on a permanent basis ever since. She couldn't see the ocean yet, but thought she heard waves breaking along the shore. As she climbed the rest of the slope, she was drawn past the cottage to the edge of the bluff and the world just fell away. "It's just like Whitman wrote," she whispered, "'. . . the tossing waves . . . the wild unrest, the snowy, curling caps—that inbound urge and urge of waves, seeking the shores forever.'" Of all the poets that she taught her students, when it came to describing the vastness of the ocean Whitman was spot on. The water stretched on and on, shifting in the light to move the horizon further away every time she tried to anchor it. It was no wonder the place was rumored to have been a hideout for pirates. Isolated, with direct access to open water, it was the perfect location for less than legal activities.

Aesop bounded up and planted himself beside her, his tongue lolling. "Nice of you to join me." She ruffled his ears. "Come on, let's see the house." When she turned from the ocean, she saw a panoramic view of the descending lane, the dunes, and the woods that separated Alden Point from the colonial village of Pocasset in the distance. The peaks of white houses and a church steeple could just be seen peeping out among the summer's trees and greenery. The view is great in every direction, she noted with a sigh. They walked back to the lighthouse's two-story cottage, gravel crunching underfoot.

When Sophie saw the cottage up close, however, it was in worse shape than she had first believed. What paint hadn't been worn off by wind-sprayed sand was peeling in strips and exposing the rot beneath. She wrinkled her nose against the smell of mold and climbed the stairs gingerly when they sagged under her weight. In one corner of the covered porch, leaves and scraps of cloth jutted out of a large hole where an animal had gnawed to build a shelter. Her heart sank. Philip Bishop and Blue Water Construction couldn't seriously want her to live here—the liability alone would be staggering. The place should have been condemned and bulldozed.

Why anyone would choose to come here was beyond her, yet it seemed that someone had. The well-oiled lock snicked open with ease, and the door swung silently on its hinges. Dust motes danced in the sunlight from the open door. She blinked as her eyes adjusted to the dim interior. The two grimy windows to the left of the large fieldstone fireplace added little light to the room. Although generous in size, the room was unremarkable except for the large silver medallion centered on the fireplace chimney and the dust that covered every surface. She would have sworn she'd been the first person to enter the cottage in decades. But the assistant at Blue Water Construction had told her that the project manager, Neal Martin, and the restoration expert, Dan Robbins, were in and out of here all the time.

She turned to find that Aesop had stopped at the doorway. "You've got to be kidding me. You charge all the way up here and now you won't come in?" He whined and shifted from paw to paw but refused to enter. "Come on, it's not as bad as the outside. It's just dirty." When he stood his ground, she shrugged and continued down the dark hallway without him.

A subtle mist built and rolled out from beneath the fireplace, a gray tongue lapping slowly along the baseboards and probing up the surface of the walls. It lazily slipped into cracks and crevices until the entire room was overcome, darker and colder than before.

She heard a sharp bark from outside but ignored it. Aesop would either follow, or he wouldn't. As she wandered from room to room upstairs, opening closet doors and peering out windows, she felt a stirring of hope. Aside from the dirt, this was the perfect answer to her housing problem. The two bedrooms and bath would provide her with more living and working space than she'd had in a long time, and Aesop would have more room to roam. Her delight abruptly vanished when she heard him franticly barking. "Aesop!" she called, bolting for the stairs. She expected to find him still outside, but he was in the living room, snarling at the fireplace. He repeatedly shoved his snout into the ash grate and snapped as if they were under attack.

"What's the matter with you?" Maybe he'd chased some rodent into the grate. She wrinkled her nose. It made her jumpy just thinking about it. "Hey, that's enough." She tried pulling him back by the collar, but he wouldn't budge. She scanned the room and shivered. Why was it so dark in here?

Curling and buckling across the ceiling, the gray mist slowly receded. It slunk over cracking plaster and pooled in corners before seeping down the walls and beneath the floor.

As hard as Aesop had pulled against her, he abruptly relaxed. He gave a few suspicious sniffs of the floor, then trotted through the front door to sit on the porch. She shrugged and followed him. She had given up long ago on understanding why he did anything. When she reached the porch, she squinted up at the sky and saw there was not a single cloud in sight. She glanced uneasily behind her and vowed to pick up mouse-traps before they moved in. Who knew what had set him off, but she didn't want to meet it at night when she was barefoot and stumbling for the bathroom. She closed the door behind her with a soft click. Yes, she nodded, things were certainly starting to improve.

Sophie balanced on the top rung of the ladder and ruthlessly vacuumed the lighthouse's fieldstone fireplace. She was determined that this lighthouse would be ready in the next few days, or she swore she'd pitch a tent on the bluff. There was no way she was spending another week in Falmouth's Harbor View Motel with its mildewed carpet and complimentary view of Ed's Gas Station.

She had already made her way around the other walls of the room, sucking up flaking plaster, dust, and more dried-up spiders than she would care to count. It had taken her the better part of two days, and numerous buckets of warm soapy water, to strip the grime from the rooms. Although she couldn't brag that the lighthouse was gleaming, for the first time in decades the windows sparkled, the walls were free of dust, and the battered hardwood floors smelled faintly of lemon. The bathroom had been scrubbed this morning, and the living room was the last of the rooms she intended to clean. The other rooms were closed off to keep Aesop out of trouble and from dragging dirt into places that were already done. The kitchen was completely useless until it resembled something more than an empty rectangle with a sink.

While she worked, Aesop explored his new home with gusto. He switched off between dashing up and down the stairwell and snuffling the floors. Occasionally he would attack the vacuum canister, rump in the air, and bark as though he was defending her life. She had given up trying to hush him and just let him bark. Who would hear him anyways?

It wasn't much longer before that question was answered. She nearly toppled off the ladder when someone tapped her on the leg. She shrieked over the sound of the vacuum and scrambled to the far side of the ladder. Hose in hand, she did not take her eyes off the tall, blond stranger who stood nearby, angrily waving a brown mailing tube and attempting to shout over the noise.

She used the tip of her worn sneaker to kick the ancient vacuum's off-button and got an earful.

" . . . completely irresponsible. Who are you and what are you doing on my site?" The man looked seriously annoyed.

"Easy." She raised her hands defensively. "I'm the caretaker. Blue Water Construction hired me. Are you Neal?" She lowered the hose to the floor and took a step backward.

"No, thankfully. I'm Dan Robbins; I'm with the restoration company."

"Oh, right." The pieces clicked into place. "Nice to meet you. I'm Sophie Tyler." She stuck out a dirty hand but dropped it when he turned away. He wasn't friendly, but definitely easy on the eyes. Fitted jeans, a red pocket T-shirt, and scarred work boots made his tall, wiry frame seem even taller.

Dan scanned the room apparently checking for damage. "I told Neal and Philip Bishop that having someone live here was overkill, but they wouldn't listen." The brown eyes sharpened. "You're the only 'caretaker,' I hope." He laced enough sarcasm into the phrase to make her wince.

"Just me and my dog." She looked around for Aesop, but he was nowhere to be seen.

"Of course, there's a dog." He planted his hands on his hips. "It just gets better. Don't you know not to mess around with restoration projects?"

"I didn't touch the half bath or your office space."

"You did." He pointed the brown tube at her, his voice rising with every word. "Otherwise, my blueprints would still be spread across the floor where I left them." He took a steadying breath. "Stay out of my space and don't touch or 'clean' or 'fix' anything. Got it?"

"All I did was tidy up and I didn't use anything stronger than Windex, Murphy's Oil Soap, and bleach."

"Bleach?" He went comically motionless. "On what?"

"My bathtub . . . " she began as he raced, boots pounding up the stairs, to check for himself. She followed at a more dignified pace and felt a pang of uneasiness that she had really done something wrong. When she reached the bathroom, she found him kneeling by the bathtub, running a calloused hand over dark orange streaks that ran down the inside walls of the tub.

"What happened?" Sophie gasped. "It was so clean this morning, blindingly bright actually."

Dan moaned softly and leaned his forehead against the tub before answering. "The porcelain finish is worn off and the tub is porous. When you sprayed on the bleach, it lightened the surface, then soaked in and oxidized."

"I'm so sorry." She was starting to agree with him about her being a lousy caretaker. "Can you get it off?"

"No, I'll have to ship it out to be sandblasted and refinished." He straightened and looked into her stricken eyes for the first time since he'd barreled up the stairs. He cursed under his breath and finally looked around the rest of the bathroom. There were new towels, small soaps, and candles all carefully arranged around the room. "At least it smells better," he admitted.

At her watery sniff, he continued rapidly, "Listen, I would have had to send it out anyways. I'll just have to send it out sooner. You can still use it, and with water in it the streaks won't show at all." His voice echoed with an optimism he obviously did not feel. When she sniffed again, he sighed. "I didn't mean to hurt your feelings. I'm just particular about my work site."

Ecstatic barking and the scrambling of paws against a wood floor erupted from a room down the hall, and Sophie bolted out the door.

Dan followed the noise to see what the uproar was about. It didn't take much imagination to see what had occurred. The dog, who looked like an enormous Jack Russell Terrier, had gotten into a box of clothes. He had joyfully flung the contents around the room and was currently shaking a black padded bra from side to side, growling every time it whapped him in the head.

"Bad boy, Aesop." Sophie made a grab for the slip of fabric in his mouth. "Drop it!" She commanded in her sternest voice, then pointed firmly to the floor. Aesop simply planted his furry butt down. He turned his head quizzically at her and refused to give up such an amazing plaything.

"Is he smarter than he looks?" Dan asked, eyebrows raised.

She felt heat creep up her neck and silently cursed her mischievous dog. She knew better than to make a grab for Aesop's new toy because it would only signal a game of keep-away. Instead, she turned her back on both the dog and the disorder, marched to the door to block Dan's view, and pulled it closed behind her. She ignored Aesop's indignant barks and quickly ushered Dan away.

"He just got into a box of old clothes," she lied, unsure of what Dan had seen, but suspecting the worst when she saw his carefully composed face.

"Hmm," Dan intoned and bit his lip. "I need to get going." He turned toward the staircase, talking over his shoulder as he walked. "I'll give you a few days' notice to let you know when to expect the work crews. I'll be in and out in the meantime to get some photos I need."

"Alright." She smoothed her hair and pasted what she hoped was a serene smile on her face.

"What I wouldn't give," he muttered on the way downstairs, "to be here when Neal gets a load of you two."

"Why? What's wrong?" Sophie called after him. She hadn't felt at this much of a disadvantage in a long time. The last time was her first teaching position three years ago. She had mistakenly passed out the answer key the day the department chair had been evaluating her. Her students' insightful, detailed answers should have tipped her off. Now there was the same undercurrent of Something Off. She didn't know what it was, but unless she was very much mistaken, Dan was barely restraining laughter. That alone was enough to make her uneasy.

She plopped down on the top stair and watched him climb into a red pick-up truck advertising "Robbins Restoration Services," then drive off down the lane.

The click, click, click of dog nails on the hardwood floor announced that Aesop had somehow gotten out of that closed room. She looked over her shoulder and bit off a laugh when she saw his version of the repentant Army crawl. His belly scraped the floor, and his ears were flat against his head.

"Opening doors now, are we? You had better look sorry, you rat! Thanks to you, that man won't take us seriously at all. We'd better pull ourselves together because we need this roof over our heads, got it?" She grabbed a hold of his face with both hands and pressed her nose against his. Aesop grumbled his agreement and licked her.

"Now, cut that out!" She laughed and wiped her face with the bottom of her T-shirt. "Come on, fuzz face. Let's get the rest of the boxes moved and settle in. We can still make a good impression on Neal when he shows up," she said and headed downstairs with Aesop trailing behind her.

A day and a half later, Sophie leaned against the living room door jamb, exhausted. "Where did all this stuff come from?" she wondered out loud, looking over the stacks of banana boxes and wine crates filled to bursting with her books, class registers, keepsakes, and winter clothing. Aesop let out a low moan and sat at her feet with a thump.

"Alright, that's enough from you, buster." She stooped to ruffle his fur, then bopped him on the nose with his toy squirrel. "I'll find a place for it eventually."

"'Eventually' would be by this Friday," said a smooth male voice behind her.

Aesop gave a sharp bark and lunged for the stranger to say hello. She just managed to snag him by the collar before his paws planted themselves on the stranger's chest. There was no way that fancy suit would survive a 'meet and greet' with her dog intact. "Aesop, sit!" she commanded.

When she was sure that Aesop had settled down, she turned her attention to the man standing in the front hall. The studied hairstyle, tailored gray suit, power tie, and dress shoes would have been in keeping with a New York boardroom, but in a decrepit lighthouse in Pocasset, he seemed comically out of place. This had to be Neal Martin. She glanced down at her grubby concert T-shirt with frayed seams and made a face. So much for first impressions.

The man pulled a business card from inside his breast pocket and motioned disdainfully to Aesop before thrusting it into her hand. "And get rid of the dog." He paused briefly. "Sophie Tyler, right?" At her stiff nod, he continued, "I told the restoration crew to get in here on Friday and start rebuilding the captain's cache, which will mean ripping up the floor."

She glanced at the card and tapped it lightly against her palm. Neal was as pushy and as high-handed as her sister. She suspected he was also as ruthlessly regimented. There looked like there was a set of bunchy muscles under that suit, probably the courtesy of some fancy health club he visited before heading to work every day.

"So, all these boxes have to go." He waved at the boxes stacked about the room, and she got a whiff of an expensive cologne called *Xelha*. She frowned reflexively. It was a scent an ex of hers had worn and ordered from an organic on-line company.

"I told Philip Bishop that we would be starting on time, and I meant it," he said.

She hesitated before speaking and wiped her damp palms on her shorts. "I was told the mechanics would be installed first." Aesop shifted restlessly against her leg, and she reached down to quiet him with a quick scratch.

"Correct, but the crews will need access to the basement to run the electrical lines and the HVAC system. And where there is no basement entrance, the cache needs to be fixed now." He craned his neck to see around her boxes and curled a lip in distaste. "It will also let me start marketing the property. Questions?" He tried to edge past her into the living room only to be brought up short by a warning growl.

"Easy, Aesop." Sophie gave him a gentle stroke across the head and tried to distract him with his toy squirrel. "Here, you go. Go, find it!" She tossed the toy into the maze of boxes, then frantically tried to think of a way to put Neal off.

She really didn't care which work got completed first, but she just couldn't face moving all those boxes again. "It seems a pain to access the basement only through the living room. How about cutting a hole in the wall downstairs and putting in a door there?" she offered cautiously and received a withering look.

"The foundation walls are made of fieldstone." He made circles of different sizes with his hands, as though she wouldn't understand without the visual. "To move some stones would unbalance the others."

"I didn't know," she said, flushing. "I hadn't explored the cellar yet." Not that she had been in any hurry to do so. Enclosed dark spaces, dampness and the things that thrived in them, like spiders, were not her strong suit. She would have forced herself below at some point anyways just to prove that she could.

"Stay out of the work areas." Neal pulled out his cell phone, swiped across its surface, then started tapping away on the screen. "The crew will complete the mechanics, ground floor, and exterior before moving upstairs." He paused his tapping and looked up. "When Phase One is finished, you'll move to the first floor, and they'll begin Phase Two upstairs."

"Alright," she agreed, but sensed that unless she pushed back, hard and right now, he would walk all over her, like Jacqueline tried to, and make her job here miserable. "But the boxes won't be completely moved by Friday." At that, his head snapped up, and he lowered his phone slowly. She hurried on before he could speak. "That only gives me one day and

I'm working by myself." She shrugged. "I was told I would have a few days' notice when the crew was going to be working. I can promise you that I won't be the cause of any future delays. And the dog stays," she said firmly. "Timely notification of work was in my caretaker contract, and there was nothing prohibiting pets." Thank goodness for contracts, she told herself as his eyes narrowed. She knew without a doubt that if it were up to him, she and Aesop would be evicted.

"You're here to satisfy Bishop's obsession with security and make the lighthouse look occupied." Neal shoved his cell phone back into his breast pocket. "But, if I had known you'd need an engraved invitation before work could start or about that mangy mutt, you wouldn't have gotten the job to begin with."

Although she knew it wasn't the smartest move to irritate him, she was starting to lose her patience. "Then why not put an alarm on the place and leave it at that?"

Neal flushed. "We've had some vandalism at other sites, and this lighthouse is a pet project of Bishop's wife . . . his pregnant wife. He's not taking any chances with this one and always wants a person on site. A person," he managed to say evenly, though it seemed to cost him, "that should have been a big guy and not you and that poor excuse for a dog."

"It's hard to mistake 'Sophie' as a guy's name," she said stiffly. "Why didn't you know who the caretaker was?"

"I was swamped with work and let my assistant handle the hire. She only said you were perfect for the job."

"She never mentioned that I was a woman and that I owned a dog?"

"No." Neal ran his hand through his dark hair and disordered his carefully styled look.

Her stomach grumbled, reminding her of her very real money problems. The apple and cheddar cheese she'd had for breakfast hadn't gone very far. Her last decent meal was a fond memory at this point. She smothered her pride and tried the brutally honest approach. "Adjunct teaching doesn't pay particularly well, so I really need this job. And if security is an issue, I would think a large dog would be welcome." She watched him closely, unable to tell what he was going to decide. Contract or no, he could make things so impossible that she would need to leave.

"Fine." He exhaled sharply. "I'll get you some guys to move your things into a room upstairs. The crew will be here Friday at 8:00 a.m. sharp to start the work, as scheduled."

A deep-throated growl from behind the boxes made Neal stiffen. He glanced uneasily toward the place where Aesop had disappeared. "The dog stays under the condition that if he threatens anyone, or chews or scratches anything, you're responsible for damages and you're fired. Do you understand?"

"Yes, of course," she replied with what dignity she could muster. "It won't be a problem."

"See that it's not." Neal turned on his heel and exited with enough energy to suck the air from the room.

She rubbed her arms against the chill he had left behind and moved to the window just in time to see his black SUV spew rocks as he turned and charged down the lane. She watched the dust settle and scolded herself at length for trusting the assistant.

The sound of claws on stone and growling finally registered, snapping her into action.

"Aesop!" she commanded. "Aesop! NO! No digging!" She rushed to make her way through the boxes. This was all she needed. That stiff-necked rump hadn't even hit the main road, and her dog was digging a hole in the floor. "You don't even dig holes outside," she said in exasperation. "What's wrong with you?"

She scrambled around boxes, then slammed her knee against the corner of a wooden crate hard enough to gash it open as she fell. She gasped and struggled to her feet, ignoring the blood that ran down her leg. She had to stop him. Between two towers of wardrobe boxes, she spotted Aesop. His nose was pressed firmly to the floor and his hackles rose as a gray mist snaked out from beneath the fireplace.

"What in the world is that?" She felt a spurt of panic. It didn't smell like smoke, but what else could it be? She tugged on Aesop's collar. "Come on! We've got to get out of here."

Aesop snarled and snapped, weaving and retreating when the mist lunged for him. It rose to float before her eyes in wisps; the tendrils reached for her like hands to stroke and grasp. 'I'm going to die' was her last thought before she slumped, unconscious, against the boxes.

Three faces were suspended above Sophie: a dark-haired pixie with sharp green eyes, Aesop's furry muzzle, and the frowning features of Dan Robbins.

"Get off, Aesop." She felt a rush of embarrassment and struggled upright, pushing against the dog's chest.

"Looks like she's okay and not too happy to see you," the pixie said with a grin. "Surprise, surprise. You must have been extra charming the last time you saw her."

"She'd scrubbed the daylights out of . . . " Dan gave up and sighed. "It doesn't matter. Could we see if she's okay?" He took a breath and turned to Sophie. "This is my sister, Chelle. Chelle, Sophie Tyler. Are you okay?"

Sophie shut her eyes briefly. Of course, Dan again, and this time he'd brought his sister. At least she seemed personable, which was more than could be said for him so far. "Did you see it?" she asked. Even through her wooziness, she caught the look between the siblings that said she was worse off than they'd imagined. She tried again. "There was a . . . fire?" she guessed, at a loss to explain what she'd seen because the house was intact and there wasn't a trace of smoke. She gave up trying to explain with a helpless shrug. "I don't know what happened. I cracked my knee on a crate." She squinted down at her knee and saw that the gash that had been bleeding now only oozed through a makeshift bandage. "Things got sort of gray after that, and I sat down hard. That's all, really."

Chelle gave her a sympathetic smile. "I hate to break it to you, but you were out cold when we came in and your knee will most likely need stitches. It would make me and my brother, Galahad, here," she jerked a thumb in Dan's direction, "feel better if Urgent Care took a look at you."

"No. Thanks, though." Sophie hoped to get rid of them as quickly as possible. "Between not eating and the cut, it made me a little lightheaded. I don't need to go to the doctors. What I need is a bowl of soup and a nap."

"You could be right, but you should really get that knee checked." Chelle stopped rolling gauze mid-loop and turned to Dan. "What do you think?"

"I hate doctors, myself, but you should be checked. Regardless of your coverage, Blue Water Construction pays hefty premiums to insure this place and its workers, and that includes you, Professor. You may as well use it. In fact, the insurance company requires that anyone who's hurt is examined." He gave her a lopsided smile. "It helps cut down on lawsuits."

"You're not funny," Sophie said, flushing to her hairline. She wasn't one of those people who sued others because of her own stupidity. She let his sister help her off the floor and guide her to a sturdy box by the fireplace. Chelle made sure she wouldn't topple off and propped open a window with a book from a nearby crate. Satisfied that Sophie was reasonably settled, Chelle went to help Dan coax Aesop into the kitchen.

Apparently, the three of them had become best friends while she'd been unconscious. Unease slid through her. How long had she been out?

A welcoming breeze whispered past the sill, carrying the scent of brine and warmed pines that cut the chill of the living room. The voices of Dan and Chelle floated through the empty house as they went about closing kitchen windows and sliding locks.

"How'd you know she was a professor and didn't have insurance?" Chelle demanded.

"All those crates with attendance registers and textbooks," Dan said. "No one moves that kind of stuff around unless they need to, so she most likely doesn't have an office. And if she doesn't have an office, she's not full-time and it's doubtful she has insurance."

"I didn't see what was in the boxes." Chelle sounded defensive. "I only saw that there was an army of them."

There was a clatter of metal, and then splashing water. "While I get the dog a drink, check on her, will you? I don't think there's anything really wrong with her, but better to be safe than sorry."

"Sure. By the way, I couldn't get that door latch to work." Chelle made her way back to the living room, the worn floorboards creaking under her feet and announcing her arrival. "How are you doing?" She hunkered down near Sophie and rummaged in a battered backpack. "It's not much, but I've got a bottle of water and a candy bar, if you want them."

"I'm fine, really." Sophie tried not to sound bad-tempered as she took the lukewarm water and slightly smushed chocolate bar. "I appreciate the concern, but you're both overreacting."

Chelle patted her on the leg and rose. "I hate feeling like I'm out of control too. We'll just get you checked out, and then you're on your own. Okay?"

"Fine." She peeled back the wrapper and took a violent bite.

Chelle returned to the kitchen and there were more sounds of windows closing. Even though Chelle lowered her voice, Sophie heard her say, "This place makes my skin crawl. Did you notice that living room was freezing and dark when we first got here?"

"You've been listening to too many of Mrs. Gladys' stories in the village," Dan hissed. "Don't start that crap. It'll make it impossible for us to hire help and any teenage idiot on a dare will be climbing all over the place at night."

"But it felt weird in here, I swear it," Chelle whispered back. "And she was mumbling about being trapped."

Dan didn't bother to lower his voice. "Come on, it's Building 101. You know houses like this were built thick to keep heat out in the summer and inside during the winter. And as far as it being dark, the sun is on the other side of the house this time of day."

"Then why were you almost as white as she was when we found her?"

Sophie had to strain to hear and bristled at his answer. "The woman's a walking headache." He sounded bone tired. "She's already ruined one bathtub and passed out cold. Now, could we please get her to Urgent Care before something else happens?"

"I hate it when you get all snotty on me," Chelle said, as she made her way down the hall toward the living room.

"All in a day's work, sweetie." He prodded his sister into the room and went to stand beside Sophie. "The dog's all set in the kitchen. Let's get you to Urgent Care."

She knew Dan was tall, but he seemed to take up even more space, crowded as she was against the window. She craned her head back and found him assessing her, as if today hadn't been bad enough already. She knew what he thought he saw: a dirty, bleeding incompetent. Why didn't he just back up and let her breathe? She grasped the windowsill for support and quickly heaved herself upright, favoring the battered knee. It would have counted as a small success, but her knee buckled, pitching her head-first into Dan.

He grunted in surprise. "Okay, you're having a very bad day."

"Week," she corrected.

"Right." There was a trace of humor in his voice. "Let's get you checked out so that you can come home, crawl back into bed, and pretend it never happened."

She nodded, stiff with embarrassment.

He slid his arm around her waist and helped her hobble across the floor as best she could. He was rather kind when he wasn't raving about his work site. When an obsessive contractor who smelled of sawdust and peppermint could get her guard down, she was in worse shape than she thought. She picked up the pace and shuffled as quickly as she could to the door. It was best to get this over with and keep her dealings with him to a minimum.

In the truck, she was distracted from her bloody bandage by the bickering of Dan and Chelle. It could have been uncomfortable, sandwiched between the two, except that the fighting was done in the easy ribbing of siblings who were also friends. It was so unlike the dealings Sophie had with her own sister that she settled in to observe the volleys like a spectator at a tennis match. She found to her surprise that she was enjoying herself. She learned more about the family business from listening to them argue than if she had talked to them one-on-one. It was clear their parents had nothing to worry about. They could enjoy their sunny retirement; the family business was in good hands.

Chelle insisted on staying with her at Urgent Care while Dan went to meet with a prospective client. Even though Chelle was easy company, the hour and a half it took for Dr. Logan to treat her knee left Sophie with a lot of time to consider her mishap. The event, although frightening, could have been much worse if Neal had found her. He could have used it as an excuse to fire her. The idea was sobering. She needed the salary as much as the place to live. She had to listen to her body and slow down. Dr. Logan, she was relieved to hear, found nothing seriously wrong with her other than slight dehydration and a knee that needed four stitches. Other than telling her to return in a week to have the stitches removed, his treatment plan echoed much of what she'd felt she needed: rest, food, and ice for a knee that was already turning interesting shades of purple.

When Dan returned, he drove them straight to *Gladys'*, a vintage chrome diner that reminded her of a burnished toaster. The red vinyl booths gave a great view of Main Street, and it struck her that the customers here all ate together, visiting with each other no matter how far apart they were seated. Chelle explained that Mrs. Gladys, at eighty-three, didn't cook anymore. She had retired seven years ago to terrorize the Senior Center into "beefing up" their social calendar. Sophie was delighted to hear that those new events included trips to Foxwoods Casino; weekly competitive card games in the church hall; and an old romance novel Book Swap once a month, as Mrs. Gladys claimed newly published ones read more like "how-to-manuals" than love stories. Despite her disappointment at not meeting Gladys in person, she was pleased to find that *Gladys'* was still a family venture. Her son comfortably wielded Gladys' spatula in the kitchen and his wife waited on the booths.

By the time Di had delivered a plastic bag filled with ice and taken their order, Sophie felt she had told her story from different starting points to almost everyone in the diner.

"You be careful there, Sophie," Di said with a wink as she expertly delivered her turkey club, Dan's burger, and Chelle's *poutine*, a pile of french fries smothered in spicy brown gravy. "If Gladys hears you've passed out cold up at the lighthouse, she'll chalk it up to the haunting and pick your brain for details."

"Haunting?" She paused with a fry halfway to her lips. "By what?"

"Nobody's ever seen anything." Dan waved dismissively. "Some people claim to have felt cold spots, and a friend of Chelle's once swore she got trapped inside. But I don't think any of the stories are too reliable."

"I don't know . . ." Chelle said slowly.

She glanced uneasily at the siblings. "There has to be some reason for people to think it could be haunted." A spoon clattered to the floor behind her and Sophie jumped. She had explained away what happened in the lighthouse as exhaustion, but something had risen from that floor like smoke. "Anybody fall off the turret or stumble over the bluff in a storm?"

"Not that I know of." Di tucked her hands into the pockets of her apron. "But," she shrugged, "it's New England." She turned toward the kitchen. "Hey, Bob, what does Gladys say haunts Alden Light?"

"You'd have to ask her," he called from the grill, then appeared in the doorway wiping his hands on a dish towel. "I know she once went inside as a kid with Auntie B and they both swear up and down there was something there. I've never felt anything, myself, but if I had to guess, I'd say the Missus."

"Whose missus?" Sophie asked, taking a sip of water and setting her glass back down in the ring of water it had created.

"Nehemiah Alden and his wife lived there, before the federal government took it over." Di served a large wedge of chocolate cake to an older man who had been silently listening to the conversation. His face scrunched by degree, depending on his level of disapproval. Most of the time it seemed as though he smelled something bad.

Bob flipped the dish towel over his shoulder. "Some people claim Alden murdered her and then set the house on fire to cover it up."

"There wasn't anything left but the fireplace and the foundation," the older man finally chimed in, licking chocolate frosting off his chin like a greedy gnome. "Never found as much as a pinkie in all that rubble."

"Now come on you two." Di crossed her arms. "You know if the town had been able to convict Nehemiah of anything they would have done it gladly."

Sophie scanned the faces around her. "Why? Was he an outsider?"

Di nodded. "Oh, he was new all right, but then they all were, jostling elbows to get their own piece of the pie. He wasn't ugly either. There's a portrait of him hanging in the library, and he's handsome as sin."

"They hated him because he was good looking?" She couldn't believe it.

"No!" The older man rapped his mug sharply against the counter, sloshing coffee over the rim. "He was as mean and twisted as he was pretty."

Di patted his tense hand. "Now, Frank. You know women of sense aren't swayed by a pretty face."

When he responded with a disbelieving grunt, Sophie leaned toward Chelle and whispered, "How long ago did all this happen?"

"Early 1700's." Chelle smiled when Sophie's eyebrows shot up.

"But they talk as if it were just yesterday!"

"I know," Chelle said. "I found it creepy as a kid when neighbors used to talk of people long dead as if they knew them." When Sophie frowned, Chelle continued, "No, really. They still give directions using the name of the first person who owned the land. Like, 'take a left at the old Crocker Place,' even though there hasn't been a Crocker in these parts for a hundred years and the house has been razed for longer."

Dan, having finished his own fries, picked a few off Chelle's plate and popped them into his mouth. "All part of living in a small New England town," he said. "Each individual belongs to the whole, the whole never lets go, and they never forget." He shrugged. "It's just the way it is."

"If you're interested," Di said, motioning to Sophie. "You should see Babs over at the library and have her show you the village records she pulled for the renovation up at The Point. You might get a kick out of what Alden's neighbors had to say about him and the town."

"Sure," she said despite a growing uneasiness. "I'll stop by after I settle in."

"I'll let her know you're coming." Di said, and turned to refill Frank's coffee.

Though it was only late afternoon, Sophie found that all that cleaning, the confrontation with Neal, and her accident had left her exhausted. Dan and Chelle agreed to drive her to the Mini-Mart to buy some more ice for her knee before delivering her to the lighthouse. When they got to the Mini-Mart, she was surprised to find Frank from the diner already there and running the cash register. She hastily paid for her ice and said a polite, but quick, goodbye to the old man when it seemed like he was ready to settle in for a long visit. She wasn't ready for any more village stories. She grabbed the ice and gratefully escaped to the Robbins who waited to return her to The Point and an ecstatic Aesop.

Despite their kindness, it was a relief when she watched them leave. the red tail lights of the pickup truck bobbing down the pitted lane and disappearing around the bend. She was grateful for their concern and help, but she was too tired to pretend she was fine any longer. She slid the door bolt home and trudged up the stairs with Aesop. She collapsed fully clothed on the bed and slid straight into sleep.

The flames licked greedily at dry fabric and sprang across wooden boards to fill the room with acrid smoke and sparks. Painfully bright against the stark autumn sky, the second floor of the small cottage was engulfed in flames. While the surf pounded in the distance, carrying the force of the oncoming storm, a man stood rigid in the tree line, watching as the house moaned and the windows shattered.

Sophie woke with a start, soaking wet and shivering. Out of the darkness, Aesop whined softly and rose to snuffle her hand.

"It's okay, boy. It's just a bad dream. A nightmare really, but just what I deserve for listening to ghost stories." She rubbed her forehead gently. "I've got a massive headache."

She swung her legs over the side of the bed and stood slowly. Her stitches strained on her knee, warning her to move carefully. With her arms outstretched, she shuffled in the direction of the bathroom, groping along the wall for a light switch. Only slight moonlight filtered in through the curtainless windows, and the longer it took her to hobble, the more unnerving she found the profound darkness. The creak of boards under her bare feet made her want to turn on all the lights to ward off whatever it was she sensed was watching in the dark.

The tingling in her arms warned of a looming panic attack, so she bore down. She inhaled slowly through her nose and said softly on the exhale, "I am peace, I am calm . . . ." She repeated the phrase until she managed to stumble her way to the bathroom and hit the light switch. The glare of the bare bulb stabbed at her eyes as she groped for the as-pirin in the medicine cabinet. She wrenched off the cap and swallowed three before sticking her mouth under the sink faucet for water. She sank gratefully onto the side of the claw-footed tub and cradled her head in her hands. Breath by breath she shoved panic away. Sensing a panic at-tack in the making was almost as paralyzing as the head pain. As time passed and the aspirin started to take effect, she was able to focus on the bathroom, taking in the yellow and rose colors of the soaps and towels.

"Whew," she blew out a breath. When she could avoid both a migraine and a panic attack it was one for the books. She shut off the light and stood, letting the night settle softly around her. The first thing she'd do in the morning was get nightlights. This stumbling around in the dark was not something she wanted to repeat.

She moved to the window and peered across a silver stretch of moonlit grass to the darkened woods beyond.

"He would have had to stand about there to see the house as I did in my dream," she said, locating a small jut in the woods. An involuntary shiver ran through her. She knew with quiet certainty that the scene that she had witnessed in her dream had not only happened, but that the fire had been deliberate. No one claimed to know what had happened to Alden's wife, but she was convinced that at least one person had known. Her gut told her that the man who had silently watched the house burn was the one.

She turned from the window chilled and felt her way back into bed.

The shadow separated itself from the side of a gnarled oak and stood immobile at the edge of the trees, watching for a long time after the woman had moved from the window.

2

Research

The next morning Sophie was roughly woken from sleep by a hand on her shoulder. She tried to focus on where she was but had a hard time keeping her eyes open. "Come on, Sophie. Wake up!" The irritated voice finally snapped her awake.

She struggled out from under the covers and batted Dan's hand off her shoulder, her heart pounding in her chest. Aesop bounded onto the bed and licked her face. "Aesop, get down! And you, get out!" She swung her legs over the side of the bed and sat up. "This space is off-limits while I'm using it. Is that clear?"

"Crystal." Dan turned for the door, then paused. "Just to clarify, I did knock, pound actually. When you didn't answer and I heard Aesop whining, I checked on you, that's all."

She curled her toes into the blue pile of the bedside rug. She hadn't heard any of it. What was wrong with her? She had left herself unprotected in an unfamiliar place. And of all the people to find her, it had to be Dan. She was torn between the self-consciousness that he had found her vulnerable for a second time and the fear that it could have been anyone else. The sense of exposure stirred a need to lash out. She was about to give in to the urge, when Chelle poked her head in the doorway, dressed for the office and as collected as Sophie was frazzled. "The moving crew wants to know where to put your stuff, Sophie. Does it matter which upstairs bedroom it goes into?"

"No, not really." She tilted her head as she thought, then held up her hand. "Wait, have them put the boxes in the room facing the bluff. I'll use the woods-side one for an office. Thanks, Chelle."

"What, no ocean view?" Dan mocked, his eyebrows raised.

"Too distracting. I'll have mounds of papers to grade this semester." She carefully clambered over the bed, looking to see where she'd kicked off her flip-flops before falling into bed fully clothed. Her knee was somewhat better this morning but still stiff. A warm shower would be first on her to-do list, after she checked on the movers. The last thing she needed was to hunt for books at the hectic beginning of the semester. It was a nightmare she was determined to avoid.

She grabbed the missing flip-flops off a growing pile of laundry and turned to find Dan still watching her. Chelle could already be heard giving orders to the moving crew downstairs. "Was there something else, Mr. Robbins?"

His lips flattened into an annoyed line. He recognized a dismissal when he heard one. "No, ma'am, but if you got yourself an alarm clock it would save us both another scene and spare you the embarrassment."

She nodded curtly, ignoring the hick-like cadence he'd adopted—clearly meant to show exactly what he felt about her attitude. She meant to steam through the doorway but had to stop short when he partially blocked the exit.

He folded his arms and leaned his shoulder into the door jamb. A slow smile lifted the corners of his mouth and lit his eyes.

Sophie blinked in confusion. Why the sudden change in attitude? She'd known he might be trouble yesterday when the clean scent of him mixed with wood and mint had fuzzed her head. But today, when he tried to be human, he was downright dangerous.

"Beautiful . . . " he said, nodding solemnly and settling more comfortably against the doorframe. " . . . even if the side of your hair is matted with spit."

She tentatively reached up to touch the side of her head and knew he was lying. She shoved him out of the way and hobbled to the bathroom. "Idiot!" she threw over her shoulder. She slammed the bathroom door shut but could still hear him roaring with laughter.

She vigorously brushed her teeth, splashed water on her face, and dragged a brush through spit-free hair. The Idiot. She grimaced and blew out her breath. He'd been out of line, but she'd had it coming. She'd sounded just like her sister, when Jacqueline was in a snit. Dictatorial and snotty. She hated it when Jacqueline pulled that routine with her, and now she'd done the same to a virtual stranger.

Only slightly more lowering was the fact she really wouldn't have minded if he had been interested in her. She thought he might have been, before he dropped her flat. She couldn't even claim that she thought he'd been joking. She was a rotten liar, and she was sure he knew exactly what she was about. Your mess; go clean it up. She squared her shoulders and headed off to find Dan.

When Sophie met two burly men wearing "Two Guys and a Truck" T-shirts at the top of the staircase, she pointed out which room the boxes should go into, then made her way downstairs. The front door stood open, revealing a glimpse of early morning sunlight playing over the grass and lightening the darkness of the woods beyond. She headed toward the noises coming from the back of the house, the rhythmic tapping of a foot with the latest hit on the radio and the occasional ruffling of paper.

Dan had taken over what there was of the kitchen counter. Large sheets of paper covered in scrawling black handwriting and detailed illustrations of a house were spread across its surface. Each drawing showed an artistic rendering of the space in question, as well as an architectural draft.

"Those are amazing." She moved to stand beside him. "They look like the notebooks DaVinci drafted his ideas into, but the period is wrong. This is colonial, isn't it?" She knew that considering what had just happened upstairs the tone and topic were wrong, but she was keeping her fingers crossed that he would ignore what had happened and move on.

"That's right." He leaned against the counter and folded his arms. "Something I can do for you, Ms. Tyler?"

So, he wasn't going to make this easy. She mentally straightened her spine and plunged in before she could change her mind. "I owe you an apology." She could see that she had surprised him and hurried on. "I had a rotten night last night, and I took it out on you. I'm sorry. It wasn't fair, and I appreciate that you checked on me." As far as apologies went, it wasn't the most eloquent, but at least it was sincere.

"What happened?" He shifted the drawings aside to find four sugar packets and a covered Styrofoam coffee cup underneath.

"Excuse me?"

"Last night. What happened?" He removed the plastic lid, dumped all four sugar packets into the coffee, and stirred it slowly with the non-business end of his pen.

Sophie blinked in surprise. Just like that. He'd forgiven her and moved on as if the incident had never happened. She was more grateful than she would have liked to admit. He seemed a steady sort, something that was rare in her academic world and something she had been without for a long time. Maybe she could push her luck a bit more and see what he made of her dream. She didn't have much to lose; he'd already seen her at her worst. Heaven knew she needed an objective opinion. Given his actions over the last few days, she knew he would be honest with her.

"I saw this house burn in a dream," she said quietly. She shifted and felt herself reddening. "I mean, it looked a bit different, but the location was identical."

"Could have been all that talk of fires at the diner." Dan gestured with his coffee cup before taking a sip.

"Maybe, but I knew what time of year it was, that there was an oncoming storm, and that someone watched this house burn and never went for help." Her voice cracked. "And worst of all he knew there was a woman still inside."

"He, who?"

"The man who watched the Alden house burn and did nothing," she said, hearing her voice rise but powerless to control it.

"How do you know it was a man or this house? It could have been anyone, and colonial houses all were pretty much built the same, especially those by the sea."

"I can't prove it. It was a dream, after all." She shrugged. "But I'm convinced that watcher was a man, and he knew someone was in this house."

"A she." He sounded as if he thought she'd lost her mind.

"It felt like he was watching a woman. Maybe Mrs. Alden. I don't know who, but I believe it was a woman." She shifted her focus to the large sheets covering the counter. Her eyes slipped over the drawings of a kitchen, bedrooms, and study before narrowing in on one featuring a living room and hearth. She recognized a fireplace with a round medallion on it as the one she had just passed on her way to the kitchen. She inhaled sharply. "These drawings are of the original house, not the current one, aren't they?" She quickly shuffled among the large sheets, searching for the woods-side view of the cottage.

"Yeah, Alden did these in the early 1700's. Bishop had them enlarged to give me a blueprint to work from. Sophie, are you okay?" He peered into her face.

She nodded stiffly. "Where's the sketch of the back of the house—the one that faces the woods?"

He shifted a few sheets and set the view in question on top.

"That's it. That's what I saw in my dream last night." She ran a shaking finger over the drawing and turned to face him.

Dan sighed. "Look, I realize this has shaken you up, but think. All colonials were built the same because the design *worked*. You could have seen any number of pictures or another real house, come to think of it, and dreamt about it last night." When her mouth opened to protest, he hurried on. "And even if you did dream of this one, it doesn't mean there was a watcher in the woods." He reached out to rub her chilled arm. "You could have filled in all that information from what you heard at *Gladys'* yesterday."

Sophie bit her lip and wondered. "It just seemed so real, you know?"

"Yeah, I've had a few of those myself."

She was quiet for a moment. "No, I still can't help but feel . . . ."

"If you want to put this to rest, hit the library and see what Babs has in the archives. There might be something that would help you prove it was pure imagination on your part."

She considered. What did she have to lose? "I suppose I could check when the fire happened. There might even be a record of the oncoming storm if it were big enough. It certainly felt like it could have been." She gave him a grateful smile. Fears were a lot easier to face when you talked with a skeptic.

He nodded and gestured toward the back door. "I let Aesop out a bit ago; he was crying to get outside. You might want to collar him before Neal gets here. He hates dogs."

"He made that pretty clear when I met him." She supposed she shouldn't ask but had to know. "Why didn't you tell me he was so hard to get along with?"

Dan's lips tightened, and he shuffled the drawings into a disorganized pile. "I'm the last person you should be asking about Neal."

"Why not?" When he didn't respond, she pushed. "What's the story?"

He checked his watch and shoved his phone into his back pocket. "I've got to get to Barnstable for a meeting. I'll see you later." He swung out of the kitchen, the screen door slapping shut behind him.

"Well," she sighed, "I certainly know how to clear a room." She shrugged and absently started to flip through the drawings, pausing over those that showed the house and woods.

When Chelle walked into the kitchen, Sophie was still muttering over Dan's quick escape. "You'd better leave things as they are." Chelle smiled to soften the words. "He can be an absolute bear about his work. It doesn't look like he's got a system, but he can always tell when someone has been through his papers."

Sophie made a face. "I think his *bearness* is a permanent condition when it comes to me. I haven't managed a normal conversation with him in the last week, and this morning was no different."

"What set him off today?" Chelle asked absently, pulling the living room drawing in front of her and glancing over Dan's scrawled notes on the border.

"Well, first I was rude."

Chelle snorted and shoved the drawings aside for a place to sit on the counter. "He very likely had it coming."

"Then after I'd apologized, I told him about a nightmare I had about this house burning, and then," she thrust her arms out before letting them drop, "I asked about Neal."

"Oh, boy." Chelle made a face. "That couldn't have gone over too well—the dream about the fire or Neal."

Sophie nodded. "It could have been worse, I suppose. At least the fire I dreamt about happened in the past. He did have some good advice about the dream but basically threw a wall up and walked out when I asked about Neal." She shrugged. "I just wanted to know why he hadn't warned me Neal was so hard to work with."

Chelle looked like she was weighing where to start and settled for, "It's complicated."

"Complicated?" Sophie echoed, frowning. "How complicated can it be?"

"Well," Chelle said, stretching out the word. "We all grew up together. But they have been at each other's throats since they were fourteen, when our German Shepherd sank his teeth into Neal's shoulder."

Sophie's hand flew to her mouth. "I'm sure you both felt awful! Was there something wrong with the dog?"

"No, I didn't feel awful, and I'm pretty sure Dan was extremely grateful."

Her stomach gave a sick roll. "You can't mean that."

"Oh, yes, I do." Chelle nodded. "That morning, Neal had picked a fight with Dan and managed to pin him down by sitting on him. When he started plowing his fist into Dan's face, I panicked." The misery was clear in her eyes, when she continued, "They had fought before, but nothing like that. I was sure Neal was going to kill him, so I let the dog out." She lifted her hands, palm up. "I didn't know what else to do, but Duke did. He cleared the fence in a leap and sank his teeth into Neal's shoulder. Duke didn't let go of him until he was finally able to get Neal off."

"And he holds that against you?"

"I don't think either of them know how Duke got out. I've never said it was me." Chelle sounded as unhappy as she must have been all those years ago. "Neal never held the bite against Dan, not really. What he did hold against him was a good home and friends that came easily. The same day Neal came after Dan, Neal's dad had started out his day by beating the tar out of Neal."

"This gets worse and worse." Sophie couldn't imagine living like that. "What about his mom? Couldn't she have taken Neal and run?"

"No," Chelle murmured. "She died when Neal was young, and Mr. Martin was always careful to hit Neal where it wouldn't show. But after gym, in the locker room, it was hard to hide the marks and word got around. We kids turned a blind eye because we were young, scared, and stupid. Neal didn't invite any sympathy, either." A shuddering breath escaped her. "Dan could have forgiven him for the beating, but he couldn't forgive what happened after."

"What did happen?" Sophie asked, unable to stop herself but dreading the answer.

"Neal waited, bid his time. A couple of weeks later he took advantage of some neighborhood kids who were easily manipulated." Anger flashed across her face. "He told them Duke was vicious and showed them the healing bite marks on his shoulder."

"Oh, no. What'd the kids do?"

Chelle's eyes filled with tears. "They threw rocks at Duke when he was in the yard and couldn't get away. He was hurt but jumped the fence anyways to chase after them." Her voice broke. "He got hit by a car."

She knew that Chelle was telling the truth as she knew it, but how could Chelle, or Dan, be sure Neal was involved at all? "How do you know it happened like that?"

"We saw it from an upstairs window. Neal was across the street, watching. By the time Dan got downstairs to stop them, it was too late. Afterwards, the kids told us what Neal had said."

"But he couldn't have known Duke would be hurt or killed." She found it hard to believe that anyone could willingly be that cruel.

"To Dan, it was, and still is, as if Neal threw every single one of those rocks. He believes that influence is power. Good or bad, the person who uses it is responsible."

"And Duke?"

Tears slipped down Chelle's cheeks unchecked. "He had to be put down."

"I'm so sorry," Sophie said. It was no wonder they hated each other. "Why do they work together?"

Chelle impatiently brushed her cheeks free of tears and hopped off the counter. "Well, there's only so much work to be had on the Cape, so we can't be overly picky. And the publicity of working with Blue Water Construction doesn't hurt. As for Neal, he really didn't have a choice. Philip Bishop was clear when he hired Blue Water that he wanted us as part of the renovation team, or he'd find someone else to manage the project."

"How do they manage?" She wiped her eyes with the collar of her T-shirt.

"They stay out of each other's way," Chelle said simply. With a nod, she headed off to the make-shift office in the front of the house.

The finality of her statement ended any dreams Sophie might have had about pleasant working conditions. She hadn't been in the same room as Dan and Neal when they were together, but she knew that the atmosphere would be strained. There was no way that she saw the rift between them could be mended. Let them fight it out and leave her out of it. She had enough problems getting along with her own sister. She collected Aesop by luring him with the promise of doggie treats and headed off to the library to dig into the archives.

Sophie gripped the steering wheel and found she was holding her breath the way she did inside tunnels. The dense woods in front of her approached and sealed off the lighthouse and the sweeping views of the ocean behind her. The damp heaviness of the air made it difficult to breathe, but she refused to give into the sensation. Instead, she imagined the sun and wind moving over the unseen marsh grass, their fine green edges whispering welcome and escorting travelers into the village of Pocasset.

When she finally turned the corner from the woods onto the open road, Aesop gave a happy bark from the passenger's seat, craned his head out the window, and let the wind flap his ears.

"Whew, me too." She flexed her stiff fingers. "There's something super-creepy about that bit of road, but nothing you couldn't handle. Right, tough guy?" She reached over to pat Aesop's back, and he answered with two sharp barks.

The smell of Dan's coffee had set her stomach rumbling, and she knew she'd better get breakfast before hitting the library. The more she considered what Dan had said the more it seemed unlikely that her research would go anywhere. She shrugged. It didn't matter; she knew she'd feel better after looking into it.

Instead of stopping by *Gladys' Diner* where she might get caught chatting, she chose *Johnson's Bakery*. It was the most convenient place for food, located at the opposite end of Main Street and closer to the library. A lanky blond youth wearing a nametag announcing *"Hi, I'm Zach"* waited on her. She selected a coffee cake muffin for herself and a few of the bakery's doggie biscuits shaped like hissing cats for Aesop.

The clerk smiled as he slid the biscuits into a bag. "The owner's got a strange sense of humor." He gestured with the filled bag. "He figures it's the only way a dog can come out on top." When she looked confused, Zach leaned over the counter and confided, "To be honest, the shape of the biscuit depends on who Mr. Johnson's fighting with that week. Sometimes it's the mailman. This week it's Edie Jean's cat because he split open Hannah's lip. She's old man Johnson's black lab." Zach scooped up the money she had laid on the counter. "One time, there was even one that looked an awful lot like John Munsford, the town administrator, frizzy hair and all."

"That can't help community ties any." Sophie peeled the paper off the muffin and took a healthy bite of the crispy sugar topping.

"You got that right, but it's hard for anyone to prove it's meant for them. Like with Mr. Munsford. When he complained at a town meeting, old man Johnson told him, 'Now John, where'd you get the idea that frizzy-haired, dough-bellied, bowl-legged biscuit is meant to be you?' All Mr. Munsford could do was stutter. Then Mr. Johnson says, 'But you're right. It *is* enough to put a dog off his chow. I'll tell the baker to come up with something else.' We had a month of different versions of the same guy." He chuckled at the memory. "People came in just to see what the doggie biscuit shape would be that week."

She smiled. "Must have been good for business."

"Oh, yeah. We moved a lot of dog biscuits that month and folks would pick up something for themselves too."

"I'll be sure to be nice to both Hannah and Mr. Johnson."

"Good idea. Although you'd be much better on a biscuit than Mrs. P." He winked. "Now there were some ugly biscuits."

She waved to Zach and made her way back to her car parked in the shade of an enormous maple and found Aesop settled in the driver's seat waiting for her. It was funny, but the ride over and that silly conversation with Zach had restored her balance. Really, she asked herself as she walked the village street lined with small shops, what difference could it possibly make if Mrs. Alden met with a nasty end hundreds of years ago? You can't change what happened. If there was a crime, the people responsible are long gone and beyond the reach of the law.

She let Aesop out of the car and walked him over to the library gazebo. After settling him with his toy squirrel, two biscuits and some water, she headed to the main entrance of the library armed with a notebook and pencil.

Sophie savored the moment as she first pulled open the front door of the library—the scent of ink and paper surrounding her and making her feel at home. That sense of home was why she loved all libraries. She enjoyed the modern ones with all the bells and whistles but had a soft spot for the historic with their carved portals and creaking stairs. Who knew what she'd find here? It didn't seem exceptionally large from its saltbox front, so she didn't think that much would come from the visit if she needed more advanced research. If she was lucky, what she needed might be found right in the stacks.

A small entryway led her to the circulation desk where she found a comfortable mix of colonial architecture and what appeared to be good computer support. She wandered past the vacant circulation desk and headed toward the back of the building. She paused at a passageway to an adjoining structure where a back wall should have been. The addition was obviously new and three times the size of the original saltbox colonial.

"Geez, Louise," she breathed as she paused in the doorway of the large central room. The walls were lined with books from floor to ceiling. "This is unbelievable." She moved aside to let a brown-haired woman, jostling an armful of books pass.

"Glad you like it." The woman stopped and beamed with pride. "Sophie, right? Di said you might be swinging by. I'm Babs."

In her stone cargo pants, faded cotton top, and hiking shoes, Babs was different than all the librarians Sophie had ever known. She was too tanned, energetic, and appeared unable to speak softly—something that seemed required in every other library Sophie had ever entered. Babs seemed more likely to be leading a safari and shouting directions to porters than reshelving books. She certainly would have the stamina for trekking, if the stack of books she was lugging around was any measure.

Sophie looked around appreciatively. "You're lucky."

"Don't I know it," Babs said with feeling and glanced about her for a place to set down the books. "Di said you were interested in The Point. What kind of things were you looking for?"

"To start with, I'd love some information on the lighthouse and the Aldens." She opened her notebook and flipped to a clean page. "And I was also curious if you had any information on hurricane activity in the area."

"The first is easy enough and a matter of public record. There aren't any more Aldens in the area, though. At least, not anyone who would want to advertise the connection. Nehemiah may not have produced any legitimate heirs, but the existence of illegitimate ones is open for debate."

Sophie raised a questioning brow, but Babs had already moved across the large room, pausing to drop her books on a rolling cart. "The second depends on how far back you want to go."

Sophie crossed the floor to follow but paused in the middle of the room. "I can't get over how big the library is. It looks much smaller from the outside."

"We serve the surrounding villages as well, so we have more resources than some." Babs moved down the shelves scanning titles. "How far back do you want to go?"

"To the first recorded inhabitants of Alden Point, I guess." She came to stand beside Babs. She knew the Aldens had lived there in the seventeen hundreds, but it wouldn't hurt to know who had come before them.

"Well, the earliest inhabitant would have been Abigail Alden's father, Captain John Hart, in the late sixteen hundreds." Babs pulled a volume entitled *New England Chronicle 1715-1731*. "This will give you news from papers during the end of the Aldens' tenancy at the point. There are no records before that."

"Then how'd you know about John Hart?" She glanced up from the volume she'd opened.

"Keeping journals at the time was quite popular. Even if the person you're interested in didn't keep one, it's likely that someone else in the village did and wrote about them. You just need to hunt for it." Babs ran a finger across some book spines, didn't find what she was looking for, and moved on to another section. "In John's case, he's mentioned in

Nehemiah Alden's journals, but you could always ask Carol. She's the current keeper of local lore."

Sophie nodded. "So, she's a historian."

"No," Babs said, without a trace of humor, "more of a white witch, if you will."

"A Witch? Is there much of that kind of thing around here?" She meant it to be a casual question, but it came out rather nervously.

A burst of laughter escaped Babs. "I'm just kidding." Her eyes shone with humor. "Honey, you should see your face."

Sophie managed a weak smile. "A witch of any kind is not normal where I come from."

"We have our fair share." Babs climbed a ladder to scan some more titles, then added, "But Carol's more of a natural healer. Her family's lived here for as far back as people can remember, and they're instinctive story collectors."

"So, she might know something the others didn't record in their journals?"

"It's possible. Here." Babs found the section she had been looking for and passed Sophie one leather-bound volume with frayed edges after the other. "This will give you records of births, deaths, and marriages. And these others are the historical events from colonial times to 1976."

"Would there be records of hurricanes in here?"

"No, unfortunately the colonists didn't track weather patterns the way NOAA does now. They focused on reading the environment for clues to predict plantings, harvest, or maritime travel, not to chart patterns of past weather events."

"That's too bad." She had hoped to confirm a storm had occurred around the time Mrs. Alden had disappeared. Now it seemed impossible to ever know.

"Cheer up." Babs clambered down the ladder. "We still have one more place to check—upstairs in the journal archives."

"Really?" Sophie shifted the pile of books in her arms and searched the ceiling hopefully, as if she could see into the room above. "Why would people have recorded the weather?"

"Pocasset was, and still is, very much tied to the sea. Quite a few old salts retired here and continued to keep records by the fireside. Besides village comings and goings, they recorded the weather."

"So, their families donated the journals to the library?"

"Some do. Others are found when walls, floors, or attics are remodeled. In fact," Babs snapped her fingers, "I've got a box downstairs Dan Robbins dropped off just the other day from a job at *The White Horse Tavern.*" She eyed Sophie speculatively. "You know, we don't get too many college professors in here. Maybe you could go through the box and catalogue what you find for me." Babs was clearly not above wrangling for some free help.

Sophie recognized a set-up when she saw one but couldn't resist the temptation of being the first to see the old journals.

"Time period seems to coincide with the early to mid-seventeen hundreds," Babs added to sweeten the pot.

She gauged the time needed to read the journals before school started next week. Maybe they weren't too long, and she'd find something to clear this whole question up. And who knew? She just might find material to develop into a professional paper, a true goldmine in her *publish or perish* academic world. "I'll do it."

"Come on upstairs and we'll settle you at a table. If you run out of time, you can take the journals Dan found home."

"Deal. '*Lay on, Macduff, And damn'd be him that first cries, Hold, enough.*'"

"*Macbeth*!" Babs raised a fist in celebration. "And properly quoted too."

As she climbed the narrow staircase behind Babs, Sophie wondered where the famous portrait of Nehemiah Alden was hung. She expected that any painting of a prominent village ancestor would be displayed front and center, but she hadn't seen any portraits yet. When she asked about it, Babs looked sheepish.

"Well, it was on loan to the Museum of Fine Arts in Boston for an extended period of time, and the thing is," Babs cleared her throat, "there was some disagreement about where to hang the painting when it was returned." As she walked, Babs dug in her pocket and brought out a handful of butterscotch candies and offered Sophie one.

"No, thanks." Sophie said, and thought there might be something else to this story. Why did it matter where the portrait was hung. "Who disagreed?"

"Tom Reed. Frank Morgan. Some of the others." Babs peeled off the gold cellophane wrapper, then popped the hard candy into her mouth where it clacked it against her teeth. "Said he wasn't much of a forefather and shouldn't be up on a wall looking over the village."

"Where did they want him?" She didn't understand what difference it would make where they hung the painting.

"Tom suggested giving the portrait to the state library or capitol building. He felt it would serve Alden right to hang in some political nobody's office. And Frank believed the portrait was plain bad luck and wanted me to burn it outright."

"But, it's a portrait." She searched Babs' face for some sign she was joking and found none.

"Uh-huh, a portrait with a lot of baggage. Even without the belief that he had something to do with his wife's disappearance, he cheated and exploited a lot of people around here."

"Their ancestors, you mean."

"They don't see it that way." Babs stopped by a long table and leaned against it, crossing her arms. "Eventually the town manager stepped in and demanded the portrait be hung in the library."

"And what do you think?"

"At first I agreed that they were over-reacting, but, then again, my people weren't colonists," Babs explained. "Although, I have to say the more I've read and researched, I think he's in the right place . . . a little-used hallway that faces the woods."

"And that satisfied everyone?"

"The town manager, Mr. Munsford, was furious. It's one of the few remaining paintings completed by Thomas Smith, the colonial portrait-ist, and quite valuable. He gave us a hard time for a while but buckled under public pressure."

"Oh, gosh," Sophie said, connecting the dots. "The dog biscuits."

"Right." Babs chuckled. "Andrew Johnson can be a pain in the neck, but it worked to the village's advantage that time."

Now Sophie was curious. "What had Alden done to the Johnsons?"

"He bought the loan on the Johnson farm, knowing they were strapped for cash. They'd almost paid it off when Johnson the Elder died." Babs grimaced. "Alden didn't miss his chance to collect and evicted the family."

"What did the family do?"

Babs lifted a shoulder. "What could they do? Legally, he had every right. So, Anne, the widow, moved the family into town and started bak-ing to support the family."

"Hence," Sophie said, "Johnson's Bakery."

"Right, but it took them generations to recuperate from the loss, and to be honest, I don't know if they ever really did. Folks born to be farmers shouldn't be bakers. Most of the people in the village have similar stories of their dealings with Nehemiah." Babs nodded in the direction of the hallway. "If you ever want to see the portrait, it's down that corridor to the left."

It was tempting, but the stack of books in her arms would take a while to plow through and Aesop was tied outside. "I'll pass for now and get to work on these books." She dumped them on the table beside Babs and plopped into a chair.

"Sure thing. Let me know if you need anything." Babs excused herself and headed back downstairs humming.

For a good hour, she slogged through record after record hunting for a mention of Nehemiah Alden. She entertained herself with colonial names that would have been right at home in an Arthur Miller play. There were names like Edward Toothacker and Deliverance Wordwell—one sounded like a real fun-buster and the other too good to be true. But who knew, assumptions could be misleading. Look at Neal Martin. Pretty average name that didn't bring anything to mind, but he'd turned out to be an intolerant rat and, if Chelle was to be trusted, downright vicious. And she did trust her. She was uncomfortable just being in the same room with the man.

Ten minutes later, she found what she'd been looking for: the marriage record of one Nehemiah Alden, age thirty-nine, to an Abigail Hart, age fifteen. Even though she knew women in the colonial period married very young, she felt a pang for Abigail marrying someone twenty-four years her senior. The age difference wouldn't have been as remarkable if Alden had been a different kind of person, but from what she had gathered from Babs and the others, he seemed an unusually hard man.

No recorded births were listed for the couple—nor was there a death certificate for Abigail, which was not surprising because of her disappearance. There was one for Alden, though, dated November 23, 1749. At 73 years old, the scoundrel had lived a remarkably long time, given the period.

In the journals, she found careful accounts detailing the financial side of maintaining a house in the 1700's. There were also pages filled with poetry on loss and faith and still others that read like gossip columns. In these last ones, the names of the villagers had been protected using initials. One entry read, *"D.K. received the Lord's swift punishment in the form of a painful and spreading rash for neglecting his chores and espying in E.C.'s window while she was unclothed."* Another stated, *"M.P. ground corn for N.A. returning to him two-thirds of the harvest and retaining the remaining third for himself. As punishment the pastor has taxed him with good works."* The situations, as well as the participants, must have been common knowledge at the time, and the efforts of the author to protect his neighbors' reputations were suspicious at best. Some fireside journals commented on the weather, but none matched the period she needed.

Sophie glanced at the clock and was surprised to see that another hour had passed. She sprang down the stairs to check on Aesop and found him snoozing in the sun. When she was unable to coax him into a game of fetch, she replenished his water and headed back to the library for one last bit of research. Over the next half hour, she plowed through the rest of the books until only one was left. She pulled it in front of her and sighed. She had set it aside, believing it dealt with political issues, but the *New England Chronicle* read like a current day newspaper. It reported on business dealings, assemblies, and local events of the time. A bi-weekly publication, it gave her less ground to cover. She focused on the year Abigail Alden had disappeared and thumbed through the entries of 1718.

The notice was so small she almost missed it. *Discovery of destructive fire at Alden Point delayed by storm.* "Oh, no." She saw her hands were shaking. She hadn't thought to focus on the fire and loss of property that would have interested the village, even more than the disappearance of one woman. The rest of the information was thin but supplied the confirmation she'd wanted. *"The fire is believed to have occurred prior to the hurricane which made land fall the evening of October 15, 1718."*

There *was* a storm on the night of the fire. She'd never honestly believed that she could confirm it. The part that was missing now was Abigail's whereabouts. The short piece did not give any more details, and though she scoured the following weeks well into 1719, there was no mention of Abigail's disappearance.

She sank back into her chair and gazed blindly into the forest beyond the far window. Was it worse to have confirmed part of her dream? Maybe not. At least she could trust her instincts—to a certain extent, that is. She still didn't know what had happened to Abigail. As Dan had pointed out earlier, it could all be coincidence. She shoved away from the table and stood. She couldn't wait to tell Dan but took the time to separate the books into neat piles before she headed for the stairs.

Just as her foot was about to hit the top step, Sophie swung instead toward the narrow hallway. It was time to see the portrait of this village ancestor the townspeople hated so much. She pursed her lips as she walked and looked about her. Babs was the queen of the understatement. Dust covered boxes, old catering racks, and discarded posters cluttered the walls on either side of the portrait. The space was downright neglected when compared to the rest of the tidy library that gleamed with oiled wood.

Sophie moved toward the heavy frame and had to stand against the facing window, her head tilted back at an uncomfortable angle to see. The portrait was an excellent example of early colonial art. If Thomas Smith's work was accurate, Nehemiah Alden had been gorgeous. The beauty of his face startled. The soft blue eyes, silvery blond hair, and sharp features reminded her of an angel. Not the cherubic kind, but an avenger, sword in hand. Smith's eerie use of light and shadow made it appear that Nehemiah could climb out of the mottled black background and into the hallway anytime he chose. Goosebumps rose on her arms as she imagined him doing just that.

"Lucifer was beautiful too," said a familiar voice.

Sophie slapped her hand to her heart. "Geez, Frank. You scared the daylights out of me. Where'd you come from?"

"Door to the end of the corridor leads to storage." He added with a sly smile, "I guess you didn't hear me." He was silent for a moment, then nodded to the portrait. "Lucifer, the most beloved, deceitful, devious, and proud of all the angels. He received his just punishment from God. Alden never did."

She spoke more harshly than she meant, "So what did Alden do to your family?"

"The villain always wanted The Point." Frank motioned out the window toward the lighthouse, jutting above the trees in the distance. "Stole my uncle's girl to get it and broke his heart."

"He forced Abigail to marry him to get The Point?"

"Must have done. That girl was in love with William Morgan—they were going to get married as soon as he returned from that voyage with her father." He nodded. "And everyone knew she was afraid of her cousin."

"Her cousin?" She felt her stomach sink. This was the first time she'd heard of a family connection, and it made the marriage all that much worse.

"Alden was a distant cousin on her mother's side." His lips thinned in distaste. "Abigail's mother married below her when she married John Hart, but at least it was a love match. Nobody could say the same about Abigail and Nehemiah."

"It was so long ago . . . how do you know this?" She glanced uneasily from the composed portrait to Frank's face twisted with bitterness.

"Family stories. Darn near killed Will to come home and find his sweetheart married to that viper. Wouldn't even explain why she'd done it. Alden had a part in that, I'm sure."

"You can't know that. Your family might have bent the story to favor your great, however many times removed, uncle." She didn't know why she was arguing but couldn't stop. "Families do that."

"I know it in my bones." Frank jutted his jaw. "The fault lies squarely on Alden's shoulders."

Sophie raised her hands in surrender. "Okay, I believe you." It was better to agree and just get away from him.

"Serves him right to look at something he could never really have." He gestured to the lighthouse again.

She frowned. "What do you mean? You said he married her to get hold of The Point."

"Yeah, he did." Frank gave a stiff nod. "But he only lived there for six months, then left her and got a place in town."

That didn't make sense at all. If Frank was right, why would Alden steal Abigail away from Will Morgan, and then leave her and The Point behind? "So, he wasn't living there when it burned?"

"No." He seemed to delight in Alden's failure. "Story goes he lived alone in town before The Point burned."

"Abigail was alone." Slowly, she let the possibilities filter through her mind.

"Abigail was always alone. Between waiting for her father to return from the sea and then Will, she spent most of her life alone and waiting." There was a strange note of pity in his voice.

Alone and isolated. Alden could have been the watcher in the woods. He could have set fire to the house to burn her out or kill her. Sophie shivered. Maybe Frank wasn't that far off the mark after all. Wedged between the two of them, she wasn't sure who was more disturbing. "I . . . I need to get my dog," she said, sliding past him to track down Babs on the first floor.

When Sophie shared with Babs what she'd learned about the fire and storm, Babs tried to give her Alden's writing as well as the other journals she'd promised. The idea of holding something personal of Alden's made her skin crawl. She was saved from making up an excuse by frantic barking from outside. She grabbed the box of journals and hurried out the door.

She imagined the worst when the barking turned into pitiful howls. She fully expected to see Aesop in a tussle with Edie Jean's cat but found him instead twisted in a forsythia bush with only two inches of leash left. After unwinding him, she stopped by the Mini-Mart for a ready-made sandwich and coffee to go.

As she pointed the car back toward Alden Light, she realized that she'd learned more than she'd hoped. It helped, in a way, to know her instincts had been right, but she hadn't found out anything about the watcher. Alden would have had the opportunity to sneak back to The Point and set the fire. But for what reason? It sounded like he'd been a cheat and a swindler, but had he been capable of burning his wife alive? Her fingers tensed on the steering wheel. The woods she passed were even more oppressive than before; it seemed her suspicions had soaked into the very branches of the trees, breathing life into what lingered there. She didn't know what she'd woken, but it felt dark and watchful. Something had waited a long time for someone to open that door, and she had unwittingly obliged. She gripped the wheel tighter and punched the gas, driving faster than was wise in her eagerness to get to the lighthouse.

3

The Cache

After Sophie bounced her way up the lane to the lighthouse, she found her parking spot taken by a large, battered dumpster. At regular stretches of time, workers appeared at a window and tossed horsehair plaster and broken laths out to the dumpster with a thunk of crumbling gypsum. Large clouds of dust billowed out of the debris and coated the grass in a fine white film. She parked at the base of the drive next to Neal's SUV. When she saw he wasn't anywhere outside, she sent Aesop off to chase squirrels in the woods.

The amount of noise and dust was a revelation. They had to be kidding. Construction noise was one thing, but the blaring music made it hard to hear herself think. How was she supposed to get anything done? When she caught sight of a familiar figure studying blueprints on the hood of a pick-up truck, she marched over. "This is insane," she yelled at Dan over the radio. "How long is this going to last?"

He turned down the radio he'd been using as a weight to keep the blueprints in place. "Hey, Professor, you're back early."

"Good grief." She rubbed her ears to quiet the ringing. "Your music's even louder than the demolition. How long is this going to last?"

Dan pulled a sheet out from the middle of the stack and smoothed it with his hands. "We're almost done with the demo. Rebuilding won't make as much noise."

"And the music?" She swatted at a cloud of plaster drifting past, attempting to keep it from filling her nose and covering her from head to toe.

"We'll keep it down while you're around." His fingers traced specifications on the paper. "We're taking advantage of the empty house to make some noise. We usually can't get away with it in town."

"I can't imagine why," she muttered. "Where's Neal?" she asked, scanning the bluff. It was hard to believe he hadn't put an end to the noise.

He shrugged absently. "He's around here somewhere."

She knew he was busy, but she had spent most the morning alone, slogging through the past, and was eager to talk to someone in the present. Frank certainly hadn't counted. The man seemed firmly anchored in ancient history. "What are you working on today?"

Dan sighed, resigning himself to her questions. "Well, we've already cut a hole in the floor to replace the old captain's cache, and the guys are in the process of ripping out the plaster walls." He nodded in satisfaction. "We're making good progress and will likely start rebuilding tomorrow or the day after when the HVAC guys are done."

Her pulse quickened. "You found the old cache? Was it empty?"

"Finding it wasn't a problem. Alden left good notes about all the rooms." He shrugged. "All I had to do was read them."

"Did you find anything?" she prompted. Geez, it was hard getting information out of him.

"Naw, unless someone buried something, the place was empty except for bugs and dust." He appeared to enjoy stringing her along. "What did you think we'd find?"

"Oh, I don't know." She was surprisingly deflated. "Babs gave me the journals you found at The White Horse. Anything like that would have been great."

"Bull. I *know* what you were hoping for." He folded his arms and leaned against the truck, a slow grin spreading across his face.

Sophie wrinkled her nose. "Alright, so I was hoping for a bit of pirate treasure," she admitted. "I bet you were too."

"You know it." He nodded. "Even though the chances were slim to none." He quickly rolled up the blueprints, leaving uneven edges on either end of the roll.

Dan might have come up empty here, but she'd had a different kind of success in town. "I found something at the library."

"Is that so?" he murmured, as he slid the blueprints into the tube and patted the uneven edges flush.

Dan's lack of interest was clear, and she suddenly suspected that he might have sent her off to the library as much to get her out of the way as to reassure her. "There *was* a hurricane on the night of the fire," Sophie said. For some reason it was important that he took her seriously. "And I almost missed it because I was looking for some mention of Abigail's disappearance."

"And this tells you what, exactly?" He pulled a white plastic cover from the pocket of his jeans and pressed it onto the end of the tube.

"Just that I had a curiously accurate dream about The Point. It doesn't tell me anything about Abigail or the watcher in the woods." She resented he'd think she would jump to conclusions, but after this morning she could see where he might.

He seemed relieved. "Glad to hear it. Wouldn't want you going off half-cocked and getting the whole town riled up for nothing."

She gritted her teeth. "I don't do *anything* half-cocked."

He gave a non-committal grunt, shut off the radio, and placed it in the bed of the pickup truck. "Just stay out of the cache and the construction area. A lot of that stuff still isn't safe." He tucked the tube under his arm and turned for the lighthouse. "Hey, why don't you go walk the beach?" he called over his shoulder. "There's a small trail that's not too steep just past those roses. I can give you a shout when we clear out."

She felt she was being dismissed, but the idea of a walk along the ocean appealed after hunching over books all day. It would certainly keep her out of Neal's way. The less she saw of him the better. She whistled for Aesop and grabbed her bag lunch. When he bounded from the woods, she walked the trailhead on the bluff with him trailing behind her.

As she picked her way carefully down loose gravel, she felt the clock turn back with every step toward the water. Past the crimson hips of seaside roses, the shifting dunes and shell-strewn beach drew her to a time when women watched the horizon for sails, waiting for their men to return—knowing they never might.

She selected smooth gray rocks and mussel shells off the beach, brushing the sticky sand free before tucking them into her pockets. When Aesop raced off to chase gulls, she sat in the sand and kicked off her sandals.

The breaking and receding waves were hypnotic. Their curl and ebb lulling her into a place of quiet being. She closed her eyes and felt the sun on her skin, warming her, bone-deep. Her mind drifted and she wondered if Abigail had come here to wait for her father and William Morgan, day after day, hoping they would return to her soon. *As gleeful as little boys setting off on an adventure, leaving their womenfolk behind to worry and wonder. Alone. A child growing inside her with no one to share the joy, and anticipation, and yes, with whom to share the fear. She didn't dare tell, not yet, and not to HIM. What could she do? What did she know of birthing or infants? Adrift, she clung to the knowledge that when this child came it would be so loved, and she would never, ever, be alone again.*

Sophie scrambled to her feet, tears streaming down her face. "No," she gasped, one hand at her throat, the other cradling her belly. "It's not you. There is no one, no baby. Knock it off."

She struggled to stay standing, but she was too lightheaded. The weight of the sorrow drove her to her knees. She fought for control, but she was too far gone for that. "Forget it," she said and dropped onto her side, letting the misery roll through her. Sand pressed into her cheek and scattered before her lips as she exhaled in gusty sobs. She grieved without restraint until her throat was raw, and a shadow fell across her.

"Are you alright?" asked a woman's voice.

She turned her head and saw Chelle crouch beside her, unsure of her welcome.

"Are you okay?" Chelle repeated and searched the beach. "Where's Aesop?"

"Chasing gulls." Sophie hiccupped, then wiped her eyes. "I'm fine. I think."

"What happened?"

"I don't know." Sophie shifted so that she was sitting and tried to compose herself.

"Come on, something must have happened. You were crying as if you'd lost your best friend."

How was she supposed to explain the tearing pain and loss to someone else, when she didn't understand it herself? "It was nothing."

"Hmm," Chelle said, not believing a word of it. "Maybe you'd feel better if you told me what that 'nothing' was."

Sophie sighed and hung her head. It was clear Chelle wasn't going to give up without some kind of answer, and she was in no shape to make up a believable explanation. "I was just lying here in the sun. Then the next thing I know, I'm waiting for a man and excited and terrified about having a baby. The feeling cut—no, tore through me. I couldn't stop it."

Chelle whistled softly. "And there's no guy? No baby?"

"Of course not." She sat up straighter and flushed. She felt ridiculous being caught like this, and by someone she had just met. "I avoid those kinds of things like the plague."

"Maybe you were in synch with one of our Point spirits." Chelle spoke as if it made all the sense in the world.

"There's no spirit, Chelle." Sophie was exhausted. "Just me and the sea and a whopping case of loneliness."

"No, seriously. Carol calls them emotional energy footprints or something like that. Supposedly, really intense experiences can leave a mark on a place, like fear or desperation. Emotionally open people pick up on it."

"I'm picking up on the feelings of dead people?"

"Sort of, I guess." Chelle shrugged as if she didn't really understand it herself. "You're picking up on the energy those feelings make. You know, like how when you're sad you're really tired or energetic when you're happy."

"Okay." She stretched out the word and wondered who was crazier, her or Chelle.

Chelle took a breath and seemed to consider before trying again. "Haven't you heard of people who visit places like Auschwitz or Ground Zero passing out from the strain—the emotional and physical strain, of being where so many people suffered?"

This, at least, was something she had heard of. "Of course, the impact of being there must be devastating."

"No." Chelle gave a sharp, impatient shake of her head. "Those people feel what those victims felt. Some of them even hear them speaking or hear their thoughts—like I'm guessing you did."

Sophie struggled past the lump in her throat. "You make it sound so logical."

"I guess I can relate. I hear them every now and then. Really scared me at first until I talked to Carol. The energy footprint thing makes sense to me."

Sophie shivered and wrapped her arms around herself. "How do you put up with it, living here all the time?"

"It's not always bad." Chelle smiled as though remembering. "Sometimes they're good feelings. Most people just don't notice because it's not as jarring as the bad."

"I'd rather not notice at all."

"I get it." Chelle lifted a shoulder. "But people who are sensitive just feel. They can't control it."

"Super." As if she needed to know how terrible the past had been. She was having a hard time just managing her own future. She stood and brushed off her shorts. "What're you doing here, anyways?"

"I stopped by to see Dan and he said you were taking a walk. I wanted to check in and see how you were." Chelle straightened as Aesop ran toward them. "There he is. He's probably been up to no good."

The "no good" had matted his fur in pointy spikes and smelled like rotten fish. "Geez, you stink!" Sophie slapped her hand over her nose and mouth. "Don't jump!" came the muffled cry as she frantically tried to keep him from rubbing it all over her.

"He must've found some washed-up fish." Chelle's eyes watered as she approached Aesop and looped her belt through his collar.

"What are you doing?" She couldn't get far enough away from Aesop and here was Chelle tying herself to him.

"You're real proud of yourself, aren't you fella?" Chelle dragged Aesop toward the sea with her belt. She motioned to Sophie. "A little help here?"

"Oh, right. Sure." She reluctantly edged forward and grabbed the other side of Aesop's collar.

"He can't go racing through the lighthouse like this." Chelle turned her head to one side so that she'd inhale less of the smell. "We'll dunk him here first and you can drag him inside for a scrubbing after."

Aesop splayed his paws and refused to budge. It took all their strength to drag him into the water and rub the stiff fur clean. By the time they were satisfied he smelled less ripe, both women were drenched and distinctly fishy. They staggered up the bluff to the lighthouse, finally releasing him from Chelle's belt when they saw that Neal had gone. Aesop wasted no time and raced off for the woods, disappearing into the undergrowth with a leap.

Sophie pushed her bedraggled hair off her face and sighed. "I'll chase him down later. I could really use something to drink first."

Chelle patted her on the shoulder. "Follow me. I know just the thing you need."

They skirted the construction and walked down the hall to find a makeshift food area in what used to be the kitchen. A toaster, microwave, and dorm room refrigerator crowded the narrow counter, but to Sophie a gourmet kitchen wouldn't have been more appreciated. "This is fantastic." she said, seeing an end of the steady stream of cold sandwiches that had made up her diet for the last week.

"We try to set up a small convenience area at each job site." Chelle opened the door to the small refrigerator and selected two cold sodas, popping open the tabs. She passed one to Sophie. "It keeps the guys from having to race to the village for lunch."

"You're welcome to use it," Dan said from the doorway, then scrunched his nose. "What's that awful smell?"

Chelle gave her short hair a toss. "Eau de Dog over a paste of sun-ripened fish."

"You need a shower . . . you both need a shower," he amended, taking in their wet and stained clothes. He paused, then frowned. "And Sophie's been crying. What happened? Did Neal hassle you?" Dan stalked over to peer into her face.

When she shrank back, Chelle elbowed him aside. "Take it easy."

"Look, if he thinks I'm just going to let him hassle whoever he feels like, he's got another thing coming."

"You don't even know what happened and you're out for blood. What's up?" Chelle demanded.

He jammed his fists on his hips. "I'll put up with his crap to get this project done, but there's no way I'll let him micromanage my crew or brow-beat her." He stabbed a finger at Sophie who watched him warily. "Can you believe I caught him trying to tell my crew what to do?"

"Relax," Chelle said, giving his arm a squeeze before she boosted herself onto the counter for a seat. "Your crew is too good not to check with you before changing plans, and this," she gestured between herself and Sophie, "has nothing to do with Neal." She took a sip of her soda. "Sophie picked up on one of Alden Point's past ancestors. It spooked her."

"That's all we need." He glared at them as if they were responsible for causing the past to resurface. "Which one?" he demanded.

"I have no idea." Sophie clutched her soda. "The whole idea of tuning into someone else's emotions or experiences is too bizarre."

"Who was it?" Dan demanded.

"How would I know?" Sophie shrugged nervously. "I'm not from around here."

"You might not recognize them, but Chelle might. Could you describe what you felt?" he asked with exaggerated patience.

She had finally had enough. "A woman, waiting for a man," she snapped. "She was pregnant, scared, and lonely. What difference does it make?"

"Sound familiar?" He turned to Chelle.

"I've never heard of that one before." Chelle shrugged. "It could be any number of women who were waiting for someone to return from the sea. The situation, heaven knows, wasn't unique. How about you?"

For all his pushing, Dan appeared uncomfortable talking about his own experiences. "I just sense the men."

"You hear them too?" Sophie asked in disbelief. "Does everyone around here?"

"Not all, but some of us do." He roughly scrubbed his face, then dropped his hands. "Sorry I lost it." He took a breath, tried for an easy smile and failed. "About the beach, you'll see that those experiences don't happen all that often and can't hurt you."

Sophie knew she must look as skeptical as she felt. She didn't know what he was talking about. It did hurt, feeling that girl's desperate hope, longing, and fear. "I wish they wouldn't happen at all."

"I hear you there." Dan stretched his neck to the side, trying to relax tense muscles. "But Chelle will tell you nothing ever really comes from them but an emotional ride."

"He's right." Chelle folded her legs beneath her and rested her arms on her lap. "No one has ever mentioned seeing or feeling anything physical."

The knowledge didn't ease her mind any. What had happened down on the beach had been more than unsettling. She deliberately avoided emotional entanglements in her own life. How would she cope with the emotional leftovers of the dead that popped up unwanted? "Well, that helps some, I suppose," she said, not sounding particularly convinced even to her own ears. She tossed her empty can into a trash bag that was tied to the doorknob. "If I want to be able to stand the smell of Aesop, I'd better track him down and get him into a real bath with soap." She inclined her head to Chelle. "Thanks for the rescue . . . both times."

Chelle lifted her can in salute. "No problem."

"Sophie," Dan called, stopping her at the doorway. "Make sure you lock up when you're here." At her surprised expression he continued, "It shouldn't be a problem, but I'd feel better knowing the house is locked when you're alone."

She nodded, wished them both a good evening, and went to search for Aesop's bath supplies. While she rummaged through boxes, she discovered that her fool-proof packing system was hopelessly flawed. By the time she decided just to use her salon shampoo on him, she heard Dan and Chelle drive down the lane toward the village. With a sigh, she gathered up her courage and went to find her dog.

The bath began with howls of outrage and continued with resigned canine grumbling. When he was finally released, Aesop tore through the second floor, racing from room to room. He bounded over her bed and then streaked down the stairs without a backward glance. Sophie looked at the mess around her and shook her head. She used her good towels to mop up the water, then washed the tub down before pouring herself a bath. She added a few drops of the lavender oil she rationed for stressful days to the rising water.

As the water trickled in, she wandered over to the window and watched the sun lower behind the woods. The sun's rays shone through the trees and created individuals out of the whole. Tall wispy pines crowded out arching maples and pin-straight oaks. The woods that Alden had looked on hundreds of years ago and coveted—plotting and scheming to get what belonged to others. And still he stared from a neglected portrait with the face of a crusading angel, gazing out at what others said he never truly possessed. Possession. It was such a cold, ugly word. She cringed as she imagined Nehemiah's unwavering stare reaching across the woods into the room. With a yank and snap of the shade, she closed him out.

Even though it took quite some time for the tub to fill, Sophie was still uneasy when she climbed into the scented water. She splashed water on her face and leaned back and rubbed her temples in gentle circles. So much damage had been done. Alden was the dropped stone in the pond whose poisonous waves continued to ripple out, tearing apart others. Hatred and fear could still taint the lives of the present as they had destroyed those of the past. *Even me. Here I am huddling in the tub to ward off . . . what? The leftover emotions of people long dead?*

The dead were buried and remained so. What did it matter? But she knew as she abandoned the short-lived idea, it did matter. Quite a lot. If she were to disappear, she would want someone to care, to search for her, and to know what had become of her. Jacqueline would look for her despite their differences, she was sure. Had anyone searched for Abigail? The papers of the time made no mention of her disappearance or that anyone had ever investigated. That had been a crime. Abigail had been only seventeen years old and alone. It broke her heart. But what could she do? She flicked at the water with a finger. *Explore. Investigate. Look for Abigail Hart. Someone must have known or suspected something. Read the journals. Of course!* She sat up so suddenly water sloshed over the sides of the tub. Start with the cache, the only original part of the cottage left. Dan had been looking for treasure, but she would look for words. Maybe Abigail had kept a journal—something she could have hidden from Nehemiah. The chances of finding anything were slim, but the cache was the natural place to start.

Sophie heard the rustle of plastic and the sounds of empty cans hitting the floor. She struggled out of the deep tub, grabbed her robe, and dashed down the stairs—leaving puddles in her wake. "Aesop! Get out of the trash!" she shouted. She ran past the living room to the kitchen and flipped on the light. Trash was everywhere, and there was Aesop comfortably settled on the floor eating a discarded sandwich. "Honestly, you're like having a two-year-old."

Aesop licked peanut butter and jelly off his muzzle, his tail brushing the floor in a well-contented arc.

"But I suppose if I'd fed you on time," she sighed, "you wouldn't have gone scavenging."

She really couldn't fault him for his taste in food. She had a soft spot for peanut butter and jelly sandwiches too. They reminded her of her childhood when she and Jacqueline had been closer. They had always giggled uncontrollably when the thick spread had stuck to the roof of their mouths. Her lips curved upwards at the memory, then slowly lowered. It had been a long time since they had done something so homey, and she missed what was once their easy friendship. A wind-driven rain and reckless driver had changed all that when he had killed their parents. With their loss, Jacqueline had found herself, at twenty-three, raising a fourteen-year-old. Neither sister had made it easy. Jacqueline had dealt with the pain by trying to rigidly control everything in her life. Sophie had known there was no point in trying. Love and caution hadn't saved her parents. She had thought it best to protect her poor heart from future pain and found comfort in her books. She knew she had withdrawn, but she couldn't live up to the standards Jacqueline had set. Jacqueline had never forgiven her for not trying.

She pushed away the memory. It was best to focus on the present and clean up this mess. She searched the kitchen for another trash bag and tidied up. She made a mental note to buy peanut butter and jelly the following day along with some other staples.

Her stomach growled reminding her she hadn't eaten either. Aesop may have made a royal mess, but he'd had the right idea. "What do you think, Aesop? Maybe Dan left something I can eat and replace tomorrow?"

Aesop lifted his head from the floor where he napped, looked at her, and settled more comfortably with a contented sigh.

Sophie snorted. "Right. It's not your problem. Your belly's already full."

She stepped over her contented dog to the shopping bags she'd seen shoved onto one end of the counter. Maybe there was something in them that could pass for a meal. There was already a sleeve of crackers on the counter, but it would take more than that to get her through the night. She rummaged through one bag after another until she hit the jackpot. "Yes!" She lifted a can in celebration. Dan had provided all that was needed for a quick meal—some canned goods, disposable dishes, plastic cutlery, and a can opener. She opened a can of tomato soup and lost no time in preparing it.

While she waited for the soup to heat, she dragged a stepstool over to the window to use as a chair, not that there was a lot to see. The slim crescent moon shed little light on the yard and woods beyond the glass. She strained to see out the kitchen window, but she couldn't see much. It felt odd that she was, for all practical purposes, blind. Dan had hung new shades on the second floor, but down here, anyone outside could see in clearly, while she saw only distorted shadows at best.

The microwave dinged and she rose to collect her soup, a plastic spoon, and the crackers she managed to carry by tucking the package under her arm. She resettled on the stepstool and crumbled a few saltines into her bowl, poking the pieces under the rich soup to coat them. It had been a while since her interrupted picnic on the beach. She wasted no time eating the contents of the bowl, scraping the last bits of the tomatoes from the bottom.

She sighed in contentment and sat back to look out the window once again. Only the first few feet of grass was visible in the harsh kitchen light. Beyond those few feet, only darkness met her eyes. She squinted once again, blinked, and thought she saw something move. Just there, on the other side in the shadows. She stood slowly, slid her bowl onto the counter, and strained to see through the night. There it was again. Something moved furtively beyond the edge of the light. She felt the hair stand up on her arms and slapped off the light switch. While the darkness eased and her eyes adjusted, she listened intently. She knew she was locked in and perfectly safe but felt threatened anyways.

There was just enough moonlight for her to make out the shapes she expected and feel her way out of the kitchen. She found Aesop by following his whines. She grabbed his collar and dragged him along with her. "It's okay. Just be quiet," she whispered, making her way down the hall. She quickly passed the living room with its hole in the floor; dark with jagged edges, the hole looked like an open mouth to her. Stop it! she told herself. By the time she reached the bottom of the stairs, she was at a dead run. She pounded up the stairs, flew into her room, and slammed the door shut, locking it behind her.

For a long time, she sat in the middle of her rumpled bed, clutching Aesop like a lifeline, listening for signs that someone had come inside. Every creak had her straining her ears. Was that the back door? The stairs? And she waited, tensed for something that never came. Eventually, Aesop struggled free from her arms and settled at the foot of the bed with a yawn.

He had been a good barometer in the past, where she had used his sense of self-preservation as the measuring stick in unfamiliar surroundings. Earlier he had sounded as distressed as she had felt. There had to have been something to set him off; it couldn't have been only her imagination. Now he was comfortably curled at the foot of the bed, sleeping the sleep of the just. Maybe she had imagined that something had been outside. After all, everything was worse at night. Tomorrow in the light of day was the time to tackle the cache and start the hunt for Abigail Hart. Tomorrow.

She tossed on the bed until she eventually drifted off into a troubled sleep. She dreamed of gaping mouths that screamed but produced no sound and of fire that raged and shattered glass, while a man slowly walked from the tree line, approaching the house that burned but offering no help.

Dense clouds crowded the sky, and the wind flung rain like needles against Sophie's window, waking her from a deep sleep. She tried to decide what time it was by squinting through the gap between the shade and the windowsill. Six o'clock in the morning? Seven? Impossible to tell. Unrelieved gray blanketed the sky and dropped its folds to smother the horizon. She groped for her alarm clock. Seven o'clock. Where was the crew? Dan had said they would be starting by now, "One of the perks," he'd explained with a mischievous smile, "of having the tenant on the payroll."

She wasn't disappointed to have a delay in all that noise, but she had depended on them to wake her up. Things absolutely needed to get done today, starting with shopping for supplies. There was no way she could continue helping herself from the kitchen. She should replace the things she'd already eaten, and then there was the cache she wanted to explore.

Rain drumming on the roof drowned out the roll of waves as they rushed to shore, despite the window she kept slightly open. Occasionally, a wave large enough to overpower the sound of the rain collapsed against the bluff with the sound of thunder. She reluctantly pulled herself away from listening and quickly completed her morning routine. When she rushed downstairs, she came face to face with Dan as he entered the front door.

"Where's the fire?" he asked, peeling off his jacket to reveal a *Brew Master* T-shirt.

"Nice shirt," Sophie stalled. "Do you really brew your own beer?"

"Yeah, a few buddies and I got into it a few years back for kicks." He hung his dripping jacket on the front doorknob. "It turns out we were pretty good at it and have been brewing ever since."

"Neat." She smiled and nodded, all the while scrambling for something else to say.

"Right," he said slowly. "Where are you headed again?"

"I was just going to the kitchen to clean up." She avoided looking at the cache and glanced down the hall to see if last night's meal was visible from where they stood.

Dan looked confused. "From what?"

"I left some stuff out last night, that's all." She wasn't going to tell him how she'd felt and have him laugh at her. She felt silly enough without him teasing her about it. And why was he so talkative this morning? The most she usually got out of him was a non-committal "Is that so?"

"What're you up to?" He cocked his head to the side and considered her carefully.

This wasn't going as she'd planned at all. "What makes you think I'm up to anything?"

"When someone tries so hard to look like they're up to nothing— they're up to something."

She shifted uncomfortably, annoyed he'd made her feel guiltier than she already did. "I kind of borrowed some soup and left a mess."

"Hmm." He looked skeptical. "You 'borrowed' some soup and didn't clean up?"

"Where's the crew?" she asked, hoping to distract him before he put an end to her search before it even began.

He moved past her into his temporary office. "The wind tore the roofing tarp off the Tavern last night and filled the second floor with water. They're trying to get the tarp back on and mop up the mess."

She imagined all the wet insulation and drooping plaster that would need to be removed and cringed. "That's got to be a nightmare."

"Close enough to cause delays here." He shuffled the papers on his desk in frustration.

"What are you looking for?" There had to be something she could do to help and be rid of him sooner rather than later.

"Reinforcements," he said, distracted. "I had a folder here with a bunch of contact numbers." He looked up. "Have you seen it?"

She pointed. "There's a stack on the floor behind you." Although she hadn't wished for a natural disaster, she was relieved she'd have the house to herself to search the cache once he left.

"Great. Thanks." He bent to search the pile, muttering to himself. After flipping through a few folders, he glanced up and asked mildly, "Don't you have stuff to clean?"

"Right. Let me know if there's anything I can do to help." She clapped, calling Aesop to her side. "Come on, Aesop."

She walked toward the kitchen and came to a sudden halt when she saw the floor covered ankle-deep in trash. Her make-shift meal was still on the counter where she had abandoned it, but she couldn't get to it without wading through garbage. As Aesop whined, refusing to enter, she managed to pick her way over to the counter. She knew she'd cleaned up Aesop's mess last night. Could it be rats? She suppressed a shudder. Rodents with their twitchy noses and scrabbling claws—all that gnawing and disease. She picked the trash liner off the floor and found it intact, no tears or gouges. Something was very wrong here. The trash was spread evenly across the floor. All the snack bags had been placed carefully with their labels face-up. There were smoothed bags of potato chips, flattened candy wrappers, and empty cans all facing the entrance like sentinels. No animal was that deliberate. Her eyes flew to the window locks and then the door. They were still locked, but someone had to have been inside. How?

Heart in her throat, she ran back to Dan's office. "Is there another way into this house other than the doors or windows? Like an access door in the turret?"

"No, the turret is barricaded." He looked surprised. "Why?"

She took a breath and plunged in, "Last night I didn't clean up in the kitchen because I felt like someone was watching me. And now there's trash all over the floor."

Dan frowned. "Let's see." He rose from the desk and followed her to the kitchen. He surveyed the organized chaos, then rubbed the back of his neck. "Well, this is weird. I'll pick up a portable alarm system while I'm out and get it installed today."

Sophie twisted her fingers together. Someone had been outside watching her and made it into the house unnoticed. "Who would do something like this?"

"Who knows?" He gestured to the mess. "There's no vandalism. Nothing's missing—maybe it was just a kid doing something on a dare."

No. He was wrong. Someone had made their way in and had taken the time to place the trash like soldiers around the room. There was a meanness to it she didn't like, as though the intruder had said, "See how long I was here, and you didn't know it?"

"So then how did they get in?" she demanded.

He lifted a shoulder. "Maybe you left the door unlocked."

The fact that she'd thought the same thing and had needed to check the locks this morning to be sure, only made her angrier. "I didn't."

"You must have," he said simply. "No one breaks into a house just to place trash around a room. It had to have been open."

She knew she wasn't getting anywhere with him and began to pick up the trash, ramming it into the liner for the second time in twelve hours.

Dan paused at the door where Aesop stood, still refusing to enter the kitchen. "I'm going to check on the crew and pick up that alarm. I'll be back later. What're your plans?"

"I have to go shopping for food and dog stuff."

He bent to scratch Aesop's ears. "How about Aesop rides shotgun with me while you're out shopping?" As the dog leaned into the scratch, Dan smiled. "It's been a long time since I've had company of the furry kind. We might even fit in some fishing if the rain lets up."

"I suppose it would be more fun than waiting for me in the car or hanging out here by himself," she agreed. There was the bonus that it would also keep Aesop out of her way while she explored the cache.

"Good—see you later." Dan turned down the hall and called Aesop after him.

Thankful for the unexpected help, she dashed for her rain jacket and keys. She hoped to get her errands done quickly and search the cache before Dan returned.

An hour and a half later, Sophie slid her key home in the lighthouse door. Who knew running a simple errand could take so long? The errand should have been simple. Pick the thing up and drop it in the basket. She'd been slowed to a crawl, not by the rain, though that hadn't let up a bit, but by advice from elderly villagers. They had swarmed the grocery store in droves, seeking company and a distraction from the weather. "No, no. Not that brand, dear. Jason, slice some Imperial Ham for her that I buy for Mr. Davis." Sophie really didn't care all that much for ham, especially at nine dollars a pound. But she didn't have the heart to disappoint the old woman. When she had asked for four thin slices, Jason had grinned, "sucker" clearly printed on his face. She'd finally escaped with most of the things she'd needed, except for Aesop's dog shampoo. She'd been told she could find that in the *Feeds and Needs* section of Reed's Hardware. What she did find on a display at the check-out counter was an inexpensive flashlight and batteries—it had almost been worth the trip.

She shoved the milk and deli items into the fridge and left the rest of the bags on the counter. Time was running out and she was worried that Dan might return before she could start her search. He would be furious if he caught her exactly where he had told her not to go. She hurried off to hunt the cache for what remained of Abigail Hart.

The rain continued to fall in thick sheets outside the windows, blotting out what light the day provided. When Sophie flicked the flashlight on, the shadows jumped away as she moved the beam from side to side. The walls lit up, stripped to the studs, and she saw the solid hearth with its large medallion coated with dust. When her light settled on the hole in the floor, she winced at the damage done to the old hardwood in accessing the cache. Fine gypsum particles crunched underfoot as she neared the hole with care and crouched beside it. She tried to pierce the darkness with her light, but the outer limits of the cache remained hidden. She pointed the light directly to the bottom of the space and could dimly see a small amount of hard-packed dirt and a few of the foundation stones just to the side. So much for cheap flashlights. This one certainly wasn't worth the price she'd paid for it.

She had to get down there but didn't want to sit on the edge and just drop into the hole. How would she get back out? She didn't even know how deep it was. She stretched out onto her belly, wriggled to the very edge of the opening, and allowed herself to hang from the waist into the blackness. No matter where she swung her light, it broke the darkness and was absorbed. It was like being hung upside-down in a black velvet bag, soft but impenetrable. The hole seemed to absorb light and air like a vacuum. When light-headedness overcame her, she flopped onto her back at the edge of the cache and forced herself to breathe normally. This wasn't going to work. She needed equipment.

As she lay there, catching her breath, she remembered the six-foot folding ladder and rope that Dan kept stored in his office. She scrambled to her feet, staggering a bit until her head cleared.

She dragged the equipment across the hall and tied one end of the rope to a cast-iron radiator and the other to the top of the ladder. She carefully lowered it into the cache, watching it disappear rung by rung into the space. Four. Five. Six feet deep, exactly. Good thing she hadn't just dropped down into the hole. She wouldn't have made it out on her own. She eyed the ladder warily and decided to keep it tied to the radiator, just in case. The last thing she needed was to knock it over and be unable to lift it out when she was done. She flipped the back legs of the ladder open and rocked it side-to-side to make sure it was steady. Shifting her weight onto the top step, she backed into the hole, flashlight trained on the cache floor.

As Sophie slowly descended, the smell of acrid earth became stronger, the dirt lifting in small puffs as she stepped off the ladder and onto the floor. Nothing could survive here. She clutched the ladder with one hand and made the first careful sweeps of the floor with the flashlight before moving higher onto the foundation walls.

She cursed the lack of good light and braced herself to let go of the ladder. Her only choice was to use the stones as a guide and feel her way down the length of the space. Cold and rough, the foundation bumped under her hand as she skimmed over its surface. She felt for depressions or hollows large enough to hide a journal, making use of what light she did have before moving on to another section of the wall.

She probed the stones, hoping for one to shift or give, but they remained as immovable as they ever were. Think! It was unlikely Abigail would have created a hiding place out of stone. If one had existed, Alden would have known about it. Abigail would have used whatever space between the rocks that had already existed. Quickly retracing her steps toward the ladder, she began again, concentrating on the gaps between the stones.

Her progress was painstakingly slow. Impatient, she tucked the flashlight under her chin to explore the rock seams with both hands. Although she covered more area this way, the result was still discouraging. Sometime later—dirty, cramped, and almost ready to accept the pointlessness of her search—she found a crack and sank her hand into the space up to her elbow. Sophie sucked in a sharp breath sure she had scraped off a good amount of skin. She gave a gentle tug, and then another. Nothing. Carefully she rocked her arm a bit and tried to wriggle out with no success. Alarm shot through her. She was stuck. Perfect, just perfect. Now she'd not only get caught exploring where she'd been told not to, but she'd add the humiliation of needing to yell for help. She flexed her fingers and brushed against something soft. Oh, no! Please don't let it be alive! She frantically tugged but gained nothing but the loss of another layer of skin. Her breath harsh in her ears, she tried angling her flashlight into the hole to see around the arm. Just enough light snuck by for her to see a scrap of brown cloth at the very ends of her fingers.

She stretched and tried to grasp the cloth between her middle and index finger. A bit more. A bit more. She strained forward, jamming her arm further into the hole. She flicked at it before managing to pinch enough between her fingertips and gather the cloth into her palm. The cloth was softer than Sophie expected and crushed easily in her hand. She had gotten it, but she was still stuck. Her closed fingers would make it harder to pull out of the crevice, but there was no way she was leaving it behind.

She tucked the flashlight once again under her chin and used her free arm to pull on the other. Treating her arm as an object, she ignored the stabs of pain that twisted all the way into her shoulder. The harder she tugged, the more the foundation stones bit into her forearm. Sophie hissed in pain as she leaned back and added her weight to the trapped arm. The arm didn't move an inch. She leaned against the wall to catch her breath and went still. There was noise from upstairs.

The front door creaked open. She panicked, bobbling the flashlight. It cracked against the stones before it dropped, extinguished and out of reach.

Footsteps made their way through the house, first climbing to the second floor and then making a circuit of the ground level.

Who was that? Dan and the crew, or even Neal, would have called out to her. Why sneak around unless it was the housebreaker from last night? She tugged fiercely on her arm and begged silently for rescue. Help me.

Be still. Be silent. He cannot see in this blackness.

Sophie fought down a rising hysteria. No! Please, not now. Already held prisoner by the wall, she was vulnerable already without layers of the past shifting over her.

It would never do to be caught with it.

Cold to the bone, she clamped her teeth together to keep them from chattering. He can't find me here. She pushed her body against the stones and tried to make herself as small as possible in the dark.

Gray wisps turned upon themselves in the corners. Twisting out toward the center, they slid and tumbled over each other as they filled the cache.

She couldn't hear clearly—every sound seemed to come from a distance. Impatient calling. *Demands.* The creak of the ladder under the weight of a threat. I'm caught . . . helpless. *Ungrateful wretch.*

She heard the shuffle of feet and felt him groping in the dark, displacing air with sweeps of his arms. Give up, go away, her mind screamed. She remained still, unwilling to alert the intruder to her presence.

It will be far worse if you defy me.

So close and such anger. Please, don't find me. Sophie flattened against the stones and prayed that he would miss her. The shuffling came closer accompanied by harsh breathing. She felt the scrabbling of fingers against her back, and she was caught. Past and present exploded as she struggled in the strong grip.

"Stop it!" a harsh voice demanded.

Wicked child.

She whimpered, then threw herself away from him, wrenching her arm from the wall and tumbling onto the hard packed dirt. A hand grabbed her leg. She frantically kicked out, connecting with something hard enough to feel it jolt up into her hip. With a howl of pain, it was over. Strong arms scooped her up, hauled her over to the ladder, and out of the cache.

"Let me go!" She struggled with little result against the man who held her in a hard grip.

"Stop it." Neal demanded, shaking her. "Why didn't you answer? You scared the daylights out of me."

"Neal?" Sophie started to cry and sagged in relief against him.

He patted her back awkwardly. "Hey, just breathe. You're okay." He looked over her head and scanned the dark room. "Can you tell me what happened?"

As she fought for calmness, the front door opened. A rain-soaked Dan walked in with Aesop by his side. He stopped abruptly at the sight of her tear-streaked face.

"What's going on?" Dan demanded, glaring at Neal.

"Stay out of it, Robbins," Neal snapped.

Dan closed the space between them. "Her arm's bleeding!" When he grabbed Neal's shoulder, the gray mist boiled out of the cache. It rolled down the baseboards and worked its way up the walls until the room filled with a rippling gray mist and two others were locked in a struggle before them.

Nehemiah Alden hunched over the kneeling figure of a terrified girl, his hand twisted in the silky black of her hair. "How dare you shame me in such a manner," he hissed, shaking her.

"Release me," she wept when he viciously yanked her upright. "I have done nothing to deserve this treatment, and I belong to another, truly." She clawed at his arm, struggling to free herself.

"No." The word fell like a stone.

"You covet what I would bring to a marriage, nothing more."

"I will not listen to such nonsense from a wicked girl!" He scanned her tear-streaked face with distaste. "I deemed it at first madness, then I saw my maker's greater purpose. I am to save you, Cousin. It appears that I am tardy, but no matter, that too can be corrected."

The girl visibly shrank at his words. "No, please. Do not . . . I will do just as you wish."

"Yes, I believe you will." He pushed her away and backed her toward the cache.

As fiercely as she had struggled against his hold, she now clung desperately, throwing herself against him. "Please, I beg you."

He set her away from him, prying her hands off his wrists, finger by finger. Calmly capturing both her hands in a crushing grip once he was free. "No, I believe this is the only way," he said, then backed her to the edge and toppled her into the cache. He quickly removed the ladder and bent to drop the boards back into place. "Yes, the only way," he muttered. He straightened and stood for a moment, breathing harshly. "Justice—and I will receive what I am due." He ignored the sobs rising from the cache and abruptly turned toward the door.

The trio, rooted to the spot since the mist had first risen from the floor, flinched as Nehemiah Alden charged straight through them and disappeared. The gray mist receded more slowly, twisting and slinking its way back through the cracks and into the cache, leaving behind it a bone-numbing cold.

4

The Plan

Sophie crumpled to the floor at Neal's feet. She'd never felt anything so cold. It cut her breath and weakened her joints so that she was unable to stand.

"I'm freezing," Dan said and bent at the waist.

Neal tried to haul Sophie to her feet, but Aesop was in the way. "Get out of here, you idiot dog."

Dan staggered to the door and held on to the frame. "Good grief, I can barely stand."

"Would you pull yourself together and help me?" Neal snapped. "She was down in the cache."

Dan's head came up. "Alone?"

"Yeah, and completely out of it when I found her." Neal struggled for a better grip and failed. "If she saw a preview of what just happened, it's not surprising she's a mess."

"You saw that, right?" She glanced vaguely between them. "That wasn't just 'emotional footprints' . . . I mean there were *people* here." She reached up to grab Neal's arm and noticed with surprise she still clutched the fabric from between the foundation stones.

"They were here alright." Neal cupped her elbows in his hands. "Can you stand?"

"I think so." With his help, she made it to her feet and saw that Dan was now upright and propped against the door frame. It took a while of hanging onto Neal before she felt steady enough to stand on her own. "I'm alright," she said and squeezed his arm in thanks.

Neal nodded stiffly and released her.

"There's no doubt that was Alden," Dan said, rubbing his closed fist against his chest. "Who do you think the girl was?"

"Abigail Hart," Sophie said softly and without hesitation. She was equally certain that the needlework she now held had been crafted by the same girl. It was the kind of work a woman in the colonies would have crafted by the fire to pass the time.

The distant rumble of thunder echoed faintly as the storm rolled out to sea. How many storms had Abigail witnessed during her time at The Point? She turned the fabric over in her hands, careful not to transfer blood from her arm to the ancient cloth.

"What'd he have on her?" Dan asked. "She obviously was afraid of him and said she belonged to somebody else. With her father gone and with that face, she could have had anyone she wanted."

"Who knows?" Neal unbuttoned his shirt cuff and tugged up his sleeve. A welt was rising on his forearm. "You're stronger than you look," he said, frowning at Sophie. He gestured impatiently toward the staircase. "Go get what you need. You're staying in town until we get this mess straightened out."

Sophie ignored him. "He was her cousin, her next living male kin. He could have forced her to do what he wanted, but he didn't have to." She opened her hand to display a baby bonnet, embroidered with exquisite birds and vines in faded silk thread. "She was pregnant."

Dan came over and peered at the tiny cap, discolored and faded with age but clearly the work of a skilled needlewoman. "Are you sure it was hers?"

"One time on the beach, and before in the cache, I felt the emotions of a girl who was pregnant and desperately afraid of a man. She hid from him in the cache and hid her work to protect her baby. The aftermath is what we just saw." Sophie made a helpless gesture and wiped at a tear that slipped down her cheek.

Dan swore and began to prowl the room. "He blackmailed a pregnant girl."

"Get that alarm set up," Neal said. "And let's get out of here. We've had enough drama for one day."

"Drama?" Sophie rounded on Neal, angrier than she'd been in a long time. "We just saw a man toss a pregnant girl into that hole. And what's worse, it's not the end of it, not by a long shot." She jabbed a finger at Neal. "Set up your alarm and get out. I'm staying." Maybe it was shock, but if she left, she knew she'd never return. Abandoning Abigail Hart was something she just couldn't live with right now.

Neal scowled. "Fine, then I'll stay too."

"Now wait a minute," Dan said, coming to stand toe-to-toe with him.

She shoved against the air, pushing their words back at them. "Work it out." She had no idea how they would resolve the issue and didn't care. Aesop trailed her from the room like a shadow, a comforting pattern for which she was grateful. She'd never been more terrified than when she'd been trapped in that cache. Now all she wanted was something normal, like her dog and to clean up the battle wounds she was collecting like a ten year-old. With the numbness from the trauma easing, both her arm and knee throbbed.

On her way upstairs, she realized neither of the two ghosts seemed to know they were there. In fact, Alden had charged right through them. She carefully folded Abigail's baby bonnet and set it on the dresser. As she ran a light finger over the tiny smooth stitches, she wondered, what had happened that night? What had Alden done? No one had ever said anything about a baby. It tugged at her heart. She'd been wanted and loved by her parents. She had a sister she could let into her life, or not, when she chose. Since her parents' deaths, she had spent most of her life avoiding emotional entanglements, yet here she was borrowing somebody else's. She knit her brows. But who else did Abigail have? Who had she ever had? It was up to her to find out. At least, she'd try. She was still unsure how to go about it, but she felt better having committed herself. She nodded decisively and went down the hall to clean up her arm.

Once the cut was free of grit, she taped on a bandage, then tended to her knee. Sounds of quiet activity reached her from the first floor. Neal and Dan must have come to some kind of agreement after all that loud arguing, but she wasn't about to investigate. It was all the same to her, and she had tons of prep to do for classes that started next week. School work would be the necessary distraction she needed to let her mind wander. She always solved problems better leaving whatever tangle she faced to simmer while she was occupied elsewhere. In time, she would work out a plan that would help her keep her promise to Abigail.

Hours later, night brought the sea lapping at the base of the bluff, the waves growing louder with the incoming tide. Sophie got up from her desk to stretch her back. At least the rain had finally ended. A flash of red brake lights caught her eye, and she turned to the window to see Neal's SUV drive down the lane toward town. Well, Dan must have succeeded in sending Neal home. She turned to face the door when she heard steps on the stairs and then in the hallway.

"Are you okay?" Dan entered the room holding a plate with a sandwich and a bottle of water. "I imagined you might be hungry."

"I'm fine, thanks. And hungry." She gestured to the window. "I saw Neal drive off toward town. Is he coming back or are you staying here tonight?"

"I'm staying and he'll be back in the morning." He hesitated like he wanted to say more but changed his mind with a shake of his head. "The alarm's installed, and I'll be in the office downstairs. If you need anything, yell."

"Count on it." Considering what had happened, she wasn't going to be shy about screaming her head off at a repeat performance. She lifted a corner of the sandwich to peek inside. "Yum, PB and J."

"Nothing else was open." He shrugged and turned for the door. "'Night, Sophie."

"'Night," she echoed. "Thanks for the sandwich."

He nodded and headed back downstairs, the house creaking around him as he made his way to the office.

As she ate, she considered ways to go about finding someone who had disappeared a couple of hundred years before. She'd visit Babs again and see if there were other avenues to follow or tackle the journals that had just been found at The White Horse. They hadn't been seen yet and might have some mention of the Aldens in them. Neither option inspired in her any great hope, but she had to start somewhere. For now, though, all she wanted was a quiet night.

The noise of Dan moving around downstairs reassured her. She settled into bed with a sigh, Aesop beside her. Usually, he slept on the floor because he was a blanket thief, but tonight she wanted him as close as possible. When she drifted off to sleep, she was thinking of Abigail and her man. The one she had chosen. The one she had told Alden that she belonged to truly. How beautiful to find someone like that . . . .

Coarse bluff grasses tugged at her woolen skirt. He'd promised to come, and she waited, watching shipping vessels and then the fishing fleet return from the open water. The wind rose as the tide shifted, lifting her hair from her shoulders. Waiting was not unknown to her. Indeed, she'd spent most of her life waiting for her father to return from the sea, but the waiting for this man tore at her.

His ship had returned hours earlier. Yet she still sought him on the beach below, yearning for that leap of recognition and joy his return always brought her. She started when she heard rustling behind her, then settled when she recognized his voice.

"You should not stand with your hair unbound for all to see," he said, brushing the smooth strands aside and gathering her close, her back settled against his chest.

"You came," she said, leaning into his warmth.

"How could I not?" He rested his cheek on the top of her head and took a deep breath. "You smell of lavender and the sea. How I wish I could take you with me when I sail."

She turned in his arms to face him and asked, "How long must we wait?"

"One voyage more. I've nothing of my own to offer you, but soon I will have a proper ship to captain. Wait for me," he whispered.

A seagull slid out over the water with a freedom she was afraid she'd never feel. She gave an impatient huff and nudged him. "I've done nothing else but wait for you, as you well know." When his eyes crinkled with pleasure at her words, she demanded, "How did you reach The Point unseen?"

"A little-known path through the woods from the village. The barkeep has a tender heart for a man in love, thankfully," he said with a smile, tugging her close.

She saw the truth of it in his eyes. "I love you," she said, laying a gentle hand against his cheek.

He gave a shaky laugh and held her tight. The sea wind murmured through the trees in approval as two dark heads bent together, caresses and gentle kisses, unsure hands and breathless whispers filling the night.

The sun rose the next morning with promise, its rays drying the last crystal drops that clung to the grass and weighted leaves of The Point. Waves washed to shore on the beach below, bubbling over rocks smoothed by winter storms.

Sophie awoke well rested, stretching like a cat and all but purring. The smell of coffee and toast teased her stomach into a growl loud enough to startle Aesop. She threw on shorts and a T-shirt and ran downstairs barefoot, following the heavenly smells to the kitchen with Aesop in tow.

Right at home in her sweats, Chelle was there toasting bread. She was flanked by Neal who was dressed for the office and Dan in his scruffy jeans and rumpled shirt from the night before. Both men were nursing stoneware mugs of coffee.

"Good morning," Sophie said, then sniffed the air appreciatively. "Who do I have to bribe to get some of that coffee?" The request was met with a baleful look from Dan, and an assessing one from Neal. "What?" she asked. "Did something else happen?"

"Ignore them." Chelle pressed a hot mug of coffee into Sophie's hands, "Milk's on the counter, the sugar too." She popped two more slices into the toaster. "They're just mad they didn't think of my solution first, and" she said, eyeing them closely, "neither of them look like they slept well last night. Maybe they were kept up by nightmares of the ghostly duo?" she said sweetly.

Surprisingly, Dan flushed to the roots of his hair and Neal pokered up even more than usual.

"Leave it alone, Chelle," Dan warned. "We've got enough problems without you taking swipes at us." He turned to Sophie shaking his head. "She's upset we didn't call her after Alden appeared last night."

Chelle slapped a plastic knife on the counter. "You're right. You guys see Nehemiah at his worst, and you don't call me?"

"It was terrible." Sophie rubbed her arms against the gooseflesh that rose at the thought of Alden. "I wish I had missed it."

"That whole thing was screwed up." Dan set his coffee down and opened a window. A breeze crisp with salt swept into the room. "I knew Alden was a snake, but to see him in action made me sick. He had some serious problems if he could treat a girl, his family, like that."

"It was brutal." Neal nodded, a little pale. "And as much as I would like to pretend that it never happened, we need to do something about it." He leaned against the counter and took a drink from his mug. "Not only because we should, but because if another apparition happened the work crew would clear out for good. If we could get anyone to stay, it would cost us a fortune."

Dan made a sound of disgust. "We'd never get this place done."

"So, what's the plan?" Sophie asked Chelle, who seemed to be the one making the most sense.

"They don't have a plan and won't admit that my idea is the only way to start." Chelle stuck her tongue out at Dan's back.

"Nice, Chelle. I saw that in the window." He glared at his sister. "What are you, four?"

Neal ignored them both with a shake of his head and turned to Sophie. "Going to Carol may be the only logical place to start. But there's a chance of the story getting out, and then we'd have a real mess."

"Carol?" She knew she should know who they were talking about, but she couldn't place the woman.

"Carol Darby, the village historian—slash—story keeper." Chelle swept crumbs off the counter and elbowed Dan aside when he started to make more coffee. "Let me do that. Your coffee is terrible." She gave the pot a quick rinse with water. "Have you met Carol yet?" she asked over her shoulder.

"No, Babs told me about her, though," Sophie said. "The Darby family has been here forever, right?"

"Yep, a couple hundred years. And in addition to story keepers, they're also natural healers." Chelle turned, the old coffee filter in her hand dripping onto the counter and floor before she could toss it into the trash. "Now that you three have seen Alden and Abigail, she might give you some ideas about what to do next."

Sophie passed Chelle a wad of paper towels she'd ripped off a roll by her elbow. "But wouldn't her ancestors have come forward years ago if they'd known something?"

"Doesn't work like that," Dan said and poured cereal into a plastic bowl, sloshing some milk over the top. He glanced at her while he reached for a spoon and said quite seriously, "There has to be someone to ask the questions. There has to be a seeker."

Sophie scanned all three faces and reflected that yesterday they had seemed like perfectly normal, rational adults. How come this was sounding more like a kid's fantasy quest, with seekers, witches, and ghosts? "I don't know, you guys. This only gets weirder."

"How's it weirder," Neal asked, "than having two dead villagers appear in the living room?"

Dan nodded in agreement and pointed at her with his spoon. "You were ready to throw us out last night because you were bent on finding out what had happened to Abigail and her baby." He looked at her assessingly, "Did you give up already?"

"No, of course not." She lifted her hands, then let them drop. "You just gave me such a hard time about that fire dream I had, but now everyone seems to be on board, even Neal."

"It's hard to deny what we experienced last night," Neal said grimly. "You were already scared witless, but Dan and I came in later and saw that apparition with you. I know we weren't suffering from overactive imaginations. Alden and Abigail were here."

He had a point. She may have worked herself up to the brink of hysteria because she'd been trapped in the cache, but both Neal and Dan had been in and out of the lighthouse for weeks and had never experienced anything. It seemed that hallucination, single or collective, wasn't a possibility. She couldn't believe she was agreeing with any of it. She lifted her hands palm up and shrugged. "When is Carol available?"

Chelle let out a sigh of relief. "Great. We couldn't have done it without you."

Sophie's pulse jumped. "What do you mean?" She certainly didn't want a starring role in discovering what was happening at The Point.

Before she answered, Chelle took pity on Aesop, who was pawing at the door, and sent him off to chase squirrels. "It's one of the things we need to ask Carol about. None of us have ever seen spirits interacting before. We've just heard or felt them one at a time." She lifted a shoulder, apparently at a loss. "We've lived here all our lives, and it's never happened. The only thing different is you."

"You think it's my fault?" She couldn't believe it. How could she possibly have that kind of influence? Up until two weeks ago she'd never even heard of Nehemiah Alden and Abigail Hart.

"I wouldn't say it's your fault," Dan said, before he scooped more cereal into his mouth and tried to talk around the milk-soaked flakes. "But it's been a lot more active and intense since you got here."

A hefty dose of reason was what was needed here. "It could be," Sophie said, "the fact that you're working on the lighthouse that has stirred things up."

"Maybe." Neal drained his cup, set it on the counter, and checked his watch. "We'll see what Carol has to say."

She studied his efficient business image and couldn't help poking at him. "You seem a bit too rational for all this."

"It's hard to explain what happened yesterday rationally." Neal spoke carefully, not taking his eyes off her. "Carol really helped me out when I was younger. I'd like to think I'm smart enough to know when I need help. How about you?"

She wasn't sure why she'd baited him, other than he usually seemed so rigid that this was totally out of character for him. She flushed with embarrassment. "I don't know enough to form an opinion."

"We should be grateful for that, I suppose." Neal paused in the door of the kitchen. "Thanks for the coffee, Chelle. Let me know when Carol can see us." He ignored the others and headed for his car.

Sophie felt she should explain. "I don't know why he brings out the worst in me. I'll apologize later."

"He always rubs me the wrong way," Dan said, and bent to give his sister a peck on the cheek. "Call, when you want me to meet you at Carol's. I'm working at The White Horse today."

"Okay." The second the door closed, Chelle pounced. "Tell me everything that's happened, and don't leave anything out, including your dreams."

"Alright." Sophie blushed, thinking of the dream of Abigail and the man who had sought her out on the bluff.

"Oh, this is going to be good." Chelle leaned forward. "And just to be fair, you can ask me anything too. You start."

She had to laugh. This was like high school, prying details from friends with the promise of delivering the goods yourself. Of all the questions she could have asked, the first one that came out was, "What do I wear to meet a healer?"

Chelle smiled. "Whatever you want. I think you'll be surprised, though. She's not what you'd think."

No matter how Sophie pressed, that was all Chelle would say on the subject. So, after she'd filled in Chelle, she opted for a sleeveless sundress and secured her hair in a clip. Nothing could be done about the bandaged arm and knee, even though they made her look pathetic. When a last look in her bedroom mirror told her there wasn't anything left she could do, she wrapped Abigail's baby bonnet in a square scarf and tucked it carefully into her bag. She hurried downstairs and settled Aesop with his toy squirrel, then went to pace the bluff until Chelle was ready.

From the moment she buckled in, Chelle's zipping through the narrow lanes did nothing to ease her nerves. "The Darby homestead is just at the end of this lane," Chelle said, ignoring an overgrown shrub that screeched along the side of the Mini Cooper. "They've been living on this property since the first Darby arrived in the early sixteen hundreds."

What would that look like? Sophie had never lived in a house older than seventy years. "The same house?" She gripped the armrest as Chelle powered through another curve spraying dirt.

"Sure, the original house is still there. But like a lot of colonial homes, each following generation built an addition to meet their needs." Chelle glanced at her before returning her eyes to the road. "It kind of sprawls now but still has the feeling of the original."

Sophie was almost afraid to ask what that feeling was. Her palms were damp, and she was more nervous than she could explain about meeting this woman. The more involved she became, the further she drifted from her comfort zone. For one thing, she couldn't trace her ancestors back hundreds of years and the people she knew didn't communicate regularly with the dead. It was like studying all your life in English, to find out the test is in German, and your classmates Dutch. She was in over her head.

5

Carol

The idea of bouncing down yet another access road with Chelle at the wheel made Sophie cringe, but thankfully, the lane ended at the Darby driveway. Under the spreading arms of an ancient elm, the little red house trimmed with black shutters was quietly inviting. Winding brick paths meandered between daylilies and rose bushes, ferns and ivy. The paths led visitors to the front door or the back garden which grew wildly, poking through the slats of the enclosing cedar pickets. Tufts of mint, long spikes of chives, ruffled parsley, and prickly thyme all bobbed in the light breeze.

She climbed out of the Mini and followed Chelle down the moss-edged path, stopping when hair-raising shrieks of children erupted from out back.

Chelle brushed away ivy that drooped from a lower branch of the massive elm and smiled. "I guess Nicolás and Alex are still here."

She didn't know why Chelle found this amusing. "Who are they?"

"Carol's grandsons. They're the cutest curly-haired rascals you'll ever meet. She watches them now and again when her daughter and son-in-law need help." Chelle grinned. "They sound like they're being skinned alive, don't they?"

A small voice complained from the back of the house, "It's my turn, Granma Carol." The voice rose in pitch. "Nicolás won't let me walk the plank."

"Plank?" The image of pirate ships and watery deaths flitted through Sophie's head.

"One of the best games around. Let's go see." Chelle led her past the garden and down a hill to a spring-fed pond, surrounded by cascading willows. On the dock, two young boys in bathing suits fenced with stalks of cattail. An inflatable crocodile floated alongside them in the water.

"Did so." The taller one yelled, then poked the cattail 'sword' into his brother's tummy. "Be quiet, or we'll get in trouble."

"Nicolás?" called a woman from the house. "Are you taking turns?"

"Yes, but Alex wants more turns than me." He poked the smaller boy again in the belly.

"Ow, stop that." Alex swiped back with his stalk.

"Hey," continued the woman. "If you boys can't get along, you'll have to come in, okay?"

As Nicolás turned to answer, his brother whapped him in the back of the head, leaving downy white fluff stuck to his brother's hair. Alex giggled and looked around frantically for a way to escape the dock.

"That's it—prepare to walk the plank." Nicolás smacked his brother, and another explosion of white down filled the air.

"Help, Granma, help!" Alex pin-wheeled into the pond, followed by his brother. Both began shrieking that the crocodile was after them.

"Are they okay?" Sophie asked with concern, watching the flailing arms. "Should we go in after them?"

"Naw, it's only four feet deep over there. If they wanted to, they could walk out."

A woman dressed in a tailored linen top, crisp red Capri's, and snazzy flats stepped from the house. She balanced a plate of cookies and two glasses of milk with ease. Sun glinted off her cropped, silver hair as she made her way down to the pond. "Okay, boys, time to get out. Your father will be here in twenty minutes. Have a snack and then shower, alright?"

"Okay, Granma." They clambered back on the dock but kept their feet dangling in the water.

"Hello, Chelle." Carol gave her a quick hug, then extended her hand to Sophie. "And you must be Sophie. I'm Carol Darby and these pirates are my grandsons." She took fluffy towels from a chair and bent over to drape them around each boy. "Nicolás is seven and Alex five." Both boys smiled shyly, revealing an endearing mix of missing and permanent teeth. "Chelle tells me you folks have had some interesting events up at The Point."

Sophie nodded. "We were hoping you could help us find out what happened to Abigail Hart." And her baby, she added silently, conscious of the bonnet in her bag, but not wanting to say too much in front of the boys.

"You can ask me whatever you want, and I'll tell you what I know."

"Are you going to help her find the baby too, Granma?" Nicolás asked from where he sat on the dock. "Abigail's pretty sad she can't find him."

Sophie shot Chelle a surprised look.

"Nicolás," Carol said, squatting down beside him. "Have you been listening at doors?"

"Oh no, Granma Carol," Nicolás said solemnly. "I heard her crying and asking where her baby is."

"When was that, Honey?" His grandmother ran careful fingers through his wet hair gently separating the curls.

"At the beginning of the summer, when we were down on the beach, near The Point. Alex heard her too."

"Yeah, she's really sad," the younger boy nodded.

"Why didn't you tell me or Mama?"

The boys exchanged a look. "Doesn't everybody hear her?" Nicolás asked with a shrug.

"No, not everybody and not all the time." Carol straightened and shaded her eyes to look toward the house. "I think your father's early. Let's see. But the next time you hear people, tell me or Mama, okay?" At the boys' earnest nods, she picked up their towels and scooted them along. She called to Chelle and Sophie, "Come on up when you're through looking around. We'll meet in the parlor."

Sophie followed Chelle to the edge of the pond and watched white butterflies flit from bush to bush. "It's so peaceful here," she said. "I can see why the Darbys came and stayed."

Chelle made a noise of agreement. "We used to come here as kids and horse around in the pond. I swear that's the sixth crocodile she's had." Chelle laughed and startled a turtle off a log into the amber water. "Carol would patch up the old croc as best she could, until it wouldn't hold air anymore. Then suddenly, Croc Number Two would go on vacation and his cousin Croc Number Three would come for a visit."

Sophie felt a twinge of envy. "So, you and Dan came a lot then?" She brushed her fingers against the tall grass growing by the water.

"Right, and Neal too." Chelle's face softened. "All the village kids came. It was the place to be. We played capture the flag in the fall, skated in the winter, and swam in the summer. Carol always had big pitchers of Kool-Aid and bowls of home-made popcorn."

"I would've imagined that Neal was a bit of an outsider."

"Well, his family, like ours, wasn't the first one off the Mayflower, but they've been here a long time." Chelle was silent for a while. "No. He separated himself when he hit his teens."

This was the first time she had heard of Neal withdrawing from village life and she wondered what had happened. "Was that when Carol helped him with his father?" When Chelle nodded, Sophie gently pushed for an answer. "Do you know how?"

"I don't know. I imagined she just listened." Chelle shrugged. "We were his friends, but he never let on what was happening."

"Then he'd already had his falling-out with Dan."

"Yeah, and nothing's been the same since. It's amazing they're even working on the same project together." Chelle deliberately set the topic aside. "Well, this is depressing. Let's see if the guys are here yet and get this ball rolling."

As they made their way around the far corner of the pond, Chelle pulled a frond off a willow and trailed it in the grass behind her, parting the blades like a snake. The moment they entered the back door into the cozy kitchen, they heard sounds of voices. Dan and Neal must have arrived at the same time as the boys' father. Right at home, Chelle led the way to the parlor where Carol and Neal flanked a bay window in matching wing chairs, with Dan opposite them on the sofa. They were bantering over some cookies and iced coffee. Sophie reflected they didn't look much different from Nicolás and Alex, but when she entered the room the laughter stopped.

"Come on in." Carol motioned for the women to help themselves to refreshments on the low table in front of her. "I was just reminding the guys of the Halloween when they were seven, and I threatened to turn them into frogs. I failed, of course. They were so disappointed." She closed her eyes and playfully tapped her chin with a finger. "I think I must have used the wrong hat."

Sophie had to smile. Carol might like to play the witch, but she looked nothing like one. At least, not the ones that Sophie had ever imagined or seen in movies. The living room, however, might raise some eyebrows. There were dream catchers, crosses, and crystals spread throughout the room, shining in windows and perched above doors. A claw-footed table hosted a deck of guardian angel cards, and two books

called *"Energy Medicine"* and *"Your Inner Physician and You."* It seemed
to her that Carol was trying to cover all the bases.

When Chelle collapsed onto the sofa beside Dan, Sophie slid into
the only remaining chair by the fireplace. "Your interests are pretty eclec-
tic," she said looking around the room some more.

"I surround myself with what makes me feel good, and I try to stay
close to nature." Carol kicked off her shoes to reveal a French pedicure
with tiny daisies painted on her toes. "There are many different ways to
wisdom and a lot to learn." She settled into her chair and turned curious
eyes on them. "Why don't you folks tell me what's been happening up at
The Point, and we'll see if we can make any sense of it."

They turned as one toward Sophie. She nervously cleared her throat.
"Well," she said, beginning with her experience on the beach, "There was
this girl—young and pregnant. She was afraid of what she should do and
afraid that her loved ones wouldn't return home to her."

"Did you get a sense of who she might have been waiting for?" Carol
asked softly.

"She was worried that whoever it was wouldn't be there for the pregnancy or for the birth." Sophie closed her eyes and summoned the feeling
of damp sand under her feet and the sun warming her face. She probed
the feelings and thoughts of that day for answers. "No," she said slowly,
shaking her head. "But she was waiting for more than the baby's father.
She called them 'gleeful little boys,' plural, going off on an adventure."

Carol nodded encouragingly. "Can you tell if it was the same person you heard, then saw the other times?"

"It seemed like the same voice. It had the same feeling as when I was
in the cache and later in the living room with the others." She tried to stay
calm but had difficulty talking through the emotion. "In the cache she
was terrified of what 'he' would do if he found her and realized she was
pregnant. She hid to protect her baby. But he realized it anyways, once
he'd hauled her out."

It was clear she needed a moment, and Carol nodded for Neal to
take over.

"I'd gone to the house to check on the crew's progress. When Sophie didn't seem to be home, I visited the second floor to plan what work
would be next. The longer I was there, the more it felt like something
was wrong, and I started to call her." He shifted, appearing he'd rather
be anywhere else. "When no one answered, I went looking and found
that groceries had been dumped on the counter, and a rope was tied to a

radiator in the living room." He glanced over at Sophie. "I finally heard noises coming from the cache and went to help. When I found her, she was rambling about spirits and needing to stay hidden."

Carol turned to her. "Why were you so afraid and confused?"

Sophie shrugged uneasily and looked out the window behind Carol where a sparrow pecked at a crust of bread under the tall elm. "I thought there was an intruder in the house because anyone else would have called to me. Then Abigail's experience started to come through, and I couldn't tell the present from the past."

"I dragged her out of the cache, and she came 'round after we got back to the living room," Neal said, absently rubbing the leg that she had kicked in terror.

Dan sat forward on the sofa, arms folded against his thighs. "I came in just after to find Neal holding onto her. She was upset, and I thought it was his fault." He shifted uncomfortably. "I tried to separate them, and the whole room filled with this gray stuff, smoke or something. It seemed alive, twisting all over the place." He gave a slight headshake as though he still couldn't believe it. "A man was bending over a girl on the floor. He was furious, and she was scared out of her mind." His lips thinned. "I didn't recognize it was Alden until later."

"She was pregnant, and he threw her back into the cache." Sophie said, and felt a leap of anger. "He left her there." She fumbled in her bag. "I found this jammed between the foundation stones. She hid it before he found her." She unfolded the bonnet from her scarf and gave it to Carol.

Carol fingered the delicate stitches. "How did it end?"

"That was the worst part," Dan muttered. "Alden said something like, 'Justice and I'll get what's mine,' then turned and charged right through us." He rubbed his chest as he remembered. "I was freezing and hunched over. Sophie had kind of collapsed on the floor. Neal seemed okay, though, come to think of it." He looked puzzled. "I don't know why. I could barely stand."

Chelle shivered. "Maybe I'm glad I missed it after all."

Outside the bay window, Sophie saw a raven swoop down from the canopy of the large elm and startle the sparrow from its food, a bully just like Alden.

"And later?" Carol prodded, standing to refill their drinks. "That night did anything happen?" she asked as she poured. "What about your dream, Sophie?"

Sophie shot Chelle an accusing glance, so much for confidences. "There really wasn't much to it," she said, beyond embarrassed. How was she supposed to share her dream about Abigail in front of Dan and Neal? That Abigail had been innocent and in love. That Sophie had witnessed the expression of that love with a man who had obviously adored her. There was no way she was going to share that with Dan and Neal. She wasn't going to say a word about it. Ever.

Carol scanned the tight, closed faces around her as she resumed her seat. "Alright, folks, this is what we've got: a story of an apparition. The meaning of the experience is what you felt at the time and what you continued to understand later, even in sleep." She turned to a surprised Sophie and said, "This whole thing is completely new to you, so we'll take it slow, okay?"

Sophie couldn't have been more thankful for what seemed like a free pass but felt she should offer anyways, "Do you want me to start?"

"Maybe it will loosen a few tongues if I explain something first." Carol tucked her legs under her. "Energy, in a person who is open and receptive, can attract like energy. Sometimes that person may experience a feeling of well-being or uneasiness depending on the event, and sometimes they experience what someone who lived long ago thought or felt. I like to call them energy footprints." She tilted her head to the side, then considered Sophie. "That day on the beach, were you feeling a bit lost and alone?"

Sophie squirmed as everyone turned to her. How was she supposed to admit that was exactly what she'd felt, despite the glorious day and knowing that she was more settled than she'd been in a long time. How pathetic. Other people seemed perfectly content to zip around their lives alone, thrive even. Why couldn't she? She returned to the question and admitted, "Yes, I suppose so."

"How did you come to be on the beach?" Carol ran her finger over the seam of the chair and waited.

"Well," she answered, remembering her return to The Point from the library and all the dust and noise that'd greeted her. "Dan suggested that I take a walk while the crew was finishing up."

"So, he dismissed you." Carol nodded as though confirming something she already knew.

"Now wait a minute." Dan sat up straight. "I didn't dismiss her. I told her she should take a walk because I thought she'd enjoy it."

Chelle snorted and nudged Dan with her foot. "You got rid of her, more likely, until it was convenient for you to have her come back." She nudged him again. "I know how you work." He scowled at her but subsided back against the sofa without a word. His silence was damning and seemed to confirm that Chelle was right.

Carol smiled at the exchange, then said, "Back to the girl. It's not too much of a stretch to think that her young man was a sailor. First because Sophie's experience occurred on the beach, and second because the girl talked of 'gleeful little boys' going on adventures. Later, after the apparition in the lighthouse, you connected her to the girl we know as Abigail Hart. Abigail's father was lost at sea. Maybe the father of her baby was with him and lost as well, leaving her alone and vulnerable."

She felt a glimmer of understanding. "If what I was feeling mirrored Abigail's feelings, it could help to bring on an emotional footprint?"

"Right," Carol nodded. "Did you sense anyone else? Say Alden or her young man?"

"No," she said, drawing out the word, "not by themselves. Only how they directly relate to Abigail."

"That's what I thought. Okay, guys, your turn." Carol gave them a pointed stare and settled more fully into her chair. "I know you two have been holding out. Time to be honest. Now, who have you been sensing?"

Neal and Dan looked uncomfortable with the change in Carol's attitude. Sophie couldn't blame them. Carol had a set to her chin that announced no one was leaving until she got the answers she wanted. After a long silence, Dan gave in first with a resentful look at Neal. "I've only sensed one guy, a sailor. He looked forward to coming home as much as he wanted to be back at sea. He loved a woman and was returning to marry her but didn't. I don't know why. When I sense him, he wants to protect her and can't. Later, he saw The Point burn and couldn't do anything about it."

"You liar," Sophie breathed. If she hadn't been in Carol's house, she would have shaken him in frustration. "I told you I saw The Point burn and you brushed it off."

"I didn't know it was anything but a coincidence that we dreamed the same thing." Dan had the decency to flush and shift awkwardly. "It was more than I wanted to get into at the time."

"And?" Sophie demanded, throwing her arms open. "What's so different now?"

"The stakes have been upped. I think he was Abigail's love, and I've seen what he was afraid of." Dan turned to Neal, eager to shift the focus elsewhere. "What about you?"

"This is a bad idea, Carol." Neal rose to leave and set his glass on the table. "It can't possibly make any difference now."

"It would make a difference to you for others to know this goes way back." Carol got up to stand in front of him and placed a gentle hand on his arm. "Please stay. I think that Sophie and Dan won't be able to find Abigail and her baby without you."

"Why?" Neal demanded. "All that monster ever did was destroy people's lives, including mine. I can't see him being helpful now."

"The only time Alden and Abigail have ever appeared is when the three of you were in the lighthouse producing the same emotion that happened hundreds of years ago." Carol tugged him back to his seat by the window. When he sat, she kept her hand on his shoulder as though to keep him in place. "The anger, the protectiveness, and the fear were mirrored in you three yesterday." She nodded with conviction. "Punishment and control, or lack thereof. You were very angry with Sophie after you got her out of the cache, weren't you?"

"I was furious." Neal pulled away from Carol but remained where he was. "I'd been calling and calling, and she didn't answer. I thought he had gotten to her too."

Too? Sophie sat frozen in her seat, trying to make sense of what Neal was saying. Who was he talking about? *Was* she in danger? The sense of being hunted she'd felt in the dark of the cache spread from her belly, filling her limbs with heat and the need to escape.

Chelle curled her leg under her, and asked softly, "Who was it, Neal, that you were afraid had hurt Sophie? Who do you sense?"

Neal's resistance slid away with a slump of his shoulders. "Alden, always Alden," he said bitterly. "I felt like I was going mad when it first started happening." He propped his elbows on his knees and dropped his head into his hands. "Would have too, if Carol hadn't helped me. But it was already too late," he said, glancing over at Dan, "for a lot of things by then."

Sophie tightly linked her fingers together so that the knuckles turned white. "Do you know what happened to Abigail and her baby?"

"No." Neal said with effort. "But I've seen more crimes that black-hearted fiend committed than was good for anyone." He gave a humorless laugh. "But what haunts me, what absolutely kills me, is that I always see them through his eyes, as though I was the one committing them." He scrubbed his face. "Last night was an exception. As awful as it was, it was a relief to be a spectator for a change. Thankfully, I'd never seen that one before."

"So why now, and why us?" Dan rested his head against the back of the sofa with a gusty sigh. "Abigail and Alden have been gone for centuries."

"I think the three of you have qualities that must be an echo of those people long ago." Carol raised her hand to quiet the chorus of denials. "Dan, you've always been a defender of the helpless. It's not unusual that you pick up on the feelings of someone who wanted to help and couldn't. Sophie's been looking for where she fits in and senses the thoughts of Abigail . . . ."

"And I see through Alden's eyes," Neal interrupted. "So, what does that make me? Some sort of sadistic monster?"

Carol gave him a level look. "Neal, I've known you your whole life and there isn't a mean bone in your body." When Dan tried to interrupt, she silenced him with a warning look. "You're proud and cautious. You don't trust anyone, not even your friends. But you are not cruel." She turned and went to sit on the arm of her own chair when it looked like he wasn't going to bolt. "The only connection you share with Alden is that you both were abuse victims." She met his eyes steadily. "Alden became an abuser. You did not."

Neal's sharp hiss of breath had everyone, except Carol, searching for somewhere else to look. Sophie focused on the breeze ruffling the leaves outside the window and wished she was back outside near the pond. Neal and Alden had both been abuse victims. She tried to get her mind around that. Could it excuse what had happened in the past? She really wasn't sure.

Chelle ignored the news about Neal and asked, "How can anyone know that Alden was abused?"

"The story goes that when he was quite old, he fell injuring his back and had Old Katherine Darby tend to him," Carol said. "During the treatment, Katherine saw that he was heavily scarred as though someone had flayed the skin off his back."

"But that doesn't mean he was a victim of abuse," Sophie objected, reluctant to put him in the same category as Neal.

"People told Old Katherine things they normally wouldn't share with others." Carol lifted a shoulder. "She had a way about her that encouraged confidences. Although, Old Katherine had said that in this case it was more of an opportunity for an old man to relive an action of which he was proud. 'Mistress,' he'd rasped, 'the marks you see are a hint of what my father did to me as a boy. When grown, I exacted payment for every curse and humiliation, every blow and kick. What you see is shameful, but only a shadow of what he suffered at my hands. When I was done, I choked the life out of him and claimed what was mine, what I had earned at his hands.'"

Neal's jaw slackened in disbelief, and he whispered, "Why didn't you tell me he'd killed his father?"

"It was bad enough you shared the same rage," Carol said. "I wasn't about to plant that seed in an unpredictable teenager's head, so I worked to get you removed from your father's reach."

"Is that why Neal has always seen through Alden's eyes? The anger?" Sophie asked cautiously, glancing between Neal and Carol. "Isn't it rare to see through a ghost's eyes?"

"Yes, to both." Carol picked a pink quartz stone off the table beside her, rolling its uneven surface between her palms. "Most people just hear or feel spirits. They don't usually see them, and they hardly ever see through their eyes. The fact that the three of you have seen Abigail and Alden shows the energy is stronger. Even Nicolás and Alex have heard Abigail on the beach, and they're very young to sense spirits. It usually takes a more mature person, one with enough life experience, to relate to the emotions or thoughts the spirit is projecting."

"What are we supposed to do?" Sophie rose to retrieve the bonnet and noted the raven outside was still greedily feeding. "I promised myself I'd discover what happened to Abigail and her baby, but I don't know where to start."

Carol nodded sympathetically. "In cases like this, people who hear or feel spirits are called to bear witness to the departed's experience." She sighed, then returned the pink stone to the table. "Realistically, that is all a person can do. And ultimately, it is all that may be required by the dead—for someone to know of, and share, their experience."

Neal gave a snort and slumped in his chair. "So, they want an audience."

"No, I think what Carol's saying is that they want acknowledgement of what they experienced or suffered." Chelle trailed a finger down her glass, making patterns on the humid surface. "Will that be enough to bring her peace? To stop the apparitions?"

Carol made a helpless gesture. "It's been successful in other cases, but I really can't say for sure."

"Back to something Neal mentioned earlier," Dan said. "He was afraid that Alden had hurt Sophie. Is that possible? Can spirits hurt people in the present?"

"In this kind of situation, no, not usually," Carol said. "And I think what Neal was picking up was the threat to Abigail in the cache, not a threat to Sophie. In fact, you said Alden charged right through you, not seeing or sensing you. I think it's a strong sign of the one-way nature of this interaction."

"So, we'll be safe at The Point?" Dan looked around the room, driving home what could be at stake.

Carol hesitated. "Life's a risk." She gave a rueful headshake. "There are no answers or growth without risk. Sometimes there is a cost, often quite high. It's up to the people involved to make their own decisions."

"Does this really need to play out once started?" Neal asked, raising a concern that Sophie hadn't considered. She already felt that the woods waited expectantly. Maybe they had released something they couldn't control.

The sun shifted, filtering into the room in scattered rays through the old elm tree. One beam lit the crucifix over the sofa appearing to deliver a silent message meant for Sophie. Sacrifice. What would she be willing to risk to find the truth? She looked at Carol who was carefully considering Neal's question. What would they all be willing to risk?

"Does it need to play out?" Neal repeated, impatient for an answer.

"Yes, I believe so," Carol sighed. "I know it's not the answer you all want to hear, but it's the truth as I know it. It's been close to three hundred years since this was set in motion." She gave an unhappy shrug. "You could close the lighthouse and send Sophie away. But at some point, the same elements which set it in motion will present themselves and set it off again."

"So, we really have no choice," Neal said. "To finish the project, we'll have to see this business through."

Sophie searched the faces of those around her and thought if they all worked together, they just might succeed. "I'd like to try," she said finally.

When Neal also gave a curt nod of agreement, Dan said, "Okay, we'll try it. If it gets too dangerous, we'll pull out."

"Is there any way to move this along?" Chelle asked, motioning with her hand. "You know, speed things up."

"Having the three of you stay at the lighthouse might initiate another apparition more quickly." Carol grimaced sympathetically. "I'm afraid you might have to stay away, Chelle."

Chelle wrinkled her nose. "I figured as much." she said, then shrugged. "Can't be helped, I guess."

"Stay there?" Neal gave a shake of his head. "I don't think that'll work."

"Why not?" Dan asked. "There are plenty of rooms to go around, and we'll never finish the project if we don't get this sorted out."

Neal swore under his breath and remained silent for a long while. "Alright, I don't see where we have much choice." He might have agreed, but he didn't sound happy about it.

"Don't confuse the feelings of the past with the present," Carol warned them as they collected their belongings and stacked the empty drink glasses on the tray. "Identifying too closely with any one of the ghosts could be counter-productive and dangerous. Sophie is not Abigail, and neither of you two are the people you sense," Carol stressed. "You three may see the same events and maybe even dream the same dreams, but the past has no direct bearing on any of you." When Dan avoided her eyes and Neal examined his keys, Carol looked like she had confirmed a suspicion. "I mean it. If you can't stay objective, this won't work."

"Right, got it." Dan gave her a lopsided smile and a hard hug. "Thanks, Carol. We'll keep you posted."

A quick round of goodbyes and a promise to keep in touch saw them out the front door. Chelle turned to Sophie as they walked down the brick path, shaded by the huge elm. "Could one of the guys give you a ride back to The Point? I have an appointment in Brewster, and I'm running late."

"Um, sure." Sophie wasn't looking forward to a ride with either Dan or Neal but didn't think she would survive another commute with Chelle, especially if she were in a hurry. "But I really need to get to the hardware store and pick up some stuff for Aesop."

"I've got a meeting on Main Street," Neal said, gesturing toward the direction of the village. "You could do your shopping, and I could run you up to The Point after my meeting."

"Thanks." Sophie was surprised at the suggestion and hoped his offer was an olive branch regarding her dog. Maybe Neal wasn't as bad as she'd imagined. The facts that had surfaced about his childhood certainly helped to explain a lot.

When they climbed into Neal's SUV and he slid the ignition key home, the loneliest jazz Sophie had ever heard drifted out of the car's speakers.

"Who's that?" she asked, her interest piqued, before he jabbed the off button.

"Miles Davis, covering an old jazz standard."

"It's haunting, and so lonely how the trumpet floats out over the rest of the quartet." She rubbed her arms. "Just those few bars gave me goosebumps."

"Mmm," He intoned and set the car rolling down the drive.

"What's it called?"

Neal's eyes remained fixed on the road, but heat crept up his neck. "Ah," he cleared his throat. "It's called, 'I Fall in Love Too Easily.'"

"Oh, well, I like it." What was the matter with him? It wasn't a crime to like sad music, especially good sad music that could make you feel as though you should be curled up in a chair, nursing a glass of wine, and watching the rain tap against the window.

The silence stretched on while Sophie racked her brain for something to say. The ghost business had been hashed out enough, at least for now. He couldn't possibly care about her teaching, and the only other topic that came to mind was his past abuse. She couldn't very well ask him about that. The longer the silence stretched, the tenser she became.

Neal finally spoke up. "You shouldn't worry. I gave up eating scrawny schoolteachers years ago." He glanced over at her in annoyance.

She felt as if he had heard every single thought that had flashed through her mind since she had buckled into the car. "Sorry," she stammered. "It's a lot to take in . . . this ghost stuff." She shifted in discomfort and turned to look out her window.

Coastal views slid by her open window as they made their way into Pocasset. Small shrubs and sea marshes graduated into taller maples and oaks that shaded the houses and store fronts of Main Street. Her gaze darted away when they drove beside a cemetery, then back again when Neal finally spoke, stating flatly, "Alden killed his father."

Neal was staring straight ahead, missing the headstones and monuments that lined the dirt paths inside the fieldstone wall. She imagined Neal trudging there where someone abused like him lay buried. Someone damaged by another's cruelty who had become a monster. In her mind, the fleshless skeleton of Nehemiah was replaced by Neal, pale and still, jammed into the narrow coffin and buried under layers of gravel and dense New England dirt. She shoved the horror from her mind and tried to breathe normally.

"It crossed my mind when my father beat me," Neal said almost to himself. "I'd think 'wait until I'm older, and then we'll see.'" His head moved slowly from side to side, rejecting what he'd thought long ago. "But it never came to that because I went into foster care."

Sophie couldn't manage a sound. What had Carol been thinking to share such personal information about him without his permission? It had put them all in an impossible position. "I'm so sorry," she said. "It's a cowardly thing for any adult to do, never mind a parent."

"Forget it," he said, slowing as another car in front of them braked to turn. "I try to."

She fell silent and thought, this ride couldn't end soon enough.

When they pulled up to the front of Reed's Hardware, Neal reached across to open her door. "Pick you up in about a half-hour." When she tried to scramble out, he held her arm to stop her. "I was a victim of abuse, but I'm not one now," he said evenly. "I don't want your pity."

She mutely nodded her understanding, got out of the car, and closed the door. She watched through tear-filled eyes as Neal reversed direction and accelerated toward the village center without a backward glance. How had a ride that had started out as a nice gesture rumbled into an absolute train wreck?

6

Abigail

Sophie pulled herself together by walking around the parking lot, sniffling and blinking until she was composed. When she entered Reed's Hardware, she had to blink again, this time in disbelief. Pine boards with the worn pattern of foot traffic creaked under her feet as she made her way down the aisles. The dimly lit hardware store still had wooden shelves and bins, but what surprised her the most were the stacks of books reaching almost to the ceiling. When she examined the stacks, she found memoirs, health books, and classics rubbing elbows with books on theoretical math, poetry, and politics.

She was so enchanted she missed seeing the man perched on the stool behind the ancient register. He was casually browsing through a book that lay open on the counter. "Hello," she managed over her surprise, "I didn't see you when I came in. I'm Sophie Tyler."

"Afternoon," the man said with a nod and a polite smile. "Tom Reed, at your service."

She waved toward the towering stacks. "Why? It's wonderful . . . but why all the books?"

Tom removed his reading glasses, absently clicking the ends of the arms together. "Babs, over at the library, used to get a lot of donations for her annual 'Friends of the Library' book sale. I'd buy the ones I wanted, and after the sale was over, I'd bring the ones that didn't sell here. I felt someone would, or should, read them. Don't you think?" He looked a bit like Oscar Wilde to Sophie, just older.

"Yes, of course." She couldn't help but agree. "You've got some great ones here."

"They started out as small piles and grew." Tom gestured grandly. "Once and future trees."

She smiled at the notion but couldn't imagine that he sold many, even if they were excellent. "Do people buy them?"

"Quite often." He indicated the Mason jar to the side of the register. It was labeled—hardcover, one dollar, paperback fifty cents, all proceeds to the Pocasset Library. It was filled to the top with loose change and singles.

"Do they find what they're looking for?" As far as she could see, there was no rhyme or reason for how the books were stacked.

"Sure, and sometimes they find something they didn't realize they needed." He tapped the book in front of him with a finger. "I've seen plenty of books on Michelangelo's painting and sculpture, but I'd never seen one about the man until now." His head tilted to the side, followed by an amazed shake. "Did you know he wrote over three hundred sonnets and poems that his grandnephew edited?" He leaned forward to whisper, "Apparently Michelangelo's view on sexuality and religion made a lot of people uncomfortable."

Sophie smothered a smile. "I knew he'd written poetry but had no idea that it was so extensive." She swept a wayward wisp behind her ear and craned her neck for a better look at the page. "I can't say I'm surprised at the grandnephew trying to protect Michelangelo's good name, though. But it does make you wonder why. You know, was it because he had some genuine affection for his great-uncle, or was he trying to keep the family from looking bad?"

"Mmm," Tom tapped his glasses on the counter. "Hard to tell. I could be convinced either way."

"It's most likely the latter, unfortunately," she said with a sigh.

His eyebrows rose slightly. "Awfully young to be cynical, aren't you?"

"Well, I deal a lot with people as a teacher." She shrugged a bit self-consciously. "And I find most of them are concerned with their own necks first, and what's ethical, second."

"Students?" he asked with sympathy.

"No, mostly the administration, some faculty. Students," Sophie sighed, thinking of the best way to explain it, "for the most part, have no idea what's at stake. They plod along like cows to slaughter, not realizing it's their chance to do something important."

"You sound like our friend here." He shifted the book so that Sophie could see the picture. "This note was found in his workshop after he died."

Dark compact script evenly scrawled with force, marched across the yellowed parchment in slightly sloping lines. She traced the words with her finger, sounding it out, "*Disegnare, Antonio, Antonio disegnare, disegnare e non perdere tempo . . . .*" She looked up. "What does it mean?"

"'Draw, Antonio, Antonio draw, draw and do not waste time . . . .'"

"Antonio was a student?" Who would have believed that Michelangelo would have had to struggle to get his students to listen? It made her feel a whole lot better about her own classroom challenges.

"One of his apprentices, I think." Tom flipped the page to check. "Yeah, an apprentice."

She rummaged in her bag for pen and paper. "That's terrific. Can I write it down?"

"Go right ahead." He seemed amused. "But it's not that hard to remember."

"No, it's not," she agreed. "It's the way it's punctuated that I love. You get the feeling that he wrote it the way he'd said it, over and over and over again." She quickly jotted down the quote in both Italian and in English. "Do you ever advertise that you have books for sale?"

"No." He gave her a crooked smile. "Then I'd miss the pleasure of seeing reactions like yours." He took a moment to look around the store. "This store is a family business; the love of books is mine. I do what makes me happy and part of that is sharing it with others." He folded his glasses and set them inside the book. "At the end of the day, you have to be able to look at yourself in the mirror. I can."

Tom had touched on something Sophie studiously avoided. How long had it been since she'd really taken a look at herself, her life? Feeling unsettled was one thing, but when was the last time she had really asked why?

"Now," he said, rubbing his hands together, all business. "Can I help you find something?"

"That'd be great." She knew she'd never find what she wanted quickly without help. "I need some supplies for my dog—food, shampoo, things like that."

"Go straight down this aisle and turn left." He nodded to the aisle closest to the wall covered in padlocks of all shapes and sizes. "The 'Feeds and Needs' section is right there in a room by itself."

Sophie waved goodbye and hurried along, unsure of how long she'd been talking with him. She was determined to be ready and waiting outside when Neal pulled up. She walked quickly down the aisle, around the corner, and crashed into Frank Morgan. She knocked several keys from his hand to the floor.

"Watch where you're going!" Frank bent awkwardly in the tight space to gather the keys.

"I'll get them," she said quickly. She scooped up the keys, then dropped them into his outstretched hand. "Sorry, I was going too fast."

Frank scowled. "Seems to be the only way you move. You flew out of the library so fast we never finished our talk about Alden."

Her heart sank. The last thing she wanted was another chat with creepy Frank. She still didn't have her dog supplies, and Neal was likely on his way. To distract him, she pointed to the keys and asked the first thing that came to mind, "Are you having duplicates made?"

"What?" He gave a sharp, emphatic shake of denial. "I made these for a customer. I fill in when Tom's short of help."

It didn't seem to her that Tom was overworked, but maybe he wanted to help Frank feel useful. "So, you're all over the place then," she said lightly. When he peered at her suspiciously, she clarified, "You run the Mini-Mart, help at the library, and now here."

"Oh, sure." He snickered as if she'd said something funny. "I get around, alright."

"I really need to get some supplies for my dog." She edged past him into the room beyond, careful not to brush arms. "Someone's picking me up in a little bit."

"I could give you a ride," he offered, following her into the supply room and shaking the loose keys in his hand.

"Ah, no thanks." She grabbed the products she needed off the shelves, piled them into the crook of her arm, and turned to find Dan standing in the doorway.

"You ready?" Dan leaned a shoulder against the doorframe. "Hey, Frank."

"Afternoon." Frank didn't seem too pleased to see him.

"I thought Neal was picking me up," she blurted out before she could think.

Dan shrugged. "He left me a message that the meeting was running long. Asked if I wouldn't mind running you home so you wouldn't have to wait."

"Thanks, I appreciate that." she said. She knew she'd just avoided another conversation or, even worse, a car ride with Frank. The way Frank was darting shrewd looks between them reminded her to be careful, or everyone would know of their housing arrangements. Getting Dan to understand it was something else altogether.

At her slight frown and glance at Frank, Dan deliberately pretended to misunderstand her. "Sorry," he turned to Frank and offered graciously, "Frank, did you need a ride?"

She swung her head back and forth in panic and mouthed 'no.' The last thing she needed was to be sandwiched in between Dan and Frank, a hostage for another lecture on Nehemiah Alden.

"What's that?" Frank frowned. "You know I've got another two hours here and my own car."

Dan nodded easily. "That's right, I forgot." He tuned to Sophie with a wicked grin. "All set to go?"

"I'm ready. 'Bye Frank." She slid past him, arms full of supplies, and stamped on Dan's foot. The sharp intake of breath told her she'd gotten the baby toe she'd wanted.

"What was that for?" Dan asked, limping behind her up the aisle.

"For being a brat at the end of a very long day. You pretended to misunderstand me!" Sophie hissed.

"And you didn't give me any credit for being able to think on my own." Dan looked as though he was willing to argue about it all day.

She glared at him over the bag of dog food in her arms. "I didn't want him to know about the housing arrangements."

"In two days, everyone will know." He took the bag of dog food from her and continued toward the register. "But unless you keep carrying on like we're up to something, they'll all think we're working on the light-house, which we should, and will, be doing."

What was wrong with her? Here she was snapping at someone she'd be living with for the foreseeable future. "Sorry. Like I said, it's been a long day."

"Apology accepted." He set the bag down on the check-out counter, nodded to Tom, and plastered an ingratiating smile on his face. "And to show there are no hard feelings, I'll let you buy me dinner."

"Not a chance." Sophie choked down a laugh. "Was he always like this?" she asked, turning to Tom.

"Pretty much." Tom rang up her purchases and put them in a bag. "He was always trying to get someone to feed him." Tom looked Dan over and said, "Don't know where he puts it, though. Been eating like that since he was a kid. You'd think he'd've run to fat by now." He shrugged like it was beyond him.

"It's good, honest living that keeps me in shape," Dan said modestly, patting his flat belly.

Tom snorted. "That'll be thirty-six dollars and forty-three cents, Ms. Tyler."

"Please, call me Sophie."

"Fair enough." Tom gathered up the money, then slid the bag across for Dan to heft. "Stop by sometime to browse. You may be surprised."

"I will," she called as she stuffed her change into her purse and hurried after Dan. She didn't know what had gotten into him, but he was moving like he was in a footrace. By the time she exited the store, he had dumped the bag in the flatbed of his pick-up and climbed in. She scrambled into the passenger's side and had just barely fastened her seatbelt when he shot out of the parking space.

"What's the hurry?" she gasped, bracing her arm on the passenger's door. "I thought only Chelle drove like a maniac."

"I want to get to *Gladys'* before the dinner rush." He tapped his fingers on the steering wheel, then checked the rear-view mirror.

"There's a rush?" It didn't seem like people in Pocasset rushed anywhere.

"Yeah," he said and gave her a sour look, "and I'd like to get some work done today. All I've managed to do was attend a meeting about ghosts and run errands for Neal. I'm not getting paid to do either."

She refused to feel bad about Neal forcing him to pick her up. "The faster we get this figured out, the sooner we'll all get back to our own schedules." Dan's disgruntled grumbling didn't sound like he believed her, and she didn't blame him. There was also no guarantee that finding out what had happened to Abigail would end the apparitions. With the events of the last few days, all work on the lighthouse had screeched to a halt. She didn't envy the person who would have to explain the lack of progress to Philip Bishop. She suspected that Dan, being a reasonable person, would leave that honor to Neal.

They managed to make it in and out of the diner before the 'rush' by ordering their food to go. Sophie added an extra turkey club in case Chelle or Neal showed up hungry. Despite Dan's claim to want to be gone quickly, he took the time to chat with everyone at the diner while they waited. It was rather nice to have this community that shouted hellos and asked after your family, good-naturedly ribbed you about your lousy performance in the softball game, and tried to set you up with their cousin.

They finally received their food and made it back to the lighthouse to find that Chelle and Neal were already there and sitting on the stone wall. Aesop was settled in the grass beside them, gnawing on the biggest bone Sophie had ever seen.

Dan bent to get a closer look at Aesop's foot long treasure. "It looks like a dinosaur bone."

"Chelle said it wouldn't be a bad idea to bring him a bone." Neal looked a bit uncomfortable. "She didn't say how big."

Chelle laughed and jostled Neal by leaning against him with her shoulder. "I didn't know they came that big, but I think it's a smart move to bribe him with the biggest they had."

Above them, calling gulls caught the shifting breeze over the woods and slid past the lighthouse to swoop and dive over the sea. They danced alone and in pairs against the fading daylight. As they watched the graceful aerial display, nobody was willing to talk about the apparitions or to go back inside the lighthouse. But someone had to be the first to mention it. They couldn't sit outside all night. "Should we give it a try?" Sophie asked, motioning at the front door. "Maybe something will happen."

"I doubt it." Dan tapped the takeout bag she still held. "We may as well eat. I've got a ton of paperwork to do before getting some sheetrock up in the living room."

Dan and Neal had agreed to keep the crew away, with the excuse of the White Horse Tavern needing immediate attention, until they had sorted out what was happening at The Point. Neal would pitch in and help with the parts of the project Dan couldn't handle alone.

Reluctantly, Chelle rose from the stone wall to leave. "Good luck. I'll be in and out for as long as this goes on, but if something happens," she jabbed Dan in the arm with a finger, "I expect a phone call."

He scowled and nodded. "Alright, alright. I promise."

They watched her climb into her Mini and zip down the lane toward town. Completely uninterested, Aesop ignored even the squirrels and continued to gnaw on his bone.

With Dan in the lead crunching up the gravel path, they walked to the front door warily. It was the first time the three of them had been back without Chelle since the full-blown apparition of Nehemiah and Abigail. Who knew what was going to happen? For Sophie, the dread came not from another event but from what she would see. What had Alden done after throwing Abigail in the cache?

As Dan pushed open the front door, she heard him inhale sharply. "What?" She craned to look around his tall frame. Neal, taller and behind her, could see well past him into the house beyond and cursed softly. "What?" She shoved impatiently at Dan. "What's going on?"

He stepped aside and gave her a full view of the hallway. It was writhing in gray wisps, lit by a dim light from the living room beyond. Her lips moved wordlessly, and the food bag slid from her hands.

She made a panicked grab for Dan's shirt when he moved forward and groped behind her for Neal, latching on to his wrist. No one was going anywhere alone. As they inched forward, gray wisps wrapped around their legs and reached out from the walls to brush cheeks and caress shoulders. Fear slicked along her skin and raised the hair on the back of her neck. She pressed her face into Dan's back and scrunched her eyes shut. It happened a long time ago, she repeated to herself, hauling in a strangled breath. *"Please, help me,"* echoed in her head, though she knew none of the three of them had made a sound. She pressed her head harder against Dan's back and felt the reassuring heat of him through his shirt.

"Help me."

Oh no. Oh no, she thought as a wave of dread washed over her. She turned her head to the side and opened her eyes a crack. She knew where she was but didn't recognize much. These walls were whitewashed. An oil lamp hung from the ceiling and a small table, scattered with shells, sat beside a carved chair near the fireplace—a large silver medallion anchored to its stones. Out of the cache rose a rough wooden ladder.

Amid the twisting gray wisps, the three of them huddled to one side of the doorway, waiting eyes fixed on the cache. She glanced from Dan's tense face to Neal's impassive one and was thankful she wasn't alone. She refused to let go of either of them, even though they pulled for more space. Neal nudged her as the ladder began to twitch and shift. The silvery blond head of Nehemiah Alden appeared over the top, his face partially hidden by a bundle of cloth. He rose one more rung, then heaved the bundle onto the floor with effort. He hauled himself out, crawled to the bundle, and rolled it over to expose the ashen face of Abigail Hart.

Sophie could not look away from Abigail's still form, although she desperately wanted to do just that. Was the girl alive? She was so pale that Sophie dreaded the worst.

Nehemiah sat back on his heels, grabbed the girl by her gown front and slapped her sharply on both cheeks. When Dan stiffened with anger and moved forward as if to intervene, Sophie hung on to his shirt more tightly. When he whipped around to frown at her, she shot him a look of desperate warning.

"Enough of this pretense. Answer me," Nehemiah growled, shaking her. When the girl remained limp, he let her thump to the floor. He chafed her wrists, then stilled, a crease forming between his eyes. He ran his hands roughly over her limbs. Pushing and prodding, he paused only once over the mound of her belly before making his way to her face. He scraped the lank black hair from her forehead and settled his hand there. "Not even three days and fevered," he bit out. Nehemiah thumped a fist against his thigh. Gathering her into his arms like a rag doll, he stood. He hefted his pitiful package a bit higher and exited the room, the girl's head lolling against his chest as he walked.

No one breathed as Alden passed them, turning for the stairs and vanishing halfway up the staircase. They remained motionless, until Sophie gasped and broke the spell.

There was a scent of acrid dirt, lavender, and cloves in the air. Her heart lurched in her chest. Unbelievable. They had been so real she could smell them. As the trio slowly separated from each other, the colonial room and the scent of dirt, flowers, and spice faded with the ebbing gray wisps.

"Everybody okay?" Neal twisted free from Sophie's grasp, rotating his wrist to get the blood circulating. She suspected that it would be a while before the blood returned to his face. She knew it would be a long time before she recovered.

She nodded shakily. She realized she was still clutching Dan's shirt and let go, leaving a damp bunch of wrinkled cloth in the middle of his back.

"I'm okay." Dan moved to the bottom of the darkened stairs and peered up. "I think the show's over for tonight." He lifted the food bag she had dropped upside down when they had entered the lighthouse. "Here, see what you can save from this."

"Are you kidding?" She said weakly as she took the bag from him. "I don't think I could eat a thing."

"Me either, but it will keep us busy until Chelle can get here. We can talk about what happened then." He rubbed at the center of his forehead. "First, we need time to settle down, and second, I only want to hash this out once."

Neal motioned toward the stairwell. "I'm going to check the second floor." He gave Dan a meaningful look. "You might want to check outside."

Dan nodded and turned to leave but blocked Sophie when she tried to follow. "I have to get Aesop," she huffed when he refused to let her pass.

"I'll get him." Dan turned Sophie back toward the kitchen with a gentle shove. "I have to get my cell phone out of the truck to call Chelle."

She wrinkled her forehead. "What's wrong?"

"Humor me?" Dan asked seriously. "Stay in the house . . . please."

"Alright," she agreed, but without much grace. "Try to take that bone away from him before he comes in, though." She peeked into the dinner bag and curled her lip in disgust; the cold food had spilled from the Styrofoam containers and littered the bottom of the bag. She sighed and went to work.

While coffee perked and water boiled for tea, she assembled plates of cold chicken tenders and fries, then toasted more bread for the soggy club sandwich. Dan was right; the busy work was settling. It also gave her time to reflect on how neatly they had maneuvered to keep her in the house and in the kitchen. She suspected that they were protecting her, but she wasn't willing to take on the role of head cook permanently.

What kind of position had Abigail held in her own household, in her marriage, if the "courtship phase" is what they had just seen? She gazed out the window toward the bluff where the sea below still rose and fell as it had since Abigail's time, yet the water had not erased the traces of that terrified girl on the beach. The house had burned to the ground, leaving nothing but the fireplace and foundation stones, but that too had not purged the trauma. If fire and water had been useless, what could they hope to accomplish as witnesses to someone else's tragedy?

Barks of welcome let her know that Chelle was back. She set the plates of food on the counter and brewed a cup of tea while waiting for the others. Unfortunately, with no chairs, they would all be standing when they talked. The clicking of nails on the floor and the odd thump told her that Aesop had won his battle to drag that huge bone inside. He entered, tail wagging, and settled himself near the turret door to gnaw once again. Dan and Chelle followed, with Neal bringing up the rear, reporting all was quiet.

"Okay," Dan said, opening the refrigerator and grabbing a soda. "It's clear that at least two of us need to be here at a time. It's too risky without someone to watch your back."

"What were you both doing outside and upstairs?" Sophie asked. She still thought they'd conspired to keep her out of the way, and she wanted an answer.

"Before you and Chelle got to the Darby place, Carol said there was a possibility of multiple or sequential apparitions in, and around, the lighthouse." Neal didn't look pleased with either possibility. "We needed to check."

"Dan told me the gist of what happened" Chelle swung her back-pack from her shoulder to set it on the floor. "It sounds just horrible." She shivered and tucked her hands under her folded arms. "What do you think? Was tonight's event random, or did it seem to carry on from the last time?"

"She had the same gown on as before, and she was still pregnant," Neal answered. "As far as we know, it was Abigail's only pregnancy—the Aldens never had children."

Sophie racked her memory for details that might help but drew a blank. She had to agree with Neal, though. It certainly seemed to continue from what they had seen the first time.

"Did she say anything?" Chelle pressed, reaching for a sandwich triangle and taking a tiny bite.

"No," Dan said, and "Yes," Sophie said at the same time.

"I didn't hear anything," Neal said with a frown. He picked cold fries off a plate without much enthusiasm. "What'd you hear, Sophie?"

"When it first started happening and that gray stuff was twisting all over us, I closed my eyes and kept saying to myself, 'It's over. It happened a long time ago.'" Sophie tried to lick her lips, but her mouth was so dry it was pointless. She reached for her mug and took a few sips of tea. "Then I heard Abigail pleading, 'Please, help me,' as if she were in my mind." She shivered involuntarily. "I heard her again a second time. When I opened my eyes, I saw we were in the old living room with a ladder sticking out of the cache." She took an unsteady breath. "That was the last thing I heard her say."

Chelle whistled softly, eyebrows raised. "So, you were in the original living room, not just in the middle of that gray stuff?"

Dan nodded. "It was like stepping back in time."

"Why didn't either of you hear anything?" Sophie glanced from one man to the other.

"Your guess is as good as mine." Dan shrugged. "Maybe Abigail can only communicate with other women?"

"I don't know." Chelle pensively tugged on her lower lip. "Let me ask Carol; maybe there's something to it. Anybody notice anything else?" She looked expectantly between them.

"This time it moved from the living room to the second-floor stair-case before Alden disappeared," Neal pointed out.

"Right," Dan said. "So, we know the apparitions aren't just stuck in the living room, although they both started there. And there was this smell too." He looked up as he tried to place the scent. "Some kind of weird mix of dirt and flowers and something spicy."

Sophie could still taste the cloying mix. "Lavender and cloves. I smelled it for the first time in the cache . . . I'd forgotten." She wiped sud-denly damp palms on her dress. "It was the same smell as tonight."

"Do you think it was Abigail? Or a combination of the two of them?" Chelle was like Aesop after his bone.

"What difference does it make?" Sophie turned sharply toward the window. In the now darkened sky, a slip of moon rising over the horizon glazed the fronts of the trees and uneven grass with a faint sheen. "She looked terrible, Chelle—sick and unresponsive. If we're right about the timeline, she survived whatever it was she caught in the cache and went on to marry Alden, but I don't know how."

"Sorry," Chelle said, looking hurt. "Sometimes, I get carried away." She made a face. "It's hard to understand not being here to see for myself."

Sophie turned from the window to face Dan and Neal. "Maybe we should have her stay. She was here earlier, and it didn't stop the appari-tion. It was already happening when we opened the door."

Dan tossed his can into the trash. "It's okay with me, but I think we've kicked this around enough for tonight." He took a bite of chicken tender and waved it, emphasizing his point. "We can't do anything until they appear again or get an idea of where to look. And" he said grimly, "in spite of all this ghost business, I have got to get some work done."

"Exactly," Neal said. "So, Chelle stays, but we need some ground rules so that we don't get on each other's nerves." He gestured to the pile of disposable dishes by the sink and the food still spread over the counter. "I won't live in a pigsty. If you cook, you clean. If you eat, you clean. Since almost all the rooms will serve a double purpose, knock. Three-minute showers only, and if I'm working, don't bother me—I won't want com-pany. Got it?"

When the women both agreed and Dan grumbled a 'yeah,' Neal nodded and turned for the door. He paused beside Aesop to trade him a chicken strip for his bone, tossed the bone outside, and snapped the kitchen door shut. "Goodnight," he said and left the room.

They listened as his footsteps climbed the stairs, strode across the second floor to the bedroom where Sophie had her boxes and heard the door swing shut behind him. Dan rolled his eyes and started collecting the used plates.

"Alright, so that went well." Chelle smiled, looking pleased. "I'll move in tomorrow." She threw the rest of the fries into the trash and began to package the remaining food.

Sophie couldn't figure out why Chelle was so eager to join them. It would have been smarter to find an excuse to stay out. But regardless of Chelle's reasons, she would be glad to have her around. For one thing, she'd need help negotiating the minefield of living with Dan and Neal. The tension that rolled around when the two men were in the same room didn't seem to bother Chelle in the least.

After the kitchen was clean, Dan stomped off to the living room to work, muttering about sending Philip Bishop an itemized bill of all the extras he was being forced to do. When Sophie looked at Chelle in concern, Chelle brushed it off. "Forget it. He got all the drama genes in the family." She patted Aesop goodbye before collecting her backpack and making her way to the front of the house. "I'll see you tomorrow. Don't worry about who goes where. I'll take whatever room is left."

After promising to keep her posted, Sophie locked the door and debated about saying goodnight to Dan. She didn't want to test his patience any further, but she decided it was better to be civil if they would be living together. She went to stand in the living room doorway and watched him measure twice, transfer those measurements to a large sheet of plaster wrapped in thick paper, and cut it with a lethal-looking knife. She almost offered to help lift the large sheet onto the wall, when he hoisted it himself and fit it against the window frame like a huge puzzle piece. "It looks like you've done that a time or two," she said, stepping further into the room.

"Once or twice." He removed a portable drill from his utility belt, braced the sheet with one forearm and knee, then anchored it in place with the whine and screech of screws against plaster and paper. "Do you need something?"

"No, I just wanted to say goodnight. Do you want any help?"

He continued securing the large sheet with more screws in a predictable rhythm that she found soothing. "If I do," Dan said without glancing at her, "I'll get Neal. Goodnight, Sophie."

"'Night.'" She ducked her head and called Aesop. As she started up the stairs, she wondered how she had become surrounded by such bad-tempered people, both living and dead. Her dealings with all of them was starting to give her a headache. Even though her teaching would keep her away a good amount of time, she wondered grimly if the time she did spend here would still be too long.

While Aesop settled at the foot of the bed, Sophie closed the door and pulled the shade down over the open window. She removed the clip from her hair and brushed it out, soothed by the long smooth strokes and wondered what simple pleasures had been left to Abigail after her marriage to Alden. There couldn't have been much joy in a life with a man like that. She tried to shake off the sadness and focused on getting ready for bed, choosing a sleeveless cotton top and yoga pants for sleeping. If the Aldens were going to make another appearance, she didn't want it to happen when she was in her nightgown.

A cool breeze ruffled the drawn shade. She felt summer winding down like the slowing of a bicycle wheel. Although the days were still gloriously warm and the shores still filled with visitors, the nights had begun to develop an edge. She rummaged in a tote she had yet to unpack and found a blanket and light quilt. She added them to the bed before gratefully climbing under them. Regardless of the temperature, she preferred to keep the window open and snuggling under the blankets. The sound of the surf and the smell of salt air that occasionally wafted in was worth the cooler room temperature.

She dozed off long before the steady rhythm of Dan's work had finished or the movement in Neal's room had ceased.

The little house on the bluff rested quietly under the waning moon. The soft rustle of leaves and the sweep of water against the shore wrapped The Point in nighttime quiet. While the people slept, one whose hands were twisted like claws slid against window frames and pressed against panes looking for entry.

Something outside the window had Aesop's ears pricking. Half-asleep, Sophie watched him pad to the window and sniff along the sill, hackles rising. A growl started deep in his chest and vibrated there while he listened intently. There was a scattering of gravel, and a bark erupted from him that brought her bolt upright in bed. He raced for the door, scratching at it with both paws to raise the alarm.

"What is it, boy? What's the matter?" She struggled out of the blankets and swung her feet to the floor. Whining in response, Aesop repeatedly lunged hard at the door. When she hauled him aside and opened it, he shot down the stairs in a scramble of legs.

Neal joined her in the hall, pulling a T-shirt over his bare chest, something that she registered with faint surprise. "What's wrong?" he asked.

"I don't know, but I'd better let him out before he breaks something." She stumbled down the stairs to where Aesop was jumping against the door, making it impossible to open.

When Neal joined her, he reached around her and grabbed the knob. "You hold him, and I'll open it." Once she'd wrestled Aesop away and planted her feet, Neal pulled the door open. Sophie let go when it was finally wide enough and staggered as Aesop shot straight to the area under a first-floor window. He sniffed for a moment, then followed the scent at a run to the woods.

"Aesop! Aesop!" she yelled. "Do you think I should go after him?" she asked, turning to Neal.

He rubbed his eyes wearily. "I have no idea."

"He'll be back." Dan came out of the office. His clothes and hair were rumpled from sleep. "Know what set him off?"

"No." She shifted from one bare foot to the other, hugging her arms against the cold. "I woke up when he was barking at the window. When I finally got him out, he charged for the woods."

"It could have been an animal." Dan stretched and yawned but went out to inspect the ground where Aesop had sniffed. "Call again and see if he comes."

Sophie called and called. Her voice reached out into the trees, but it was absorbed by the dense growth. She moved across the rough gravel to the damp grass and tried again. "Aesop! Come here, boy. Come on." She shouted as loud as she could, moving closer to the tree line. A clear yelp and frantic barking had her running for the woods. "Aesop! Come, boy. Come on."

"Dammit, Sophie! Wait!" Dan called after her.

She could see him gesture urgently to Neal, dark shadows in pantomime against the lighthouse, before she plunged into the trees.

The forest swallowed Sophie whole. Dense shrubs and towering evergreens blocked out every scrap of moonlight. She hadn't taken her bearings when entering the woods and had no idea where she was. She hoped Aesop would continue his baying. She ducked under the branches and tried to place her bare feet on flat, smooth surfaces, but it was impossible. Twigs and rocks jabbed at her soles. When I get a hold of his scruffy hide, she complained silently, but called in the sweetest voice possible, "Aesop, good boy. Come on out, and let's go home." As if in answer, the baying stopped and she froze, listening. There wasn't a sound. Unsure whether to call again, she leaned back against the rough bark of a tree, straining to hear familiar sounds.

For the longest time, there was an eerie quiet as though the trees were listening and waiting with her. Fear slid through her, leaving her skin cold and prickling. She pressed her lips together to quiet her ragged breathing and dug her nails into the tree behind her. There was something out here besides her and Aesop. It was biding its time, patient to see if she would venture further into the woods.

Downwind, like he had been taught when hunting, he flexed his misshapen fingers and listened. If she had continued walking, she would have passed close enough for him to stroke her hair. No matter. The dog was now lost, having dropped his scent in the marshy woods. It could be hours before it found its way back. He could go to her and be quick about it. They wouldn't find her until daylight when he would be long gone.

A branch snapped and leaves rustled near to where she stood, moving in a line toward her. She kept her eyes fixed on the movement and backed away, stumbling slowly backward from tree to tree. Bushes nearer to her began to sway and terror surged through her. She tensed, filling her lungs to scream, when Aesop bounded out of the shrubs and barked a joyful greeting.

"Aesop!" she gasped, torn between relief and anger. "You just took ten years off my life." She sank onto her knees and grabbed him to her. "Where have you been?" she demanded. "You scared me, and now we're both lost." She continued talking while Aesop tried licking her face and crawling into her lap.

The sound of movement in the fallen leaves had them both tensing. Aesop struggled to free himself, but she held on tight.

Her breath escaped in a whoosh when she saw Dan emerge from the undergrowth.

"Good, you found him." He turned, then shouted, "Neal, over here."

The watcher pulled back behind a tree to stand still. He could have delt easily with the woman, but the dog and men made things more complicated than it needed to be. He would be patient, waiting to find her alone.

Sophie stood and gave Dan a shaky smile. She was genuinely relieved to be with someone who knew how to get back to the lighthouse. "Thanks for coming after us."

"Neal's bringing a flashlight. I know where we are, but it'll make it easier if we can see the path." He eyed her warily. "You're not going to cry, are you?"

She made a rueful face. "No, but my feet are." She winced, shifting from foot to foot. "I should have put shoes on like you did. Running off without them is not the smartest thing I've ever done."

He shook his head as if he were dealing with someone particularly dense. "Especially if you come down with a roaring case of poison ivy."

She raked her memory for what she knew about poison ivy but could only call to mind pictures of the oozing rash. "Seriously?"

"Yeah." He bent down and slung her over his shoulder, ignoring her squeak of alarm. "We'll meet Neal on the way. Better get back to the house and wash those feet. If the plant oil stays on long enough, you'll breakout, guaranteed." Aesop jumped around them barking, wanting a part in the game.

They must have made an odd sight staggering toward the edge of the forest—the tall hunchbacked shadow, stumbling over rocks and lurching against trees, and the leaping dog. Neal caught Dan before he toppled into the field. "Is she hurt?"

"No. She's barefoot and been walking through poison ivy," Dan said in disgust. "What took you so long?"

"Couldn't find the flashlight in that pigsty you call an office." Neal played the light over Sophie's inverted face. "You okay?"

"I'm fine." She thumped Dan on the back. "You can put me down now."

"Knock it off or I'll drop you on your head," he threatened. "I'll put you down in the tub where you can wash off and not track that oil all over the house."

She resigned herself to being carried like a sack toward the lighthouse. The house soon blazed with light as she was carried upstairs and dumped unceremoniously in the shower. Dan gave her a gritty cleanser that smelled like gasoline. "Hurry up," he said. "I probably got some on me too."

Later, when movement no longer made shadows on the shades, the watcher slunk from the woods. He skirted along the outside of the house and crept through the damp grass for something he had seen near the kitchen door. He swung his foot, sweeping the ground in the dark, and struck it. Quietly hefting the bone under his arm, he loped off toward the woods, using the overgrown path that would lead him back to the village undetected.

7

Nehemiah and the Crone

The slip of moon that had barely lit the dense woods two weeks ago had passed its cycle, and Sophie observed with mixed feelings that since Chelle had moved in there hadn't been a single apparition. It was as if the lighthouse had exchanged ghosts for plants. Chelle's clothes had fit neatly in the small closet with room to spare. However, her plants had taken over almost all the flat surfaces of Sophie's office. They lined the floor, balanced on windowsills, and sat on boxes. It gave her the ridiculous sense of having dropped her desk into the middle of the tropics where quickly growing vines and foliage covered everything in their path. Chelle's excuse had been that there were just too many, and their needs too different, to trust their care to someone else. Sophie had learned the pickiness of those plants the hard way. One day she'd mistakenly misted a fuzzy plant with cheerful purple flowers sunning under her desk lamp. Chelle's shout of horror and the following lecture on watering African violets, "from the bottom or the leaves will rot and drop," had sworn her off touching them altogether.

Despite what Sophie saw as a tendency to be plant-obsessive, Chelle was an important presence in the house. She diffused difficult situations with a joke and lightheartedness Sophie was often too tense to manage. Surprisingly, the four of them didn't fight over things she had imagined they would need a panel of judges to settle—like Aesop's nighttime waking of the entire house and the following search of the woods.

The men hadn't held the late-night trouble against either her or Aesop. They preferred lack of sleep to vandalism or theft. In fact, it had shown them some holes in their security. It was fine to have an alarm on the house to protect people and the restoration work inside, but since the project was in its beginning stages there wasn't much finished work to protect. Most of the equipment would be delivered shortly and stored outside in a temporary shelter. To get ready for the delivery, they had set up spotlights to discourage thieves. They reasoned that it lessened the appeal of sneaking onto the property if it could light up like a shopping mall.

So, an event that Sophie thought would have Neal packing his bags was a non-issue, but the smaller things had them close to drawing blood on more than one occasion. Chelle had set up a rotating shopping schedule for groceries and posted showering times outside the bathroom. Dan had refused to stand in line and had constructed a make-shift shower outside with a tarp, smooth stones from the beach, and a hose connected to the kitchen sink.

Today it was her turn to shower first because she had an eight o'clock class to teach in Falmouth. After she let Aesop out, she shuffled to the bathroom but found Neal already inside. Although the delay hadn't made her too late, she stomped down the stairs, balancing an awkward pile of textbooks, class registers, and purse. Breakfast would now need to be eaten in the car, thanks to Neal. When she quickly swung around the newel post, her armful tumbled onto the floor and the entire contents of her purse spilled.

"Oh, for Pete's sake." She got down on all fours. The wallet, old receipts, tissues, and keys got shoveled into a pile, then rammed back into her bag.

"Missed one." Dan crouched beside her, offering a lipstick that had rolled the length of the hall.

"Thanks." She reached for it, but he didn't let go, forcing her to look at him as they stood.

"What's the matter?"

"Neal was in the bathroom when he shouldn't have been, and then I dropped my stuff, and now I'm going to be late." It sounded so ridiculous when it was said out loud.

"We can both be thoughtless, but that's been the case from the get-go." He cocked his head to the side. "What's really the problem?"

She took a shuddering breath and let fly, "I've got to go teach this class, and I don't want to. A good number of my students are completely messed up—kids really, with adult problems. Single parents, abuse victims, addicts coming to school to make a better life. They write about it, and it breaks my heart." The words tumbled out one after the other. "I've even got a 'locker tapper,' this big blond kid. He missed the first six sessions and has now started showing up a half hour early for class. He walks the hall outside the classroom, tapping every third locker and listening as if someone will answer. He's completely out to lunch, and he believes coming early now will make up for what he's missed. It won't. It can't."

"But you like teaching."

"I do," she admitted, then her shoulders slumped. "It's just . . . it's not really the kids." She blinked quickly, fighting tears. "It's been two weeks. When do you think Alden will appear again?" She pressed her hand to her forehead. "Every time I open a door, I brace thinking 'this could be it' and there's nothing there. The waiting is wearing me out."

"It's wearing us all out," he said. "Maybe it's over."

"No." She knew that couldn't be true. "I can feel it coming. It's not done."

"Okay, then we'll deal with what comes together." He shrugged. "You're not alone here, you know. We're all feeling the same thing which is why we're getting on each other's nerves."

"You might be right," she said with a slight nod. There was nothing she could do at this point to help Abigail. All she had done so far was wear herself out with worry, and now she was going to be late on top of everything. When she noticed that he still held a scrap of her scattered papers she asked, "Can I have that?"

Dan glanced at the Michelangelo quote she had copied and read out loud, "'Draw, Antonio, Antonio draw, draw and do not waste time . . . .'" He turned the scrap over and considered. "Michelangelo, huh? Did he really say this?"

"If he didn't, he should have." She smiled faintly, taking it from him. "It was in a biography Tom at the hardware store was reading. Apparently, Michelangelo wrote it to prod along a procrastinating apprentice."

"Speaking of which, I need to finish priming the walls." He tucked his hands into his jeans pockets and nodded. "It'll be okay. You'll see." When she was silent, he turned down the hall. "See you later."

"Bye. And Dan?" She stopped him before he could disappear into the living room. "Thanks."

He brushed it off. "Let it go for now . . . it'll come soon enough."

"Be careful what you wish for," she whispered when he'd gone. She gathered her things and headed out to see if the 'locker tapper' had beat her to class again today.

The following weeks developed a steady pattern. Blue Water Construction was hauling the lighthouse out of disrepair and showing a vision Sophie had been too short-sighted to imagine. Dan had finished painting and had moved the make-shift kitchen into the newly renovated living room. He had set up a long folding table to hold all the appliances. Usually kitchen spaces were completed last, but with all four of them living in the lighthouse, they needed a fully functioning kitchen as soon as possible. Neal and Chelle were in and out, managing the lighthouse project as well as other jobs. Sophie, too, had gotten into a pattern at the college and was beginning to see progress in some students. The rhythm had a sense of cautious ease settling over the group, enough to have them questioning the value of all remaining under the same roof.

Chelle was the first to suggest a change when they gathered for dinner a few days later. As they sat around the living room, surrounded by creamy vanilla walls and white trim, it was hard to imagine any more drama happening in this welcoming room. Chelle toyed with her sandwich and half-heartedly volunteered to leave first. "Maybe I should go. Maybe something would happen if I wasn't here." Aesop whined and crawled closer, licking her hand as though he understood.

"Or," Neal added, "it might be over, and we can get back to our own lives."

"Sophie says it's not," Dan said, shaking his head. "And I don't think it is either."

Sophie sat crossed legged opposite the cache, a bowl of cereal cradled in her lap. She had chosen breakfast food over another salad or sandwich. "I don't know for sure, but I feel like it's not. And it's not just wishful thinking on my part. I'd be disappointed not to find out what had happened to Abigail, but in a way I'd be relieved."

Neal shrugged, "At this point I don't think it matters if you stay or go, Chelle. Give it a few more days. If nothing happens, we can all clear out, except for Sophie, of course, who needs to stay." When Dan started to disagree, Neal cut him off. "Nothing's happened since Alden carried Abigail out of the cache and none of us have seen or dreamed anything or we would have said so." He gave a dismissive wave. "I think it has run its course."

Sophie eyed the recently enclosed cache with its proper trap door and heavy brass hardware and felt the clench in her stomach that had accompanied every single apparition so far. Being alone once again in the lighthouse didn't appeal in the least, but she couldn't blame the others for wanting to get back to their own lives. She also had no way of forcing them to stay.

Stop it. What had happened had scared her, but she'd never been in any danger. "Well," she said with forced lightness. "Why don't we see how it plays out and go from there?" When no one commented, she jumped on the first thing that came to mind. "Aesop finally remembered where he buried that bone you gave him, Neal. He showed up yesterday with it and wanted to bring it into the house." She wrinkled her nose. "It was absolutely disgusting."

Chelle said quietly as she scratched Aesop's ears, "He must have done that a long time ago; I haven't seen it in a bit."

"Can't beat a moldy bone," Dan said and tossed limp fries back into his plate. "It'd be better than this."

Neal flicked salad around its container as if looking for something edible. "I think we've bankrolled *Gladys'* for the last month. I'm ready for something different."

"We could go out for Italian," Chelle suggested, sitting up straighter.

"Or have one last clambake of the season." Dan seemed to perk up at the prospect of real food. "We could have it down on the beach like when we were kids—fire pit, seaweed, corn on the cob, clams and lobsters."

"I suppose it wouldn't hurt," Neal agreed, "before we all get back to life as we know it."

There was no doubt in Sophie's mind what he was talking about . . . a few more days at best was what was left of their current housing arrangement. She drank the rest of the milk out of her cereal bowl, the dissolved sugar making the milk too sweet for her stomach. Alone again. Well, it wasn't the first time, and it wouldn't be the last.

She rose to toss her plastic bowl and spoon into the trash. "The sooner things get back to normal the better," she agreed. Saying it was one thing, but believing it was another.

How would she manage here by herself? She didn't have the luxury of just moving elsewhere if the Aldens acted up. She was stuck. She wished them a quick good night, escaping to her room before she made a complete fool of herself by begging them to stay.

Sophie curled up on the bed covered in her school stuff. She had a stack of grading to do but found herself reaching for her phone and calling Jacqueline instead.

"Sophie?" Jacqueline asked from the other end of the call. "Hold on a minute and let me pull over. I'm in the car." There was a short pause, and then she was back. "Is everything okay?"

Sophie toyed with the metal spiral of her grading register and shrugged. "Sure, why wouldn't it be?"

"Well," came the dry reply, "You're calling me, for starters."

Sophie sighed. "I promised I would call when I got settled and I am."

"And are you . . . settled that is?"

She thought it over, rocking her head from side to side. What could she tell her? What would Jacqueline believe? Sophie had seen the apparitions herself, and it still sounded unbelievable. She settled for the superficial and a memory she hadn't thought of in years. "The lighthouse is great and really coming along. You'd love it. It reminds me of the one in York, Maine."

There was a silence, and she thought Jacqueline would resist the reminder and begin harping about coming home, then Jacqueline said quietly, "That was a special vacation: two weeks of sun, surf, and Nubble Light. We were in heaven."

"Mmm," Sophie agreed in gratitude. It was stupid that such an ordinary remark would mean so much. Just that small acknowledgement of common ground had her eyes filling.

When the silence stretched on, Jacqueline asked, "What else is going on, Sophie? I know you, and something's up,"

Sophie stumbled on. "I don't know how to explain it." That, at least, was the absolute truth. "I came across the mysterious disappearance of a colonial girl in the village, and it's kind of getting to me." A shadow . . . of a hint . . . of the truth. "I don't know if I want to find out what happened to her, or even if I can."

"You're upset about a girl that's been missing for three hundred years?" Jacqueline said, her confusion and disbelief obvious.

This was a mistake. Sophie found she just couldn't tell her what had happened at The Point; Jacqueline would think she'd completely lost her mind. "It's . . . complicated," she said, finally and winced. Even to her ears, she sounded lame.

She thought she heard her sister mutter, "For goodness' sakes . . . " before Jacqueline cleared her throat and said in even tones. "Listen, I'm really trying here. I don't know what's going on, and you don't seem to want to tell me." Although Sophie tried to interrupt, Jacqueline talked over her, "But I only really need to know two things: one, are you safe, and two, if you need me, you'll call."

She felt a surge of relief and grabbed at the escape Jacqueline had given her. If Jacqueline was willing to take Sophie's word that things were fine, it was clear that Jacqueline was uncomfortable too. "Yes, of course, I'll call if I need you. And I am safe. Thanks, Jac."

"Alright, I'd better get going. I'm not in a great spot to be parked."

"Okay, bye." She swiped the phone off and tossed it onto the bed.

She flopped backwards and pressed the heels of her hands to her eyes. What had she been thinking? The last person she should have called was Jacqueline. Their relationship had never been based on confidences, and what was happening with the Aldens demanded a kind of trust that hadn't existed since their parents had died.

She allowed herself to wallow in self-pity for a while, then sat up suddenly and squared her shoulders. She pushed her hair from her face and took a deep breath. "Get a grip." She slapped her pillow against the headboard, settled back, and pulled her class papers from a canvas tote. Resting against the pillow, she grabbed a red pen and dove into her students' third essays.

Sophie was first aware of the cold. She groped for blankets and scattered the papers still cluttering her bed. A light shone on her face she couldn't place. She frowned and tried to think. The only lamp in the room was across the floor, right next to the only outlet in the room. *"Please, help me,"* begged a woman's distant voice. She lifted her hand to rub her eyes and felt it pass through frigid air that smelled, somehow, of cloves. Cloves. Her eyes flew open, and she stared straight up at Nehemiah Alden. Candle in hand, he bent over the bed to peer into her face with hard assessing eyes.

Prey faced with predator, she pushed back into the pillow. His coldness became a weight pinning her to the mattress. As the tallow candle came closer to her face, she tried to turn her head away, but she couldn't move. She tried to call for help, but no sound came out. For airless seconds he hovered, searching her face. He straightened slowly and turned from the bed—the gray wisps slinking after him as he disappeared down the stairs.

Her heart pounding, she struggled upright and saw Chelle across the hall through the open doorway. Sophie launched herself from the bed with a strangled cry and began to pace. She could hear Neal and Dan pounding up the stairs, but Chelle got to her first and snapped on the floor lamp. "Are you okay? Did he hurt you?"

Sophie gave a negative headshake. "Don't touch me," she said avoiding Chelle. "I just need to move."

"Alright." Chelle backed up and let her pace. "Just let me know what you need."

Sophie nodded gratefully and concentrated on breathing.

Dan and Neal appeared with Aesop, who barreled into the room and hopped around her, wanting some sign she was okay. "What happened?" Dan demanded, crossing to the window and peering out.

"Alden was here," Chelle answered for Sophie. "I was in my room and saw that gray stuff you told me about coming up the stairs." Chelle's eyes were wide, and her cheeks were drained of color. "Before I could do anything, Alden appeared carrying a candle and went into her room. He stood over her for a bit, and then turned to go downstairs." She lifted her hands in a helpless gesture. "I'm so sorry. I didn't know what to do; I just . . . ."

Sophie waved off the apology. "I don't know what you could have done, to be honest. He really didn't do anything but look at me." She rubbed her arms to warm her chilled skin. "I have to say that was enough though. He creeped me out completely."

"Do you have any idea what he wanted?" Neal asked from the doorway.

She gave her a head shake. "No, I was asleep. I woke up because I was cold, and the room was too bright."

"Yeah, well, having a candle stuck in your face might be why." Chelle jammed her hands into her pockets. "Sorry," she looked at the others in apology, "I hadn't expected it to be so . . . ."

"Terrifying?" Sophie offered. She could hardly blame Chelle for freezing. She'd done the same with Neal and Dan the last time Alden had emerged from the cache. It was one thing to hear about ghosts appearing and another when you saw them yourself.

"Did you wake up because he was standing over you? You know, like you could sense him or something?" Dan turned from the window, satisfied all was quiet outside the lighthouse.

"No, I woke up because I heard Abigail calling for help, and I was freezing." She shuddered. "When I opened my eyes, Alden was right over me."

"Did he say anything?" Dan asked.

"Not a word." She looked puzzled and shrugged. "He seemed like he was coming to check on me."

"But not on you, not really," Chelle said. "As far as we know, there's no connection between the past and the present, so he must have been checking on Abigail."

"That sounds right," Sophie agreed. "The last time we saw him, he was carrying her upstairs. He could have put her in this room, or rather this space in the old house." She pulled the sheets and blankets from the bed and headed for the door. "I know two things for sure . . . one, I'm not staying in this room tonight, and two, he was obsessed."

"With Abigail?" Neal stopped her before she could walk past him.

"Absolutely with Abigail." She knit her brows, finally registering that all three of them were still fully dressed. "Why weren't you guys in bed? What time is it?"

Neal checked his watch. "Ten o'clock. You've been upstairs for about three hours."

"And Aesop?" she asked, watching as the dog wound his way around her legs as if he'd been caught napping and were trying to make up for it.

"He came down about an hour after you went up. He was watching the ball game with me in the office." Dan looked sheepish and lifted a shoulder. "I didn't see or hear anything until you screamed."

"This is definitely not over." Her eyes singled out Neal. "I think we should talk to Carol and see what she has to say about it."

"I'll do it," Chelle offered before Neal could answer. "I never followed up the last time you saw Abigail. Things have been so quiet that it didn't seem important."

Dan pulled down the shade, turned off the light, and followed the others into the hallway. "See if Carol has any other suggestions for how to move this along."

"That should be it for the rest of the night." Neal paused at the head of the stairs. "We've never had more than one apparition at a time." He slowly tapped the banister as he thought. "It was just luck Chelle saw what was happening. Why was your door open anyways?"

"I fell asleep correcting papers and never closed it." She wrapped her arms around herself because it made her feel like she wouldn't fall apart. "Somehow I don't think a closed door would have stopped him though."

"Most likely not. You were lucky he was only checking on Abigail." Dan ignored Chelle's low warning with a shrug. "Who knows with any of this stuff?"

Neal ran his fingers against the banister reflectively. "I think that if anyone is going to have a ghost standing over them, it's better to have someone else around." He frowned. "As much as I don't like it, I think the doors should stay open and we should sleep in shifts until we talk to Carol."

Sophie thought the night patrol a bit much but agreed about the open doors. She wished the others goodnight and dragged her bedding into her office. Curling up on the floor behind her desk, she was asleep in no time, surrounded by Chelle's plants.

Midmorning the next day, Sophie returned from teaching to find the others still at the lighthouse. She followed the sound of voices coming from the office and was relieved to hear Carol's voice mixed in with Dan and Neal's. She found both men leaning against the heavy wooden desk like bookends. Carol was seated in the room's only chair. Only Chelle was missing.

"Anything different about these last two events?" Carol asked the men.

"There were smells too," Sophie answered as she entered the room.

"Smells?" Carol sat up straighter. "Like what?"

Sophie described the new apparitions and the smells she had identified while Carol nodded attentively. "But last night it only smelled strongly of cloves," she finished, giving Dan and Neal an apologetic look. "I didn't remember that until I was teaching this morning."

"Hmm, anything else?" Carol prodded.

"Abigail asked me for help, both times." She lifted a shoulder. "No one else heard her, but I swear both times she was begging for help. It's what forced me to open my eyes."

Carol considered, then asked, "Were your eyes closed when he first carried her out of the cache?"

Sophie nodded. "I heard her twice then, the second time more urgent than the first."

Carol settled back and gave a small shake of her head. "It seems that Abigail desperately wants you to bear witness to her story in a very real way."

"What do you mean?" She spread her hands in frustration. "I couldn't have been more involved than when I was sandwiched between Dan and Neal, and then with Nehemiah looming over me."

"Yes, but for some reason she needs you to see, not only hear. She wants you to be physically present to what happened."

Compared to what had already occurred, it wasn't the strangest thing she'd heard. "Okay, that makes some sort of sense, I guess."

Dan stretched out his legs in front of him. "Is there any risk of Alden confusing Sophie with Abigail?"

Carol weighed the question. "I don't think this is that kind of situation. For some reason you three have been selected, chosen, whatever you want to call it, to see this play out. And as you told me before, they are unaware of you."

"But she asked me for help." Sophie knew she must appear as uncertain as she felt. "She must know I'm here somehow."

"I think her spirit is aware on some level, but the Alden and Abigail you see?" Carol said, framing her hands into a square like a movie screen. "Look at them as actors in a film . . . the action was real at one time, but only the image remains."

At the sound of Aesop scrabbling down the hallway, Sophie quickly warned Carol, "Hold on, here comes my dog."

Aesop entered in a whirl of sun-warmed fur, making the rounds to greet everyone, including Neal who tried hard not to look pleased. Aesop plopped down in front of Carol and raised a paw to introduce himself as a gentleman should.

"Isn't he the cutest thing?" Carol ruffled his ears and beamed. "Aren't you a handsome one? Yes, you are."

"He's a complete ham," Dan laughed. "And knows how to get around the ladies."

A breathless Chelle arrived in the doorway. "Sorry it took so long. I had to get that bone away from him." She collapsed onto the floor beside Aesop and rubbed his side. "What'd I miss?"

After the others had filled her in, Chelle was silent for a moment. "If Abigail is asking for help, could Sophie force these apparitions to happen just by wanting them to?"

"It's possible the more open she is to them, the more frequent the apparitions may be." Carol agreed, then shrugged. "It's not an exact science."

Neal stood. "I'm sympathetic to what's happened here, but I need to get this job wrapped up. Any ideas the rest of us could try?"

"Try some of the journals Babs has at the library," Carol suggested. "Maybe there's something in them that might be helpful."

"You know," Sophie said, drawing out the words. "Babs gave me the journals Dan found at The White Horse. Nobody's seen them since they were stuck under those eaves eons ago. It might be worth the trouble to see what they say."

"I'll look at them," Neal quickly offered. "They might have something useful I can use for the restoration."

"All good places to start." Carol stood and slung her pocketbook over her shoulder. "And you, Sophie, try inviting Abigail and Alden to appear in different locations in the house at different times of day and see what happens. You never know, it might encourage more apparitions."

She could feel her cheeks warming but bobbed her head in agreement. She would feel a complete fool inviting ghosts to visit. She wasn't sure she wanted them to come anyways. Except for her dream of Abigail's young man, the rest of the apparitions had been traumatic, and she dreaded that what followed might be worse.

"Maybe while I run Carol back to town, you three should try to scare up some ghosts." Chelle gave Aesop a final scratch and dug in her pocket for keys. "The more information we get, the better."

None of the three seemed particularly thrilled with the idea, but what choice did they have? After they watched Carol climb behind the driver's wheel to "test out" the Mini, they returned to the office.

Dan checked his watch. "Do you want to give it a shot now? I've got some time."

"I suppose so," Sophie said without much enthusiasm, "but I don't know where to start."

"Well, I don't think we'll have to hold hands," Neal said sarcastically.

Sophie gave him a dirty look. "That's not helping."

"My apologies." He gave a mocking bow. "We wouldn't want to mess up the atmosphere, now would we?"

"Knock it off," Dan said without heat and turned to Sophie. "How about we try in the living room? It always seems to start there anyways."

"It's as good a place as any," she agreed.

When they filed into the living room, she sat against the fireplace and faced the men who hunkered down against opposing walls. "What if we start by thinking about what's already happened and inviting them back?" She felt ridiculous saying it, but how was she supposed to know what to do? She hadn't consciously done anything to produce the apparitions before, and she was at a loss for how to start them now. Dan nodded and Neal rolled his eyes, but they sat, eyes closed, reliving the past experiences with Abigail and Nehemiah and inviting them to return.

After a time, Sophie shifted uncomfortably. Were they even trying? She snuck a peek at Dan and frowned faintly. He sat loose-limbed against the wall, propped comfortably as if preparing for a nap. It didn't look like he was trying too hard. She swung her gaze to Neal and found him watching her, eyebrows raised mockingly. She flushed and quickly shut her eyes. She exhaled and resettled against the fireplace, concentrating on the past and the drama that had happened at The Point. Abigail and Alden alone, and together, paraded through her thoughts, but nothing happened. Time stretched on and on. She fought the urge to check on the men, convinced all the while that Dan was sleeping and Neal openly watching her.

"This isn't going to work," she said finally, opening her eyes. "I'm spending more time thinking about what I'm doing than I am about Abigail and Alden."

"Right," Neal sighed in relief and rose quickly to his feet. "I think diving into those journals might give us more useful information." He didn't wait for them to agree and crossed the floor. "You keep at it, Sophie," he said from the doorway. "And when you get a chance, drop those journals in my room. I'll start them when I get back. I've got a meeting in town I've got to get to soon."

"Sure, I'll do that now." She was just as grateful to have the session over with. "While I'm upstairs, I'll try inviting the Aldens and see what happens."

Dan straightened his lanky frame with a stretch and yawned. "I'd better hang around. I don't think you'll have much luck rounding them up, but I still think you shouldn't be alone."

"It's the easiest way to build in some safeguards," Neal said over his shoulder as he walked down the hall. "Nobody stays in the lighthouse by themselves."

She didn't have a problem agreeing to that. She had already decided that if she was going to be the only one left at The Point, she would find an excuse to go to the village until she knew someone was back. She was committed to finding Abigail, but taking unnecessary chances was an entirely different ball game.

Dan stopped Neal at the front door as she was climbing the stairs. "I heard from the structural engineer. He says the inspection of the turret showed no problems. So, we can start the restoration whenever we want."

"Good." Neal checked his pockets for cell phone and keys. "I'll take a walk up when I get back, and we can make a plan of where to start while the weather holds."

"Can I take a look?" Sophie asked, turning on the stairs. She had been eager to see the view from the turret since first setting eyes on the lighthouse.

"Alright," Neal agreed, "as long as one of us is with you. We don't want another repeat of what happened in the cache."

Although she had wanted some time alone in the turret, she understood the risk.

When Dan asked for fifteen minutes before taking her up, she made her way to the kitchen to wait. Even though she knew the demolition had started, the room was still jarring. With the counter and sink ripped out, and plaster torn off the walls and ceiling, all that remained was a stark skeleton of a room. Cloth-wrapped wires drooped from the ceiling, ran down the walls, and through the floor in two places. One of them was dangerously close to the only remaining pipe that jutted from the wall and dripped slowly into a battered bucket. It was an accident waiting to happen. She steered clear of the area and walked toward the turret door, grasped the knob, then paused. She had promised to wait, but what was on the other side was so tempting. Just one little peek was all she wanted. The knob turned with the stiffness of unused metal but didn't squeak. She smiled and took it as a sign to continue. When she eased the door open, dust lifted in the hallway and swirled in the sunlight filtering through the windows of the narrow passage.

She hesitated only a moment, before cautiously stepping through. Decades of debris on the floor forced her to pick her way down the hall. The wide plank boards led her to the bottom of a curving staircase. She stood on the first stair, fingers lightly resting on the hand-smoothed rail, and craned to see around the bend. The curve was sharp enough so that all she could see were the next few foot-worn stairs and nothing more.

Slowly, she climbed up the staircase. Her eyes were trained on what would come around each bend, until she arrived at a small landing. A wooden farmer's ladder, anchored to the floor between two windows, rose roughly twelve feet to a trap door.

She grasped the ladder and gave it a vigorous shake. When it didn't so much as creak, she kicked off her shoes and climbed, rung after rung, until she could touch the trap door. She pushed against it, and it lifted easily, locking open. She braced her elbows on either side of the entrance to scan the hexagonal room.

The turret's rusted metal roof and lower walls were joined by wide panels of clear glass, assuring the central beacon could be seen all along the coast. From the ladder, Sophie saw only a brilliant blue sky unmarred by clouds. She took her weight onto her arms and crawled up onto the floor. Grasping the metal sill of the wall, she pulled herself upright and finally saw the water.

The small strip of bluff that normally separated the lighthouse from the ocean disappeared with the turret height, and she had the peculiar sensation of standing on water. Everywhere she turned, she was surrounded. To the left and right, the ocean rolled in vast sweeps of blue, sometimes frosted by white foam or speared by the silver glint of sunlight. The width of this sea hinted at a horizon that would shift with the waves and spray, teasing with a boundary that didn't exist.

Her reverent sigh was interrupted by the stomp of booted feet up the access ladder. A few moments later Dan's angry face jutted into view. "Is there something the matter with your ears?" He grasped the edge of the floor and pulled himself into the lantern room.

Sophie couldn't help flushing. "No. All I wanted . . . ."

"And all I wanted," Dan interrupted, "was to make one phone call and have you listen for a change."

She'd never seen him this angry. "I do . . . listen, that is." When her attempt to defend herself seemed to make him even angrier, she knew something besides her bad behavior was the problem. "I wasn't in any danger from Nehemiah—this part of the lighthouse didn't even exist when the Aldens lived here. Structurally the turret is sound. You said so yourself." When she saw him relent a bit, she was honest. "I wanted to experience that jolt of recognition first-hand." For some reason, it was important for him to understand. She gestured to the expanse of blue stretching out beyond the salt-abraded glass. "You see, I teach these authors who write about the sea so clearly that I know what the water looks and feels like just by reading the page. Some of what I use in class was written not far from here, and I wanted to see it for myself."

He watched the sea and horizon shift in the light. "So, when are you going to write your own version?" he asked, as if it were as simple as that.

Surprised, she searched his face for signs he was joking. "I don't know. I might, but I think the most moving things are the ones most difficult to write about. With loss, it hurts too much to make any sense of it." She shrugged. "And with love and life, it seems that the best has already been said."

"But not by you."

His simple observation caught her off guard. "No, you're right. Not by me." She let go of the regret of the unwritten and turned to him with forced brightness. "If Neal had caught me, I'm sure he wouldn't have let me off so lightly. Thank you."

Dan nodded. "Come on, let's get out of here." He motioned her toward the ladder. "I need to find out what happened to the rest of my materials. Chagnon Lumber delivered only half of what I ordered."

"Okay." She scooted to the edge of the trapdoor, letting her feet dangle. "And I'd better get those journals for Neal while I'm thinking of it." She lowered herself into the hole, carefully placing her feet on the nearest rung and descending slowly with Dan following behind her.

Sophie left him grumbling on the office phone and went up to change out of her grimy clothes. Aesop was stretched out on her bed, his head on the pillow, snoozing. "Been a rough day already, buddy?" She dropped down beside him and stroked his head. He sighed in contentment and wriggled closer to lie partially across her lap. "Cradling you was a lot easier when you weren't so big. Alright, alright," she laughed when he nudged her to continue, "but you've got to help me find a way to call up those ghosts. If we don't, we'll be living here alone, and Neal won't be able to sneak you food when he thinks I'm not looking."

She stretched out beside Aesop and draped her arm over his back. How to call a ghost, she mused. Inviting them downstairs hadn't accomplished much but make her feel ridiculous. And she couldn't see Nehemiah responding to a request from any woman, never mind a demand. Abigail might be a different story, but what she needed to know involved both the Aldens. What about imagining? What would she have done if she were Abigail? What had Abigail felt? Sophie closed her eyes, welcoming the fear and weakness she had sensed when Alden had hauled Abigail out of the cache. She let herself sink into what it must have meant to be that girl long ago. Dark and oppressive, a blank slate with vague images floated before her. There were tiny birds stitched in silk thread, violent ocean waves that rolled over each other without direction, and a black prison so parched it absorbed all air and light.

Sophie gasped for air and snapped her eyes open. There was someone downstairs. Not Dan. She'd heard him moving about earlier. This was different. It had an urgency about it—something was wrong. She felt a prickling sensation across her skin and clutched an already alert Aesop like a shield. She sensed someone climbing, closer and closer, until the first gray wisps crested the stairs. Nehemiah Alden appeared, carrying a flickering candle and darting sharp glances about the upper floor. He moved past her to the other rooms, searching, a hunched crone dogging his footsteps.

"But I left her downstairs on the cot, sir. The lass was too weak to stand and the doors barred. Where was she to go?" the old woman rasped, shrinking away as he raised an arm as if to strike.

"You were to watch her, stupid woman," he hissed, "so that something like this did not happen."

"But the babe," she said, wringing her hands, "You demanded that I rid the house of it. I could not do both."

"You did neither! And now both the girl and the child are missing." He stretched to his full height and dashed toward the far room as if he'd seen something. The crone shuffled after him.

The tendrils of gray mist followed the figures, twisting around their feet. Sophie held her breath and clamped Aesop's muzzle closed. The other times the ghosts had appeared no one had made a sound. She wasn't going to test their hearing now. She was too terrified to move and stayed anchored to her bed, eyes fixed on the scene outside her door. Where was Dan?

"We'll be needing hallowed land." The crone made the statement a hopeful question.

"Don't be daft," he sneered. "He's illegitimate and unanointed. He'll be returned to his father."

"Oh no, sir," the old woman cried. "It would be a mortal sin," she said and crossed herself.

"Not of my making."

Sophie moved on unsteady legs toward the door for a better view and dragged Aesop with her. Dan was halfway up the stairway, pressed to the wall, and completely absorbed in the scene before them.

Nehemiah leapt forward to a darkened corner of the room. "There you are you wicked girl." He squatted down in front of where Abigail lay cowering, deathly pale and delirious. She cradled a newborn in her arms. "Here, take him." He roughly pried the child out of her arms and passed it to the old woman stooping beside him. The girl made a mew of distress before he scooped her up and moved toward the staircase.

Sophie ducked back as Alden approached, keeping the door open only wide enough to see out.

Abigail's feverish eyes searched around her. "My babe," she wept, "my babe."

The old crone shuffled after, gingerly clasping a too tiny newborn with a thatch of black hair poking out of the swaddling.

Sophie strained to see the baby's face and only saw the curve of a cheek and a perfectly shaped mouth. Then she gasped, her heart sinking. The crone turned black eyes toward her and stared to pierce the darkness as though she knew someone was there. Sophie shrank back and held her breath. The crone stared for a long moment, blinked twice, and followed Alden down the staircase. The gray mist slipped down the staircase behind them.

She sagged against the doorway, releasing her grip on Aesop. That had been too close. If she were going to come face to face with a ghost who could see her, she wanted somebody else there besides her dog.

Dan bound up the stairs two at a time and arrived outside her door, eyes wide. "Did you see that?"

"Yeah," she managed. "Did you recognize the old woman?"

"No. She wasn't someone I've seen in portraits, but she didn't look like the portrait type."

Sophie pushed past him on unsteady legs into the hall and looked around. "You must have gotten pretty close."

"When Alden headed for the stairs, I ran for the living room and got there before them. They passed within a foot of me." Dan followed her into the front room where Abigail had been discovered. "And neither of them was any better up close."

She crouched, passing trembling fingers over the floor where Abigail had cowered. "It was so real, you'd expect there to be something left behind." She grabbed onto Dan's arm to pull herself upright and hung on for a moment.

He searched her face. "Did you invite them?"

"Not really," she said and released him. "I just imagined what it must have been like for her, what she must've felt, and it happened."

"I thought you might have done something to bring it on." He didn't look pleased. "She had her baby."

Sophie felt a pang of sadness for the poor girl. "Yes, a boy." She sifted through what she'd seen and knew that what Abigail had desperately wished for on that beach had never happened. "He didn't survive."

"How could you possibly know that from what we saw?"

"His skin was gray." She forced words out around the lump in her throat. "He was too premature, if we go by what we've seen of Abigail. She wasn't that far along in her pregnancy. Maybe six, seven months tops. That length of pregnancy can be touch and go nowadays depending on the baby; it was impossible in the 1700's."

Dan was grimly silent, then asked, "Do you think Alden had a part in his death?"

She walked slowly to the window and looked out on a perfectly calm day. There was no wind, no sound, even the waves came to shore in gently collapsing arcs—so different from the scene that had just played out before them. She leaned her head against the wooden frame.

"I don't think he directly injured him or ordered it done." Her voice was quiet. "But he's responsible. Definitely responsible."

"It doesn't give us much to go on. He could have buried the baby anywhere." Dan joined her at the window and looked toward the woods.

"He said he was going to return it to the father. He must have known, or strongly suspected, who Abigail's lover was."

"I can't see him going out of his way to be a stand-up guy. The baby must be buried around here somewhere." He pushed away from the window. "Besides, admitting there was a child would have been social suicide. He had too high of an opinion of himself for that."

"Frank claims Will Morgan was supposed to marry Abigail, but she already had married Alden when he got back. Maybe he's the baby's father."

"Could be," Dan agreed, then fell silent for a while. "Are you done for the day?"

She didn't know what he was up to but hoped he had a plan. She was fresh out of ideas. "I don't have to be back on campus until tomorrow. Why?"

"Why don't you head over to the library and see what you can dig up in the nautical records or the journals about William Morgan's travels. Maybe his whereabouts will match the timeframe of Abigail's pregnancy. I'll stay here and go through the journals I found. Neal can help when he gets back."

"That sounds like a plan." As she geared up for another afternoon hunched over books, she considered what Dan had said before about actively seeking answers. "While you're waiting for Neal, could you give

Carol a call and see what she has to say about the old woman?" she asked. "She might be able to identify her for us."

"Good idea," he agreed and followed her back into her room to collect the journals.

She pulled open a dresser drawer and gave them to him. "And Dan?" She caught him before he could descend the stairs. "Be sure to call Chelle. We can use all the help we can get."

"I'm on it." He saluted and jogged down the stairs.

Sophie grabbed Aesop before he could sneak after him. "Oh, no. You stay here and out of the way. And no more begging for food." Aesop resignedly flopped onto the rug, head between his paws. She grabbed paper, pen, and book bag. "Be good." She bent to tap him on the nose. "I'll make it up to you later."

8

Aesop

"Later" was longer than Sophie had expected. Cramped and headachy, she had missed dinner and been the last one to leave when Babs locked up the library. She hoped that someone had put Aesop out while she was away. As an apology for leaving him alone for so long, she'd bought him some doggy biscuits at Johnson's Bakery. This week's treat was shaped like what appeared to be a troll. She wasn't sure who had gotten on the baker's bad side, but the biscuits were hysterical.

Even though it had been a grind, she had found some useful but unsettling information. William Morgan's sea voyages had matched up neatly with the timeframe of Abigail's pregnancy. The nautical records had shown that the *Moira* had set sail from Massachusetts on April 7, 1716, bound for the West Indies, listing a crew of forty-six, including first mate William Morgan. The passenger logbook named one hundred and thirty people, John Hart among them. The *Moira* was reported missing and assumed lost three months later. William Morgan, the ship's only survivor, returned to Pocasset aboard a merchant ship, eight months after the reported loss. His return had been delayed by a lengthy convalescence from injuries suffered in the sinking of the *Moira*. Morgan had been swept off the deck when the ship had foundered off the coast of Hispaniola and had survived by clinging to a piece of the ship's wreckage. Most of the crew, and all the passengers, had been below decks—they hadn't had a prayer of surviving.

If the colonial journal she had found was to be believed, Morgan had been unaware of the pregnancy, birth, and death of his only child. He had quit the sea and never married. He spent the remainder of his short life either drunk or shadowing the Aldens about town. She might have taken the tale with a grain of salt if the story had been clearly for, or against, either Nehemiah Alden or William Morgan. Instead, the balanced tale told of a beleaguered Nehemiah, a haunted Morgan, and a disturbing description of Abigail as "broken."

When Sophie returned to the lighthouse, she found the others sprawled about the living room floor, looking exactly how she felt—drained. "Any luck?" She nudged the journals aside with her foot and flopped down beside Aesop.

"Not yet." Chelle rubbed her eyes with both fists and groaned. "The handwriting in these last ones is torture."

"Are they all by the same author?" She dug a biscuit out of the bag and frowned when Aesop gave it an uninterested sniff and lay back down.

Dan poked the nearest pile. "These are by a guy named Marsh. The rest are by a Stephen Parker." He motioned to the stack closest to Chelle and Sophie. "Both of them were retired seamen. Although Marsh seems to have been just passing through and left his journals behind, Parker lodged above The White Horse for a good ten months before moving on, to the 'other side.'"

"Parker was a villager," Neal continued. "After he retired from the sea, he spent his time either in the tavern or down on shore waiting for ships to return." He rolled his shoulders and stretched. "He kept busy by collecting gossip—some of what he recorded was tattle in the village, the rest he picked up from drunken ramblings in the tavern."

Chelle gave a tired smile and let her head drop back against the wall. "In vino veritas."

"Absolutely." Sophie nodded. "No better way to find out what someone really thinks than to ask when they're plowed—not fall-down drunk, mind you, but trustingly pickled."

Dan eyed her speculatively before shaking his head. "Anyways, we haven't hit on any dirt about either of the Aldens or William Morgan, but we got further with what Carol had to say."

"Really?" Sophie looked up from trying to entice Aesop with broken bits of biscuit. "Did she know who the crone might be?"

"Yeah." Dan's face lit up, showing he was particularly pleased. "She said the description sounded like Alice Goodwin, an old mid-wife and pseudo-herbalist who lived on the outskirts of the village. She thinks Alden could have gotten her when Abigail went into labor because he never went to Old Katherine Darby for help."

"Birthing is a messy business." Chelle said, wrinkling her nose. "I can't see him doing something he considered beneath him and delivering another man's child would have definitely fallen into that category."

Neal picked up a journal and fanned the pages slowly. "He must have wanted Abigail pretty badly to overlook the baggage she came with."

"Greed and spite will make people do crazy things," Sophie said. "Besides, he believed God had sent him to save her. If he believed that, he could have justified anything." She slid her hand along Aesop's side and jumped when he yelped. "Sorry, buddy." She shot Dan and Neal a narrow look. "Have you guys been sneaking him food again?"

"Not tonight." Dan shifted, embarrassed. "I mean . . . I tried to, but he didn't seem interested. He did drink a lot of water though."

Chelle pushed off from the wall and crawled over to examine Aesop carefully. "You'd better keep an eye on him. He's never had problems like bloat before, has he?" she asked, sitting back on her heels.

"No, never." Sophie stroked his head. "But he's a canine garbage can. He could have eaten something that didn't agree with him." She pushed the worry away with a silent promise to call a vet in the morning if he wasn't better. "What else did you ask Carol?"

"I asked if she knew where Abigail's baby had been buried." Dan winced at the memory. "It didn't go over too well, but the answer was no. Carol said Old Katherine would have turned Alden in without batting an eye if she had known or suspected. She agrees with me that the baby is buried around here in an unmarked grave."

"So now what?" Neal snapped shut the journal he'd been thumbing.

Sophie considered carefully before answering. "I guess we'll have to wait and see what Alden shows us before we can find the grave. So that's a dead end for now, but I did find out that William Morgan is a prime candidate for the baby's father." While explaining what she'd learned, she kept a watchful eye on the faces of the others, hoping their reactions would confirm her suspicions.

"Seems to fit," Chelle said. "The timeframe works, and if he had known about the baby, he'd have done more than just shadow them around town. He'd have confronted them for sure, and somebody would have heard of it in a village this size."

"That's what I thought." Sophie looked at Neal, then Dan. "Well?"

"Sounds right to me," Dan said, pulling in his legs to sit cross-legged and bracing his arms on his thighs. "I think the man I've sensed is William Morgan. Not only does the timeframe fit, but it's what I feel when I get those left-over emotions from the past. The helplessness, the loss, it all fits."

Neal picked another journal from the pile and said without looking up, "But that could be any man from that time who went to sea."

"Right, but my guy also saw this house burn." Dan spread his arms wide. "A house the Aldens were living in, and Sophie has a source that states Morgan used to follow them around. That connects the dots for me."

"It's still no smoking gun." Neal challenged.

Before things could get out of hand, Chelle quickly interrupted. "Why don't we call it a night and keep after the journals tomorrow?"

Sophie was more than ready for bed. It had been a long week, and she was teaching first thing in the morning. The men appeared reluctant to stop but agreed, insisting that they all take turns keeping watch. When they started to bicker about who would go first, Chelle settled it by taking the first watch herself and assigning Sophie, Dan, and Neal the following shifts.

Hours later when Sophie took over the watch, she saw that night had settled softly across The Point. The stars were spread across the sky like scattered seeds, a pale haloed moon emerging among them. Gently arcing waves slid in toward shore, frosting the hard-packed sand with foam as delicate as lace, whispering stories of sailors who had loved and lost. She turned from the living room window and shivered. Despite the peacefulness outside, it was eerie to walk about the lighthouse alone while everyone else slept. Every creak had her catching her breath and looking over her shoulder, even though she knew the biggest worry came from the Aldens and not an intruder.

She checked the window locks in the living room before moving down the wide plank boards to the back of the house. When she paused in the office doorway, she saw Dan sprawled halfway out of his sleeping bag, sound asleep, and completely clothed. He apparently wasn't taking a chance of being caught unprepared. A small smirk lifted one corner of his lips. She rolled her eyes. Whatever he was dreaming, he seemed quite pleased with himself, which usually didn't bode well for somebody else. He could be a horrible tease when the mood struck him, and she had seen him harass Chelle without mercy. It seemed to annoy his sister to no end, but Sophie was envious of the exchanges anyways. She wondered what her life would have been like if she had been blessed with a brother instead of Jacqueline. She frowned at the direction her thoughts had taken and gave the room a final look before turning for the stairs of the second floor.

Chelle's door, like Dan's, was wide open. Although Sophie still fully expected her to be awake, Chelle was snoring softly. She was curled up on her side like a forest sprite asleep amongst all her plants. Sophie smiled. There were no problems here. Maybe it was all the greenery, or Chelle herself, that kept the Aldens at bay. Sophie turned and padded down the hall to Neal's room.

Even though everyone had agreed to the watch, she was uncomfortable peeking in Neal's door. It was barely cracked open, but she could see him well enough, flat and straight as a board on his back. She made a face. The man couldn't even relax in sleep. She began to back away, but he woke up as if he had sensed her standing there. He lifted his head and froze her in place with a look that made her flush to the roots of her hair.

"I'm sorry," she whispered, backing away. "Everything's okay. You can go back to sleep."

He stared at her for several unreadable moments, then laid his head back down as still as before.

She let out a shaky breath and tip-toed away to continue her rounds. She'd like to have said that for the rest of her shift she was thorough in checking all the rooms for ghosts, but when it came to Neal, she gave his room a quick glance and moved on. She wasn't willing to risk waking him again.

She hadn't slept much during Chelle's shift. She was self-conscious not only with the open door but also knowing that Chelle, and eventually the men, would be patrolling the hall. By the time Sophie's shift was over, the mix of tension and fatigue had taken its toll. She gratefully turned over her shift, checked briefly on Aesop who seemed to be resting comfortably, and tumbled into bed. She was asleep the moment she closed her eyes.

Warm gentle fingers brushed against her forehead, shifting the long layers of hair off her face and resting briefly on her cheek. Murmuring, Sophie turned into the wide palm and sighed, content to lean into the warmth until a sudden jerk left her deprived of the comfort. A small crease formed between her eyes. She shifted restlessly, finally settled, and was soon once again deeply asleep.

Through the open window, the watcher had seen him enter the girl's room and stand by her bed. Fool. A weakness, a tool, to be used sometime in the future. The first part of the plan was underway and showing effects. The dog hadn't barked while he had sat under the window eavesdropping. It was a good thing he had taken the chance, or he wouldn't have learned of their plan to set a watch. It would have been awkward to explain why he was in the house, but not impossible. Glee bubbled up within him with such force that he clamped a dirty hand over his mouth to keep it in. He'd rid himself one by one of those who stood in his way for what was rightly his.

Sophie slapped her alarm clock, knocking it onto the floor where it went silent.

"A bit violent, but it gets results." Dan stood in her doorway holding a cup of coffee. "You've already turned that off twice before throwing it on the floor. It's seven-thirty. Aren't you going to be late?"

"Yes, most definitely late," she mumbled, then pried her eyes open. "Any coffee left?"

"Nope." Dan clearly enjoyed telling her, pronouncing the "p" with a pop.

"Bite him, Aesop." She leaned over the side of the bed when the dog didn't respond. "Aesop?" Instantly alert, she scrambled off the bed and crouched beside him, placing a gentle hand on his head. Listless eyes rolled toward her, watching with what she felt was a plea for help. She felt a surge of alarm and everything inside her tightened. "Dan, something's wrong."

Dan set down his coffee, skirted the bed, and bent down over them. "He most likely ate something that didn't agree with him." But concern etched his face when he saw Aesop's shallow breathing. "Get ready, and I'll call the vet. Maybe she can see him before you have to teach."

The knot that tightened in her stomach was one she knew all too well. It was the one that had curled in her gut when a state trooper had walked deliberately through the driving rain to her front porch and shared the news of her parents' accident. The news had ripped love, security, and a place of belonging from her fourteen-year-old life. It was the one that only made itself known when something was very, very wrong.

Sophie rushed to get dressed, while Dan carried Aesop to her car and laid him gently on the back seat. She met him outside just as he was closing the car door.

"Dr. Collins won't be in until nine o'clock. But the vet tech is there and will start the exam," Dan said, guiding her to the other side of the car.

"I won't be able to stay." She panicked. "He hates the vet's. It reminds him of the animal shelter . . . all that disinfectant and fearful animals." She held onto her purse with tense fingers. "What am I going to do?"

Dan wrapped an arm around her shoulders and gave her a quick hug. "It'll be okay. It's not that kind of office. You leave when you need to get to class, and I'll stay with him until you get back."

She nodded mutely and gave him the keys. She climbed beside a panting Aesop. He had his belly tucked in as though it hurt. "Poor guy." She stroked his head. "We're going take good care of you. I promise."

Dan drove carefully down the lane so not to jostle the back seat and headed toward town. "While you were getting ready, I told Chelle and Neal." He glanced into the rearview mirror as he talked. "They said to let them know how he's doing."

"Alright," Sophie murmured, then turned to look out the window. Thick shrubs and the curving coastal road blurred past her window. She felt a surge of guilt. This was all her fault—she hadn't paid enough attention to him while she'd been focused on the dead. She'd left him too much on his own, and he'd gotten into something that had made him sick. Hot tears spattered on her hand and Aesop listlessly licked them off, resting his head on her lap.

When the car finally pulled to a stop in front of a large Victorian house, Sophie asked, "This is it?"

"Yeah. Dr. Collins has the examination rooms on the first floor and her office is on the second." Dan opened the door and gently lifted Aesop out. "Should I carry him?"

"Please. He's in a lot of pain." She followed him up a walk lined with red geraniums and into a reception room that had the scent of tart apples. Leather chairs and a sofa were spread around the room, inviting dogs and cats to flop wherever they wished.

After settling Aesop on the sofa, they sat on either side of him. While she filled out paperwork, Dan talked to the tall assistant in purple scrubs named Brooke. "Not feeling so good, are you, fella?" she said, stroking his head. Her brown ponytail swung over her shoulder as she bent to listen to him breathe. "We'd better get a chest x-ray and draw some blood. When Dr C comes in we can hit the ground running. Will you be staying?" Brooke asked.

Sophie felt the knot clench tighter. "I can't, but I'll be back in about an hour and a half." She felt the need to explain. "I have to give a class at the college."

Dan gave Aesop a reassuring pat. "I'll be here, though."

"Thanks so much," Sophie said, and passed the leash to Brooke.

When Brooke tried to lead Aesop away, he wouldn't budge. Instead, he stood rooted to the spot, peering hesitantly over his shoulder at Sophie.

"It's okay," Sophie sweet-talked, getting down on one knee to hug him. "Go ahead." Aesop, head drooping, followed the assistant down the hall. He paused once to look over his shoulder, then disappeared from view.

All the way to the college, she re-ran in her mind the image of Aesop standing in that hallway struggling for breath, painful fruitless breaths rasping in and out. He had gotten into things before, but he'd never been this sick. Never.

Class was a blur that stretched on forever. She heard herself lecturing, responding to questions, even laughing at a few students' jokes, but her mind was at the vet's and what was happening there.

She finally escaped from student questions with promises of answers by email and bolted for the door. When she got to Dr. Collins', she saw Neal and Chelle climbing the stairs to the office. Their arms were full of Aesop's things: his favorite blanket, his toy squirrel, and even that ridiculous bone Neal had bought him. Her mouth went dry. "What's going on?" she said as she struggled out of the car. "What are you doing with Aesop's stuff?"

Chelle opened the door and ushered her inside. "Dan thought Aesop would feel better with some of his own things around," she said with a hitch in her voice.

"What are you talking about?" Sophie turned to Neal in confusion. "What's happening?"

Neal looked miserable. "Aesop's sick. He got into some engine coolant somewhere, and it damaged his organs. His body is shutting down."

Sophie groped for the sofa and sank onto it. "I told him it was going to be okay, and then I left." Her eyes filled. "I told him he was going to be alright."

Chelle caught Sophie's hands in hers. "I'm so sorry, Sophie."

"How?" Sophie demanded. "None of the cars at the lighthouse leak. I checked. I always check. I know it's poison."

"That's just it," Neal said. "Dr. Collins doesn't think it was an accident. She thinks he was poisoned, slowly, over several weeks. There isn't enough in his blood for it to have been an accident, or the symptoms would have been more obvious."

"But *why*? We don't even have neighbors."

"We'll figure it out after we take care of Aesop." Chelle got up and helped Sophie to her feet. "He's in the first room on the right."

They were met at the door by a petite blonde in a white lab coat. "Ms. Tyler?" A warm hand clasped hers. "I'm Dr. Collins. I'm sorry we needed to meet in this way. Please, come in."

Sophie entered to find Dan sitting on an examination table with Aesop cradled in his lap. They were both draped by a fleece blanket. She crossed the room to Aesop and said, "Hey, buddy. I'm back." She bent and kissed him on the nose. "Do you mind?" she asked Dan, motioning to the table.

"Of course not." He slid off, so she could take his place.

"Ms. Tyler, you'll need to find the source of the coolant so that another animal isn't sickened," Dr. Collins said. "And I would strongly recommend reporting it to the police."

"Is he in pain?" Sophie tried to keep her voice even.

"No, I gave him something to ease it until you could get here."

"How long?" She left the rest of the question unsaid.

"It's hard to say," Dr. Collins said. "Unless you want me to give him something to help the process along?"

"No, I need some time with him." She felt selfish and small, but she wasn't ready to say goodbye. "Is that alright?"

"Of course. I'll be outside if you need anything."

She spoke to the others without looking up. "I think I'd like to be alone with him now, if you don't mind."

"Sure," Neal said, holding the door open for Chelle and Dan. "We'll be at the lighthouse. Call us if you need anything."

Sophie nodded, then tugged Aesop into her lap and smoothed his ears back. "I'm so sorry, baby dog," she whispered. "You've made it home for me wherever we were, and I let you down." A slow tear slid down her cheek and landed on Aesop's muzzle flattening the fur with its wetness. When another one fell joining its twin, Aesop grumbled and tried climbing further into her lap despite his labored breathing.

She gave a watery laugh. "You always wanted to be right here with me, didn't you?" She hugged him to her and buried her nose in his neck, inhaling deeply. He still smelled of the forest and sea, things he would never see again. Sophie brushed her cheek against his fur and fought against despair. She wouldn't make this harder on him by breaking down. "Do you remember when I first rescued you and the ruckus you rose every time I had to leave you alone?" She sniffed and wiped her hand under her nose. "I snuck you into more faculty meetings than I can remember." She gave him a light stroke. "But you were so good. You would just curl up under my chair and sleep until it was time to go."

Aesop's breath rattled in his throat. Oh, no, she thought, not yet. Just a little longer, please. She spoke quickly, brightly, hoping to postpone what would happen with her words. "And remember how you learned to walk off-leash when we played hide-and-seek?" He rolled his eyes toward her and blinked, his tail twitching in imitation of a wag. "When you used to get too far away, I would hide behind a tree and call, and you would come find me." She rocked slowly to comfort them both. "You always came back," she whispered, smoothing his fur with gentle fingers.

Sophie held him and softly sang "You Are My Sunshine" until Aesop's breathing slowed and became shallower. She held her own breath as she listened for his and willed him to take another, and yet another. But she knew it was selfish to hang on when the kindest act would be to let go.

"I love you. I will always love you," she said softly, kissing his nose.

And as though he understood, he licked her and closed his eyes for the last time with a gentle sigh.

She hugged him closely and released the anguish that was choking her with quiet sobs.

Outside the door, Dr. Collins called, "Ms. Tyler, are you okay?"

Lifting her head at her name, Sophie sniffed and roughly rubbed her eyes dry. She carefully placed Aesop to the side and covered him in the fleece blanket. She walked unsteadily out of the room. "He's gone," she told Dr. Collins. "Could you arrange to have him cremated? I'd like to bury him myself."

"Certainly." Dr. Collins gestured to the room where Aesop lay. "And his things? Do you want to take them now?"

"No. Please." She put her hand to her head; she couldn't think. "Could you use them here?"

Dr. Collins placed a comforting hand on her arm. "Yes, of course. It will all be put to good use. Some of the dogs that are brought in are strays and don't have anything."

Tears welled in her eyes again. Aesop had been a stray. She nodded mutely to the vet and walked past Dan. She walked out the door, then down the street in the direction of the lighthouse, gravel on the side of the road crunching underfoot.

"Sophie, your car's here," Dan said gently when he caught up, shortening his stride to match hers. "Let me give you a ride home."

"No. I'm going to walk."

"Sophie, please." He stepped in front of her, stopping her. "It's five miles, easy."

"I'm fine, really." What was he still doing here? Why hadn't he left with the others? "I just need to walk." When she tried to step around him and he blocked her again, anger flicked through the numbness. She gave him a shove. "Get out of my way."

He swore in frustration. "So that you can wander into the road because you're not watching where you're going? I don't think so."

Anger flared and she hung onto it. "I'm sad, not stupid. And I need to think."

"Fine, then give me your keys and I'll see you at the lighthouse."

Moments later, peeling tires and a cloud of dust swept by her. That was the fastest that car had moved since she'd bought it with Aesop. Aesop. Her heart gave a twist. Now what was she going to do?

Sophie cried herself out on the way home. They were steady, trickling tears that didn't soothe the hurt. When she finally had no more tears to cry, the sun dried her cheeks, leaving them stiff and burning. What do you do when you don't know where to start? She thought of her mother and swore she heard her speak as clearly as if she were whispering in her ear, "You put one foot in front of the other, Sophie, and do what needs to be done first. Sometimes it's enough." Foot after foot, she trudged back along the five-mile road toward the lighthouse. By the time she reached the marsh, the lack of shade trees and midday sun had sweat trickling down her back and plastering her thin blouse to her shoulders.

It was almost too easy, he wouldn't even need to hide. They'd believe him. She'd wandered in front of his car, he'd say. There was nothing he could do. And she'd be gone, and the past and The Point would remain exactly where he wanted them . . . in the past.

Sophie blinked the sweat from her eyes. She was vaguely surprised to see The Narrows bridge stretched out before her. It would take her across the canal to the lighthouse. The old trestle structure was just wide enough for one car and a pedestrian to pass, if they both were careful and stuck to their own side of the bridge. She started across, the rough wooden beams of the bridge scraping underfoot. Who would want to poison Aesop? It made absolutely no sense. He'd never bothered anyone; he hadn't even been a good guard dog. His only guard talent had been his ability to make a lot of noise.

The roar of an engine and the rapid bumping of tires over the uneven beams caused her to snap her head up. A car came hurtling down the center of the bridge. There would never be room for them both. By instinct, she vaulted the bridge railing, dropping fourteen feet into the canal below. Cold black water smothered her, stopping the air in her lungs as she broke to the surface. She fought the current that raced her sideways in a swirl of foam and seaweed. Riptide. She drew in a breath to scream for help but choked on saltwater. Stop it. The surest way to drown would be to struggle—swim at an angle—it was pulling her *in*, not out to sea. She let water drag her along a jutting bank. She was near enough to grab at thick roots, but as she seized them, they splintered in her hand. Canal banks blurred as she was swept further from the bridge. She kicked and stroked with the force of the tide, angling toward tough grasses that lay anchored, just out of reach.

Kick, reach, kick, and reach. As her fingertips brushed the shore, she clutched at a branch to pull herself free from the current and climbed up the slippery bank. She grabbed handfuls of sharp grass and hauled herself forward. Pulling hand over hand, she finally reached the top, then collapsed on the gritty sand to cough and vomit seawater.

Over the sound of her coughing, she thought she heard a car door closing but couldn't be sure.

She crawled to her feet and struggled to keep her balance once upright. Her palms were raw, and she was nauseous. But she was alive. The bridge, the only landmark she would recognize, was no longer visible. Where was she? If she could locate a path, it would save her cutting her now shoeless feet on the uneven ground. The problem was finding a way through these towering cattails. She plunged into the cattails and hoped to make it through without getting covered in deer ticks.

False start after false start had her backtracking until she finally hit the path that led to the main road. She scrambled up the steep embankment and poked her head up just as Dan drove past in his pickup. Brakes screeched and the truck reversed with a squeal of tires. "Sophie!" He jumped out and ran to her, steadying her with his arm around her waist. "What happened?"

"Someone didn't see me on the bridge." Bending over, she spat. "I jumped the guardrail to get out of the way."

Dan's face went blank. It would have been funny at another time, but the last thing she felt like doing was laughing.

"Are you out of your mind? It could have been low tide. You could have broken your neck or drowned."

The ugly possibility of falling into shallow water and rocks played in her head, and she straightened slowly. "I really didn't have a choice. I would have been crushed if I hadn't.

"Did you recognize who it was?" He automatically brushed aside her hair to check for ticks, peered closely at her neck, then examined her arms and legs. When he was satisfied she was free of the disease bearing parasites, he asked again, "Did you see who it was?"

"No, just a flash. Mid-sized car. Could have been white or light blue." She tried to remember and swayed. "I think I need to sit down."

Dan swung her up into his arms before her knees could buckle. Cursing, he quickly carried her to the truck and tucked her into the passenger seat. He reached across her to buckle her seatbelt but paused before clicking it home. Nose to nose, he said quietly, "Don't say another word until I get you home, or so help me . . . ." He slammed the door shut, rounded the front of the truck and climbed in, giving her a final glare before setting the truck in motion.

Sophie leaned back against the seat and closed her eyes. Instead of helping, it made it worse. She could still see Aesop gasping for air so clearly it made her chest tighten. Who would cruelly poison a harmless animal? A fat tear slid down her cheek. She opened her eyes to look out at the last curving view of the ocean before the woods blocked it out. No longer greedily dragging her along, this ocean lapped at mussel-covered rocks, bathing them in gentle tidal waters and gurgling away again.

"Chelle sent me after you," Dan finally said. "She expected you to be back before now."

She toyed with the door handle. She hadn't been very nice. "How long has it been since we were at the vet's?"

"Close to three hours." He shot her a glance before turning his eyes back to the road.

She knew from his clipped answers he was still angry. "Thanks, for coming after me . . . " she faltered and turned to face her window. "I didn't mean to be rude."

"Forget it." He swung the car around in front of the lighthouse and came to a stop as Chelle ran out to open the truck door. It felt wrong to be returning to the lighthouse and not have Aesop racing toward her. One of the many broken patterns that would leave an emptiness now that he was gone.

"What happened to you?" Chelle asked, pulling her toward the lighthouse. "You're soaking wet and filthy."

Dan saved her the trouble of explaining. "She's lucky she's alive. She nearly got herself run down crossing The Narrows and hopped the rail into the water. Where's Neal?"

"Out looking for the engine coolant." Chelle called over her shoulder as she propelled Sophie up the stairs to the bathroom and sat her on the edge of the tub. "You could have killed yourself," she scolded, but softened when Sophie's face crumpled. "Oh, honey. It's been a really bad day." Chelle wrapped her arms around her and gave her a hard hug. "Go ahead and shower. I'll get you some clothes and heat up some soup. We'll find who did this."

"It's too late to help Aesop." Sophie turned on the water, missing what Chelle might have said, if anything.

When she got out of the shower, a pair of leggings, T-shirt and underwear lay stacked on the side of the sink. She dressed slowly, muscles complaining with every movement. She shook two aspirins into her palm and took them by sticking her mouth under the sink and washing them down with the metallic water. She bundled her damp hair into a loose knot, as she headed for the stairs. The smell of chicken soup led her to the living room where everyone sat on the floor, their bowls already empty.

Sophie settled down beside them and refused Neal's offer of food with a shake of her head. She asked, "Did you find anything?"

"Nothing obvious." Neal shrugged and ticked off on his fingers, "No bowls, no empty containers, and no obvious spills on the ground."

"Whoever it was could have taken the container away or cleaned up afterwards," Chelle pointed out.

"But that doesn't fit." Dan shook his head and discarded the idea. "Dr. C. said he'd been poisoned in small doses over a long period of time. They needed some way to get it to him regularly. One of us would have noticed a strange bowl hanging around."

Sophie toyed with the hem of her T-shirt and followed the conversation without contributing. It was hard to scrape together the attention needed for clear thinking when all she saw in her mind's eye was Aesop struggling to breathe.

"We know he didn't roam far enough to harass any of the neighbors, and he didn't attack anyone in town. So why didn't someone want him around The Point," Chelle asked.

"So, he wouldn't bark his head off when they showed up?" Dan suggested. "It doesn't make any sense though. There won't be anything to steal in the house until it's done, and we had already set up the extra lights. Aesop was a distant second, security-wise."

"I'm not sure." Chelle glanced at her phone when it rang. "But it's the only possibility that makes sense right now." She struggled to her feet. "Hold on a sec while I get this," she said, and walked into the hall. Her conversation didn't last long, and she returned, a bleak look on her face.

Neal slowly rose to his feet. "What's wrong?"

"That was Dr. Collins," Chelle said. "Her assistant was cleaning up Aesop's things for donation and found small holes in the bone Aesop had been chewing. They were regular enough that she showed them to Dr. C., who ran some tests. The bone had been drilled and soaked in engine coolant. The marrow acted like a sponge. She thinks it's how he was poisoned."

Dan leapt to his feet and shoved Neal with enough force to back him up a pace. "You haven't changed at all, have you?"

Neal shoved him back. "What are you talking about?"

"You know exactly what I'm talking about," Dan ground out. "What's one more dead dog to you?"

"Hey, now wait a minute." Chelle held her arms out and stepped between them. "You need to calm down, both of you."

"Get a grip, Robbins." Neal's face twisted in derision. "You're delusional, as always."

With a snarl, Dan shoved Chelle aside and pinned Neal to the wall, both fists twisted into his shirt. He gave Neal a shake and rammed him against the wall once more.

"Dan, that's enough!" Chelle yanked at his arm with both hands.

"I didn't do anything—either time—you lunatic," Neal gasped. He tried to wrench out of Dan's grasp but couldn't. "Let me go."

The violence jolted Sophie from her numbness. "Stop it," she said, jumping to her feet to help Chelle separate the men.

"Stop it!" She thumped Dan on the arm. "And you, too," she said, when Neal stuck out his chin as if daring Dan to hit him. "It might make you two feel better to beat the heck out of each other—but stop and *think*."

When Dan shoved Neal away from him, Sophie exhaled in relief. "Think about it. When Neal bought that bone for Aesop, we all saw it and there was nothing wrong with it. It disappeared for a while, remember? It could have been poisoned then. When it reappeared, it was so dirty it looked like it had been buried. None of us paid close attention; it was too gross."

"Doesn't mean he didn't do it," Dan said, glaring at Neal for good measure.

"No, but why call attention to it by bringing it to the vet's for Aesop? I don't know who did it, but it wasn't Neal. He liked Aesop, you all did." She looked from one to the other, then lifted her hands and dropped them. "Whoever did this is an outsider. I agree with Chelle—it must have something to do with this lighthouse. And where an unfinished house isn't worth much, and the construction equipment is well-protected, there must be something else we haven't considered yet. Maybe someone doesn't want the lighthouse restored."

"Who?" Dan demanded, irritably tugging his shirt straight. "The place was abandoned for years. Any investor could have snapped it up and didn't. This project, when we're able to work on it," he added bitterly, "brings money to the village. And will continue to bring money when it's taking renters. For the village, it's a win-win situation."

Neal slowly re-tucked his shirt and nodded. "He's right. The Point's been an eyesore with undeveloped potential for years." He spread his hands. "I can think of several people who will gain. But I can't think of a single person or business interest who would benefit from it staying the way it is. There's no motive."

"Possibly." Chelle lifted a shoulder. "But what else could it be?"

Remembering this was their village and friends she was accusing, Sophie said cautiously, "Maybe, someone doesn't want us to find out what happened to Abigail and her baby."

"After all this time?" Neal looked doubtful and she didn't blame him.

"Look, you guys are the ones who insist on talking about the dead as if you know them," she pointed out. "It's not so strange some crackpot would take steps to make sure that something terrible didn't come out about their family."

"Alden's dead and has no living relatives." Chelle shrugged. "There's no one to care what people think or know about him. He was as bad as they've always said."

Sophie searched the faces of the people she had begun to consider friends and wondered if they hadn't all been blinded by the village prejudice against Alden. "Right, but what if he didn't murder Abigail, and someone else does know what happened. It could be worth their while to keep the truth hidden."

"Well, the only way to keep it hidden would be to make sure the apparitions stop," Dan walked forward as he talked it out, "which would mean emptying the lighthouse because nothing really happened until . . . ."

" . . . Sophie moved in." Chelle nodded as though she'd seen the truth of it. "It's been ghost central ever since."

"Not just me." She pointed to the two men standing next to her. There was no way she was taking ownership for all of this. "It took the three of us."

Neal brushed the thought off. "But no one had ever *seen* what had happened between Nehemiah and Abigail before. That took you."

"What if the bridge wasn't an accident?" Dan asked.

Sophie balked at the idea and pushed down the anger that was starting to replace the numbness. "That's crazy. It's one thing to poison Aesop, and another to run me down in cold blood."

"Wait a minute. When did this happen?" Neal demanded.

"On her walk home from the vet's, someone forced her over the rail on The Narrows bridge." Dan couldn't have looked grimmer. "She had to jump into the canal to get out of the way."

"It was an *accident*," she said. But could somebody be that desperate?

Dan was ready to hammer the idea home if necessary. "If the car didn't kill you, the water could have."

"He's right," Neal said and earned a surprised look from Dan. "If we agree that clearing out the lighthouse is the goal, maybe the close call on the bridge was intentional." Neal gestured with his hands, weighing the outcomes. "Either they run you over or force you over the side where you are injured or killed." He spread his hands. "In either case, you're out of commission and out of the lighthouse."

Chelle rubbed her arms, then shivered. "If that's what's going on here, then we're all in danger."

Sophie had to agree. "So," she said, knowing they really had only one option, "How do we find them?"

"The only people who know we've been having apparitions are us four and Carol, and I'd trust her with my life," Chelle said.

Sophie knew Chelle was right. The problem or the threat lay with what had happened at the lighthouse hundreds of years ago—facts someone didn't want to come to light today. "So, do we make what we've seen common knowledge? It might be the best way to stay safe."

"And get no work done," Dan said, rubbing his eyes tiredly. "We could try keeping it quiet a little longer, but we'd have to be careful."

"No more walks alone." Neal looked directly at Sophie, and she nodded. "Nobody stays by themselves in the lighthouse, and we keep up the night watch." It was common sense advice they couldn't argue with. "Maybe we'll see an apparition that sets the record straight about the Aldens. Maybe the truth will be enough to stop whoever is targeting us."

"We can only hope," Sophie muttered, and began to clean up the empty bowls while the others scattered. She wanted to put off the moment she'd need to climb the stairs without Aesop behind her for the first time.

When she had run out of things to tidy and couldn't avoid it any longer, she headed upstairs for the night. As she climbed, she thought she heard a dog padding behind her, nails clicking on the stairs. She paused on the landing to look down, saw nothing, and wrinkled her forehead.

Chelle emerged from the second-floor office, stopping when she saw her. "Forget something?"

"No, I could have sworn . . . never mind." She gave a weary shrug and turned to her room. "Wake me in two hours when it's my turn."

"You got it." Chelle trotted downstairs to begin her rounds, armed with a flashlight.

Sophie went to the dresser and dug for the cellphone in her purse. That she found herself for the second time in as many months calling her sister spoke loudly about the state of her heart and good sense.

It rang four times before Jacqueline answered in a hushed tone from the other end.

"Hello?"

"Hey, it's me." Sophie exhaled in relief. "Can you talk?"

"I'm at a client's house in the middle of an appraisal. Can it wait?"

Sophie looked up and blinked rapidly before speaking. "Aesop died today. He was poisoned." The words tumbled from her lips, even though she knew the acceptable thing to say was 'of course.'

"Oh, no," Jacqueline breathed quietly into the phone. "Okay. Give me a sec."

Sophie paced slowly across the bedroom as she waited. She heard Jacqueline make excuses, referring to a "family emergency." Then there were footsteps and the closing of a door.

"Alright, I'm back. But I don't have much time," Jacqueline said breathlessly. "What happened?"

As Sophie explained in stops and starts about the bone and coolant, she heard Jacqueline catch her breath.

"Oh, Sophie. I'm so sorry." The clear compassion in Jacqueline's voice helped to dull the sharp edges of loss that scraped at Sophie's heart. "Are you okay?"

She discarded the lie of "I'm managing" for the truth. "No, I'm not. I'm so angry and confused and sad. So incredibly sad, Jac, it's choking me." She dropped to sit on the edge of the bed and pressed her fingers to her lips to keep from crying.

"That's totally understandable. You and that dog were inseparable." Jacqueline's voice shifted from compassion to outrage. "How could anyone be so cruel?"

Sophie latched on to the phrase 'that dog.' He wasn't 'that dog' to her. He was Aesop, her best friend. She ignored the pang of hurt her sister's words caused and blinked back tears. Jacqueline still didn't get it, still didn't understand her or what she and Aesop had shared.

"He was family." Sophie heard an edge to her voice but couldn't help it.

"I'm family, Sophie. Aesop was a pet," Jacqueline huffed. "Let's not fight about the dog. Isn't it enough that I understand what he meant to you?"

"That's just it. I don't think you do." The things that drove Jacqueline mad about Aesop, like his frantic energy and those tufts of fur he could leave behind, were some of the things Sophie would miss most. She closed her eyes and hung her head wearily. "Never mind. Thanks for taking my call. I appreciate it."

"Sophie," Jacqueline interrupted with a trace of impatience.

"I'd better go. It's been a long day." She rubbed at the spot between her eyes that was starting to throb. "And you need to get back to your client."

"Sophie, don't you hang up on me," Jacqueline warned.

"'Night, Jacqueline. I'll be in touch." Sophie swiped off the phone and powered it down. Her sister would be furious, but she'd had all she could manage today. Thank goodness they'd never gotten to discuss the bridge incident. She could only imagine what Jacqueline would have had to say about that.

She stretched out on the bed fully clothed. What was the point of changing? She'd showered earlier and would be up in two hours, anyways. One arm slung across her eyes, she breathed slowly, trying to relax stiff back and leg muscles. The trauma of the day and the phone call with her sister had done its damage. She felt battered and ancient.

When the stretching and breathing didn't help, she lay on her side and stared through the window she'd neglected to close, watching the wind drag jumbled clouds across the moon. As a child she'd enjoyed the sight of clouds backlit by moonlight. Feet peeking out from under her nightgown, bare toes gripping the floor, she used to lean out from her window to watch. It had been her own private puppet show playing across the sky: knights on white chargers rescuing the helpless from snarling dragons and warlocks. The stories had always worked out—the peasant saved and the knight triumphant. Things had made sense. As an adult, she'd learned no knights would ride to the rescue, the helpless were often trampled underfoot, and, now especially, it could be difficult to find things that made sense. The death of her dog, the possible attempt on her life, how could she begin to understand that? A tear slid over her nose and dropped to the pillow with an audible *pat*. Then another, and another followed, until she buried her head in the pillow to cry herself to sleep.

9

The Bluff

Sophie knew she had risen to teach, corrected student papers, and kept her night watch at the lighthouse, but she had no conscious memory of any of it. It was like driving someplace you were familiar with but not remembering the journey. The fact that she didn't remember made her uneasy. What was even worse was what she kept imagining in the lighthouse.

On more than one occasion, she caught herself blinking to clear her eyes when she saw Aesop trailing around the house behind her. It was not his physical form, but the essence of him just a few paces away from her. She was either going crazy or . . . . Well, there was no 'either.' She was going crazy. What other answer could there be? She'd been purposefully avoiding the lighthouse since the last time she'd seen him standing uncertainly by her bedroom door. But even without the Aesop apparitions, there hadn't been a reason to stick around. Neither of the Aldens had been seen since the apparition of Nehemiah and the crone.

Four days after Aesop died, she pulled up Carol Darby's dirt lane and came to a stop under the giant elm. Its leaves were taking on the tinge of fall gold. The calm day had birds singing and squirrels scrambling in the branches as if they too knew autumn was coming and were making the best of it. As she turned off the ignition, she rested her head on the steering wheel. She'd driven here instinctively, not even knowing if Carol was home. She sat up and shoved hair out of her eyes. She didn't know what she needed, but she needed something.

She climbed out of the car and circled round the garden, past the fading summer herbs. Only the tufts of lemon balm and mounds of

Black-Eyed Susans still thrived. As she passed, she pulled a leaf off the lemon balm and lifted it to her nose. The clean, tart scent made her mouth water. She absently brushed the leaf against her nose as she inhaled and slowly wandered behind the house to the pond. She could have checked the house first but had a feeling she'd find Carol outside on a day like today.

At the back of the house, willow branches arched over the pond. The tree shaded the now-dry dock and battle-weary crocodile that Nicolás and Alex had defeated the last time she came. Carol sat in an Adirondack chair, watching the pond and a solitary white butterfly that floated from flower to bush. Carol called without turning, "Come on over, Sophie."

Sophie slipped off her shoes and felt the cool grass press between her toes. "How'd you know it was me?" she asked, walking across the grass and coming to stand besides Carol's chair.

Carol smiled slightly and looked up at her. "Who else would it be?" She was quiet for a moment. "Chelle told me what happened, and I'm sorry for it. He was a good dog."

Sophie shredded the leaf, covering her fingers with the sticky lemon-scented sap. "Thanks. I'm here about that, I think."

"Alright." Carol nodded and settled back. "I'm listening."

Sophie dropped onto the grass and drank in the serenity of the pond and trees before she spoke. "Aesop . . . " her voice cracked, and she started again. "Aesop was the only family I really had left. He always accepted me just as I was." She tossed away the battered leaf and wiped her fingers on the grass. "And now that he's gone, I have this emptiness inside me that aches. How can emptiness ache?" She shrugged helplessly. "And worst of all, I keep seeing him everywhere around the lighthouse. I mean not him physically. I can see through him, but he's there. Or I picture him because I expect him to be?" she asked. "I'd rather not be losing my mind."

Carol sighed. "You're not losing your mind. Sophie, you're grieving."

"But I see him where he should be—walking around the lighthouse, napping on the rug." She rubbed her eyes wearily. "I didn't see my parents after they died. Why Aesop?"

"First of all, you're more open to that kind of experience now, and Aesop is not just a dog. Animals," Carol searched for the right words, "enhance the human experience. They bring a richness to life humans have nurtured and developed for thousands of years. You know, when we sense loved ones who have died it can be in dreams, as apparitions, or internal conversations. I visit whenever I want with my mom who's been gone fifteen years, just by talking to her. I hope when I'm gone my daughter will be able to do the same with me." Carol lifted a shoulder and smiled. "Who knows what I'll get. Animals, though, are a little different than people. Their spirits tend to linger for a time before they move on."

Carol slowly tapped her armrest with her thumb and watched Sophie. "Maybe your Aesop's still around," she said softly. "I know that people claim to hear or see companion animals long after they've passed. I've got a friend who had two cats. When one of them died, the remaining cat used to bat at nothing, just like it used to do when it had a playmate to tangle with. Rose swears up and down her first cat's still around lurking under chairs waiting to pounce on the other." Carol nodded, a serious expression on her face. "I've also heard people insist they hear their deceased pets or continue to find pet hair long after the animals are gone."

Maybe Sophie wasn't the only one who was unhinged. "That's impossible."

"Is it?" Carol raised an eyebrow. "And this is from someone who sees people who lived three hundred years ago?"

Sophie gave a humorless laugh. "The only thing I'm perfectly sure of is that I'm sad and lonely and feel like I'm losing my mind." She leaned against the side of Carol's chair. "What am I going to do?"

Carol placed a gentle hand on Sophie's arm. "All who have passed are not lost if we seek them with open minds and hearts."

"People or pets?"

"Both." Carol turned and watched the breeze finger its way through the fronds of the willow, moving over the surface of the pond like an unseen hand. "Use your imagination when you seek Abigail and her child, wonder what Nehemiah was feeling, and you'll find the answers you are looking for. Do the same with Aesop."

As far as advice went, it was some of the vaguest and most unusual she'd ever been given. Oddly enough though, she felt a little better. She sat with Carol for a long while, watching her solitary butterfly flit about the yard. Sometimes it was close enough to feel the flutter of white wings, and other times it was out of sight. But it always returned. Perhaps spirits were like that. She closed her eyes and lifted her face to the sun.

Hours later, she returned to the lighthouse and found it empty. She tucked her school things on the staircase and sat on the floor. Taking the parting advice Carol had given her, she took the time alone to really mourn. She wept for both herself and Aesop, for what they had shared, and for what had been taken from them.

When at last, she dried her eyes, she let out a shuddering sigh. Arms crossed on her bent knees, she gazed down the hall. As though he'd been called, she saw Aesop's spirit, head and ears down, tail drooping, walking tentatively toward her. *He's as lost as me.* She suspended reason, held out her arms, and called to him. "Come on, boy. It's alright. You can stay with me as long as you want. Unless you have somewhere better to be?" She sniffed and dragged an arm across her eyes. Ignoring and avoiding him hadn't helped at all. Maybe it was better to reach out spirit to spirit.

Haltingly, Aesop's spirit made his way to her and crawled into her lap, like he'd done too many times to count. It had been his most comfortable and secure place to be and their favorite way to pass time. She closed her arms around the space he would have taken, drew it to her, and felt whole. *Not all was lost.*

Slowly, like the sifting of sand through her fingers, Aesop slipped away as gradually as he had arrived. She was alone again, but not lonely—sad, but not devastated—knowing he would stay close.

When Chelle lugged two bags inside a short time later, Sophie was still there, seated on the floor. "What are you doing?" Chelle asked.

"Communing with the dead." Sophie tilted her head back to look at Chelle.

"Well," Chelle mused. "It can't be the Aldens because you look too peaceful."

"No, not them. I was visiting with Aesop." She waited for a flip response from Chelle and got none. She looked at her curiously. "This is where you tell me I'm off my rocker."

"Soph, after what we've seen together," Chelle said, shifting the bags in her arms, "if you tell me you visited with your dog's spirit, I believe you."

"Thanks." Sophie struggled to her feet and dusted off her pants. "It helps to be surrounded by the like-minded." She peeked over the edge of the bag. "What do you have in there?"

Chelle jiggled both bags with a grin. "Fixings for tonight's clam bake."

"Will the weather hold? We're supposed to get that nasty storm up the coast from North Carolina."

"Yeah, Dan checked the forecast. We should be able to get dinner in before it hits." Chelle looked at her with a mischievous glint in her eye. "But you got drafted to help with the prep. Dan's on the beach right now tending the fire, and Neal will be home later to help haul the food down to the fire pit."

Sophie tugged one of the bags from Chelle. "In that case, let's get busy."

With loose gravel sliding underfoot, the women skidded down the bluff to the beach where they found Dan raking coals out of the stone-lined pit. "Where's the seaweed and food?" he demanded, jamming the rake, tines down, into the sand and dropping the handle.

Chelle kicked off her sandals and settled onto the sand beside her battered bag. "Neal should be right down with the cooler." Sophie followed suit, pulling out a bag of chips she'd flattened by falling. Smushed or not—she intended to eat them.

When Dan tried to sneak some chips, Chelle playfully slapped his hand and told him, "How about you help Neal first?" It certainly looked like Neal needed help. He was lifting a giant cooler, walking a few steps, then setting it down. He adjusted his hands and tried again. He wasn't making much progress down the bluff path.

Dan called out, "Neal! Hold up a minute. I'll give you a hand." When Chelle wasn't looking, he snagged some chips on his way past and jogged over to the path.

"Is it really that heavy?" Sophie asked, a little surprised that Neal really did look like he needed help. "I lifted one side in the kitchen, and it didn't seem so bad."

"It wasn't, at the time." Chelle smiled slyly, then popped a chip into her mouth. "The watermelon must weigh more than I remember."

Sophie smothered a burst of laughter and turned to watch Dan and Neal wrestle the cooler to the bottom of the path.

When the men finally joined them, she listened to the good-natured bickering around her. Who would have imagined just a few short months ago they would be rubbing along as well as they were? Granted, along with most rubbing came friction. But nothing compared to the snarling fights that had happened when they first moved into the lighthouse. She let them battle it out and watched the ocean rise and ebb, gulls sweeping into the surf for fish.

"Hey, Sophie. Help me out," Dan said. In the next few minutes, he showed her how to spread seaweed over the rocks without getting burned by steam. Next, they laid the bundles wrapped in cheesecloth and covered the pit with a large canvas tarp, weighing it down with extra stones.

As seaweed hissed, steam rose from around the edges of the canvas. "Terrific." Neal rubbed his hands together. "In two hours, we can eat."

"Most likely sooner," Dan said. "That fire is seriously hot." He gave Sophie and Chelle a nudge, following Neal's lead down the beach. "Come on, let's collect some driftwood to burn later. Dinner will be ready before you know it."

The four of them wandered over the sand, seeking wood washed to shore by storms. There were broken branches stripped of bark and splintered boards, perhaps from ships, all returned to the land from where they'd come. Dry and bleached by the sun, they made quick-lighting fires that burned hot and fast. They would make the perfect heat for sitting around after the meal and toasting marshmallows.

"You haven't been around much," Dan said as he fell into step besides Sophie. "Are you doing okay?"

She took her time answering and bent to pick up a thick section of dried wood. "Yeah, I've been busy. And it's been kind of weird around the lighthouse without Aesop." She sighed, then shrugged. "I'm doing as well as can be expected, I suppose." She avoided the sympathy she saw in his face by glancing past him to the bluff. The late sun gilded the small plants and shrubs clinging to its eroding sides. She tilted her face into the light and thought for a moment. "You know, with all the excess emotion I've been giving off around the lighthouse, it should have been enough to coax the Aldens out by now." She turned to Dan to gauge his response. "I'm surprised we haven't seen them."

Dan nodded in agreement. "Maybe you should ask Carol about it."

"I did." Sophie shifted the wood for a better grip. "She said to imagine what it would have been like to be in Abigail or Nehemiah's places."

"Have you?" He stooped for a twisted piece of wood, gray and light as air, and tucked it under his arm.

She rubbed her cheek against her shoulder, brushing aside a strand of hair that had blown into her face. "Not yet, I haven't had the chance."

He bent for another piece, then straightened. "Maybe we could kick ideas around the fire later."

"I suppose," she agreed, but was reluctant to have the Aldens intrude on the evening's peace.

Neal and Chelle returned, their arms already full of craggy drift-wood. "It's a good thing you two have us to do your share," Chelle teased, when she saw their pitiful collection.

"Over-achievers," Dan retorted and made a show of scrambling for more wood to catch up.

On the way back to the fire pit, the four talked easily of the ocean and the lore it created. They shared stories of 'surf men' who risked their lives to rescue shipwreck survivors, Ocean Born Mary and her bolt of green fabric, and the sinking and reappearance two hundred years later of the cursed *Sparrowhawk*. Sophie shared her favorite story. It was not about the ocean, exactly, but what was found besides it—a skeleton dressed in ancient armor. "It inspired Longfellow's ballad, 'The Skeleton in Armor.'"

"A ballad . . . " Neal made a face as though he couldn't imagine any-thing worse. "It sounds painful."

Sophie rolled her eyes. "It's just a poem that tells a story." Sophie felt like she was lecturing and shut it down. "But really, the beginning is unbelievably creepy. There's lots of swordplay by a fearless Viking for a chieftain's daughter. I think you'd like it." When he made a noncommittal grunt and walked ahead of her, she gave a half laugh and turned to the others. "What'd I say?"

Dan shrugged. "I like Vikings. It's the poem part that gives most people the willies."

Sophie had to reluctantly agree. Poetry in any form was always a tough sell to her students. Even the most approachable poems made them squirm. But tonight wasn't about work, or ghosts, or loss. It was about good food and an ocean that stole your breath away with its beauty.

This evening's ocean had the deceptive calm of water before an on-coming storm. Waves collapsed lethargically against the shore and pulled away with the hiss of retreating foam. Kneaded under the next curl of wa-ter, the foam spread repeatedly against the wet sand in a placid rhythm, soothing the four who walked beside it.

When they reached the picnic spot on the beach, they stacked the wood beside the fire pit. Plumes of mouth-watering vapor escaped when Dan and Neal peeled back the thick canvas tarp. Chelle helped by skew-ering the steaming bundles with a long fork and serving them in large enamel bowls. While she passed out the dinners, Dan raked out the sea-weed and prepared the pit for a campfire.

"Ow, that's hot." Sophie blew on her fingertips, sure she'd removed a few layers of skin.

"Hold on a second," Neal said, and helped her cut open the cheese-cloth to reveal corn on the cob, potato, lobster and perfectly steamed clams.

"Beautiful. Thanks, guys." It was a nice change of pace to be on the beach away from the lighthouse and the Aldens. Nothing had happened since Nehemiah had appeared with the crone, but Sophie knew that Neal and Dan were determined to get the apparitions resolved. Philip Bishop planned to give the lighthouse a trial stay with his wife and newborn daughter. By both men's accounts, he was delighted with the baby and doted on both his girls. She raised her voice over the call of gulls and asked, "I wonder what it was like for Abigail? There was no one to watch over her, to share the joy of that baby."

"I know," Dan agreed, pausing as a series of waves crashed onto shore. "What she had, from the looks of it, was a jailor. On the times we saw her, she was desperate and terrified."

Chelle gave voice to the most essential question of all. "What state of mind was she in when the baby disappeared? How could she have gone on to marry Nehemiah, knowing he'd been responsible for the death or at least the disappearance of her baby?"

The question hung uncomfortably between them. Sophie set her food aside, no longer hungry. "I don't know if she had much choice. Options for single women at the time were limited, especially for ones as young as her."

Dan rose to place a few pieces of driftwood in the pit and lit a fire, feeding the small flames with broken bits of wood. "Still . . . ."

"What about Nehemiah?" Sophie asked the others, watching the firelight flicker on their faces. "What do you think he felt?"

"I don't want to know," Chelle said, then shivered. "He was a monster."

"Well, he must have felt something," Sophie said. A change in the sound of the waves caused her to cast a wary eye toward the water. Angry clouds had blown out of nowhere to cover the remaining sun. The ocean began to shift to high tide, growing in force as the waves took on an ominous green tinge in the fading light. That storm must be charging up the coast faster than the Weather Bureau had anticipated. She hoped the fishing fleet had all returned to the harbor. People with few ties to the water tended to forget how brutally unforgiving the ocean could be. A harsh gust of wind stung her face with sand.

"No worries," Dan said, assessing the clouds that were starting to boil toward them over the ocean. "We've got a couple of hours before it hits." He settled back on his elbows and nudged the fire with his shoe. "I think the only emotion Alden ever felt was greed." When the wind whipped the fire to lick at his jeans, he cursed and batted at the frayed edges that had caught fire.

"What about desire?" Chelle turned to watch waves begin to crash against the sand, inching their way up the shore. "He was willing to force Abigail to marry him, even though she loved someone else and was most certainly, in his mind, damaged goods."

Sophie tilted her head as she considered. "Maybe, but it seems more likely that he convinced himself that he was saving her . . . after the required penance of course." A fat drop of rain splattered against the sheet. She assessed the sky. "I don't think we're going to have a couple of hours before that storm."

Neal, who had been unusually quiet, spoke up. "Absolute, self-righteous rage is what he felt." A roll of distant thunder echoed with his words. "Alden wanted Abigail beyond all reason. He pursued her and was rejected. When he finally ran her to ground with her father gone, he found her not only in love with someone else but pregnant too." He closed his eyes briefly and said in a rough voice, "It would be enough to drive him to measures most people wouldn't be able to justify."

"Yeah," Dan agreed grimly. "Like what he did with the baby." A gust came howling down the beach, spraying sand into their faces and blowing large raindrops sideways. "Ugh!" Dan spat sand out of his mouth. "We'd better pack this stuff up."

"Forget carrying anything up the trail," Chelle shouted over the rising wind. She turned, grabbed the bags, and shoved them into the cooler. "Weigh it down with rocks. We'll get it all tomorrow."

While the women struggled to kick sand onto the wildly swaying fire, Neal and Dan moved the cooler higher up the beach, using rocks to wedge it in place.

"Line squall!" Chelle grabbed Sophie's arm. "Let's get up the bluff before it's too late."

The wind whipped Sophie's hair as she sprinted for the trail, following Chelle and Dan. She glanced back to be sure Neal followed and saw he was only a few steps behind. Clutching at wind-twisted shrubs for balance, she stumbled forward and fought to keep from tumbling off onto the black rocks below. The ocean slammed the shore like a fist, echoing until the next blow rammed home. Sand blasted her face, and she lowered her head to protect her eyes. When she stumbled, she felt Neal's hand in her back propel her forward. She shot a quick glance at the sky and saw fierce clouds devour the last dregs of daylight. They were clambering up the bluff near-blind, and she felt a wave of panic. Dan's eyes had better be sharper than hers.

Near the top, the wind rose in a keening wail so human all four of them stopped dead and looked up. Over the crest of the bluff gray tendrils reached out and descended, twisting and winding downward to cover the path around their feet. Dan turned to shield Chelle, and Sophie stepped back into Neal.

Sophie let out a strangled cry when Nehemiah appeared at the outermost point of the bluff, arms outstretched over the churning ocean. He had the still body of a naked infant balanced in his hands.

The water that raged to shore and greedily wrenched rocks and shrubs from the bluff would serve his purpose well. No trace of the illegitimate child would remain. Let him seek out his father in the ocean's depths. His coat flaps slapped against his legs as he lowered his arms and tilted his palms, letting the small bundle roll off his fingers down to the merciless waves below.

"No!" She tried to wrench free from Neal, who held her shoulders tight. "It's too late," he shouted over the wind, holding her in place. "There's nothing there. It happened too long ago."

"It's wrong." She slapped at his hands, then tore away suddenly to bend at the waist. "I'm going to be sick."

Chelle grabbed Sophie by the arm and pulled her upright. "We have to find Dan," she shouted. "He went after Alden; I couldn't stop him."

When they struggled up the rest of the trail, there was no sign of either Dan or Alden anywhere along the bluff. The wind howled and the skies opened, dropping sheets of rain. Sophie squinted through the downpour and saw a faint glow from the lighthouse. Its front door was open and swinging against its frame in the wind. "Over there," she said, pointing and pulling Chelle with her.

They half stumbled and ran to the lighthouse, slipping on water that had fallen too fast to soak into the ground. Sophie was wet to the skin and shivering when she finally threw open the front door. "Quiet," she whispered without turning to Neal who had caught up. "It's not over." They edged their way forward and eased toward a feeble light coming from the living room. Time stretched out so slowly that Sophie clenched her hands against the building tension. Goose bumps rose on her skin when the room finally came into view. A gray mist twisted about the floor, partially covering the body of Dan as though eating it greedily.

Dan appeared as if he'd been cut down in battle, his limbs sprawled at impossible angles. Neal made a grab at Chelle as she rushed forward, snagging her by the arm. "Wait. By the window." He motioned to where Abigail stood barefoot facing the storm in a linen nightgown, her hair hanging straight down her back.

"I'm not just going to leave him there," Chelle hissed, yanking her arm away.

Neal forced the words through his teeth, "You don't even know if it's safe. What if the same thing happens to you?"

Sophie ignored them both and stepped forward, calling softly, "Abigail?" She held out her hands. "I'm so sorry. Your baby's gone." Her eyes filled as she groped for words. "He was too small, and you were so sick when he was born. He never had a chance." She took another step closer to Dan, keeping her eyes fixed on Abigail's back. "Nehemiah buried him at sea where he thought the baby's father had died." It was a sanitized version of what the monster had done, if there ever was one, and she hoped it didn't backfire. Silence. None of what she said had any effect on the girl looking blindly out the window. Sophie desperately groped for something that would move the ghost before her. "Dan tried to grab Nehemiah, to punish him for what he did to you, to your baby."

She sidled up to Dan and crouched beside him, checking him carefully for wounds. Her hands trembled with the coldness she felt coming through his wet clothing. He was practically hypothermic, but alive. "Abigail, please," she said, her own teeth beginning to chatter. Abigail remained mute and still. Sophie didn't know what had happened to Dan, but she knew without a doubt that he wouldn't get the help he needed until Abigail was gone. "Please . . . go!" Sophie frantically rubbed Dan's chest to revive him and get the blood circulating. Chelle and Neal finally joined her and chafed his arms and legs.

Abigail slowly turned from the window with vacant eyes and walked past where they were huddled over Dan. She was a beautiful broken shell, disappearing into a trail of twisting gray mist.

Crouched on the stairs, the watcher passed a shaking hand over his face. If he hadn't seen it for himself . . . . He wagged his head back and forth. They were prying where they had no right. He'd have to be bolder in how he dealt with her, with them. Accidents were easy enough to ar-range. He'd managed to loosen the turret ladder, but then the storm had broken, trapping him inside. While they were busy reviving the fool on the floor, he'd make his escape and come back for the journals. He had to give him credit though, the boy had guts . . . he'd seen it from the turret. He had given chase to Nehemiah after seeing him drop the infant over the bluff. Alden had felt it too and had run like the hound of hell was chasing him and snapping at his heels. The fiend had quaked in his boots when the boy's fury had crossed time, reaching out to him. Alden had sputtered and clawed at his own throat for relief, with Abigail standing passively by the window. He'd been forced to intervene and clout the boy on the head. He grabbed the banister and hauled himself to his feet. If he'd been thinking, he'd have finished the fool off and saved himself the trouble later. A real pity the boy had to go. They all had to go. He nodded resolutely and slipped out the open door into the storm.

10

Neal

Neal hurried back from the kitchen and dropped an armful of scrap wood by the fireplace. "Chelle, get those wet clothes off him. Sophie, grab Dan's sleeping bag and whatever blankets you can find and wrap him up." He stooped to build the fire as Sophie bolted from the room.

Chelle wiped the water from Dan's face with a corner of her shirt. "Will he be okay?" her voice wobbled.

"Yeah, he's not hypothermic . . . yet." Neal balled up the newspaper and laid the strips of wood across it. "But he's got a good-sized knot on the back of his head. He probably hit it when he fell."

"How did he fall?" she demanded, as she struggled with Dan's shirt buttons, a note of hysteria replacing the wobble. "The ghosts have never bothered you guys before."

Neal struck a match, lighting the paper. The flame flared, licking the wood and singeing the edges black. He bent his head low and blew on the struggling fire. "I have no idea. But," he paused to look at Chelle steadily, "I'm sure he'll batter us with the details when he wakes up."

"Right." And then more strongly, as if convincing herself, "Right." She rolled Dan on his side to pull off his wet shirt.

"Here, let me help," Sophie said, and knelt beside Chelle. When they were able to peel the wet shirt off, she handed Chelle a blanket. "Wrap this around his shoulders, and we'll work on the jeans next."

Between the three of them, they managed to get Dan down to his boxers and over by the steadily growing fire. They wrapped him in the jumble of blankets, quilts, and outdoor gear Sophie had gathered.

Rain drummed heavily on the roof. "'Rescue' will be long in getting here with the storm the way it is." Chelle glanced anxiously out the window. "What else should we do for him?"

"Tell me," Dan moaned, "that Neal didn't undress me."

Chelle dropped to her knees and kissed both his cheeks in relief. "Don't you scare me like that again." She thumped him on the shoulder and angrily swiped at her damp eyes.

He placed his hand over Chelle's. "I'm fine. And I don't need an ambulance."

"It was a stupid thing to do," Sophie snapped. He'd been so pale and cold—she'd believed the absolute worst. "And you do need to be seen by a doctor."

He brushed aside the suggestion and gave his sister's hand a weak pat. "Call them off, Chelle. They'll be busy tonight with real emergencies." He gave a weak smile. "How 'bout some coffee, instead?"

"Tea." Sophie put her hand on Chelle's shoulder to keep her from rising. "You cancel the ambulance, and I'll get the tea. I'll get a cup for you too, Chelle. You could use one." She looked over at Neal. "How about you?" When he declined, Sophie nodded and headed to the kitchen.

Thankfully, the kitchen was almost completely renovated which made pulling together the hot drinks easy. She rummaged in the cupboards for tea bags and honey, found exactly what she needed, and put the kettle on. Through the rain still pelting the window, she saw a movement near the tree line and went to the door. She pushed her nose against the glass. Furtive and bent, it looked like a person moving into the trees. Who in their right mind would be out there? Lightning pierced the sky. The field and the first edges of the forest lit in a sickly green light. Empty. She exhaled the breath she'd been holding and turned to remove the whistling tea kettle. Knock it off. It's spooky enough around here without imagining a figure in the woods.

By the time Sophie returned with two mugs of strong English tea, Dan was sitting up and scowling at the others standing over him. His chin was set in a stubborn line. "I know it was stupid."

She handed Chelle her mug and crouched to give Dan his. He sniffed it suspiciously. "At least it doesn't smell like flowers," he said, and took a cautious sip. "That's hot!" He whistled and winced in pain. He glanced at his sister and sighed. "Look, I'm sorry, Chelle. It was reflexive when I saw him drop the baby."

"He's a GHOST." Chelle sloshed tea over the rim of her mug as she waved her arms in exasperation. "What did you think you were going to do? Beat him?"

"Yeah, that's exactly what I had in mind," Dan shouted, then blanched, squeezing his eyes shut until the pain passed.

Neal bent to tend the fire. "Listen, as crazy as it may have been, I get it." He placed a few small logs on the fire before straightening and dusting off his hands. "It's hard to remember it happened hundreds of years ago, when it's playing out in front of you."

"We keep saying it's not real. But . . . it is or was at one time." Sophie watched lightning split the sky, and the lights flickered in response. "We saw a man drop a baby into that ocean." Her voice wavered. "What kind of evil person does that?"

"A calculating one," Chelle said, and sat cross-legged next to Dan. "If the baby were ever found, the lack of clothing or swaddling would have made it impossible to trace him by his mother's needlework."

A gust of wind battered the seaside wall of the lighthouse, causing the timbers to creak in protest. Sophie instinctively hunched her shoulders and hoped the lighthouse would stand strong. "I'm glad you went after him." She touched Dan's shoulder. "Do you remember what happened?"

"I was too late to stop him. When I reached the top of the trail, he was half-way back to the cottage, so I started running. I might have yelled." He shrugged. "I don't remember, but I do know I was furious and running flat out. He kind of glanced behind him and started to run, like he knew I was after him. I caught him just inside the living room . . . Abigail was over there by the window, just watching the storm."

"Did he react at all?" Neal tossed some more scraps on the fire to keep it going.

Sophie was grateful for the fire's light and heat. They'd lose power sometime during the night. And no one, after what had happened on the bluff, wanted to sit in complete darkness waiting for dawn. At least, she didn't.

"Did Alden react at all?" Neal repeated, when Dan didn't answer.

"No, and it didn't look like he could see me. He kept swinging wildly." Dan held his hands out in front of him, contracting the fingers until the knuckles were white. "I tried grabbing him by the throat and squeezing. There wasn't anything there to grab, but it seemed like it was enough. He stopped swinging and seemed to claw at his throat. This crippling cold vibrated up my arms. It was like I was freezing, part by part." He spread his fingers and let his hands drop into his lap. "Then the back of my head exploded. The last thing I saw before I hit the floor was Abigail by the window."

"Maybe you blacked out from the cold," Chelle suggested.

"It felt like I got clobbered." He fingered the bump on the back of his head and flinched. "I think I can feel my heartbeat in my head."

Sophie didn't see anything that Dan could have hit his head on. What was in the room was too high or far away to have done any damage. But who knew with ghosts, maybe it was enough for them to will something to happen?

"Abigail didn't hit you." Neal straightened from tending the fire. "She was practically catatonic. If she couldn't muster up energy in the past, it's doubtful she would be able to now."

"Right," Chelle agreed. "She didn't look like she was alert enough to take care of herself, and I doubt she would have been defending Nehemiah. Do you think he kept her drugged?" She was quiet for a moment, and then warmed to the idea. "It could be the reason she stayed with him."

Sophie felt the eyes of the others on her, as if she were the authority on Abigail and her thoughts. "Wait," she said. "Remember that journal passage where Abigail is described as broken? Maybe, that's polite colonial-speak for mentally unstable."

Neal grabbed a towel off the floor and rubbed it briskly against his chest and legs, removing the excess water from his clothes. "So, she snaps when she sees Alden throw the baby from the bluff?"

"She could have." Chelle nodded and tilted her head to the side. "But if that were true, she would know what had happened to the baby and wouldn't be looking for him."

"Hmm, I wonder." Sophie shifted closer to the fire to dry her own clothes. "Carol felt Abigail wanted me to witness her story first-hand, and we didn't know why. Maybe she needs me to see because she doesn't know what happened. If she was harmed somehow by the fever or labor, it would explain why she's so lost."

"Poor kid," Dan murmured, and shed a blanket. "She can't move on because she can't understand what happened to her. She can't see the whole of it."

Chelle gaped at her brother in surprise. "That was very insightful."

He flushed, shifted uncomfortably, and said, "Well, it rubs off after listening to you go on and on."

"Now what?" Neal spread his hands. "Is it over or are we waiting for the next matinee?"

Chelle pulled one of Dan's discarded blankets over her so that only her face showed. "It could be . . . we finally know what happened to the baby."

"But we don't know what happened to Abigail." Sophie had come this far, and she wasn't willing to leave without the answer. And to be honest, she didn't think the others would be satisfied either. "It seems to me like these events are building, not winding down."

"I agree." Dan turned to Neal. "Did you ever get any further with those journals?"

"Not much farther." He looked like he was going to say more but shrugged. "I'll take a look at them again tomorrow and see what else he has to say. But in the meantime," he said, turning his back on the storm still howling outside the windows. "We should take advantage of the fact we still have electricity and hot water."

"Seriously," Chelle agreed. "I thought we were getting a stretch of bad weather, but this is more like a hurricane."

"Except that it came on so fast." Dan struggled to his feet, clutching the remaining blankets around his waist. "Someone's going to get fired at the Weather Bureau."

Sophie felt ridiculous suggesting it but charged ahead anyway. "Maybe we should get some supplies together and spend the night down here," she motioned to the fireplace. Since her parents' deaths, storms like this always unsettled her, and the lighthouse's location on the bluff made her feel especially vulnerable.

A shutter began to bang regularly against the side of the house. "I'll shower, then get that." Dan pointed overhead from where the sound came. "Sophie's right. It's a good idea to stick together tonight. I'll grab an oil lamp and flashlights on my way down."

"Make it snappy in the shower." Chelle snatched his trailing blanket, stopping him. "I want electricity and hot water when it's my turn."

"Right." He yanked the blanket from her grasp and stomped up the stairs.

"Sophie," Neal said, as she moved to follow Dan for supplies, "I need to talk to you. Alone," he added pointedly when Chelle remained seated.

"Sure thing," Chelle said, giving them both a curious look before she rose to her feet and left.

"That was kind of rude." Sophie frowned at Neal. "What's so important?"

He was silent for a moment. "I need you to move out of the lighthouse."

"What . . . why?" she asked.

Neal shrugged. "I think you'd be safer, we'd all be safer, if you weren't here. I'm thinking of calling Bishop and advising him to hold off on the restoration for a while."

Her eyebrows rose. "If that's what you think, why don't we all clear out?"

"Because somehow you're the key to all of this." He stepped forward, and she reflexively stepped back. "I was watching you on the beach, Sophie, and you called Nehemiah and Abigail up."

"I did not." She felt a small spurt of panic. She had no control over the dead. No one did.

"You did, and I'm pretty sure you called up the storm too."

"You're wrong." Sophie took another step away from him. "I can't call up a storm any more than you can. And all I did, what we all did, was imagine what it would have been like to be the Aldens."

Neal shook his head slowly, rejecting what she'd said. "It hinges on you, and I want you out."

"You want me out?" she said, some licks of irritation threading through her surprise. "Forget it. It's not happening."

"Don't be so stubborn." He released a long breath. "You could get hurt."

"What about Chelle and Dan?" she demanded.

"What about me?" When she looked at him blankly, he lost what patience he had. "I've been trying to get you out of this house from the start. First, I used Aesop and then the ghosts as excuses."

She frowned. "Why? Aesop was never in the way, and you needed me here."

He took a breath and said in resignation, "You . . . you got to me in a way I didn't expect." When she continued to look at him in confusion, he stiffened and stepped away. "I see."

She didn't see. She hadn't seen at all. What a mess. "Neal, wait!" She grasped his arm. "I didn't mean . . . ."

He eased away. "My mistake." He turned to the doorway and walked out without a backward glance. "I've got the turret to check."

Wind slashed through trees and whistled past the lighthouse, driving rain and torn leaves against the windows. Sophie hoped the glass would hold. Warily making her way past them, she followed Neal to the kitchen. She called herself twenty times a fool when the lights flickered—once, twice, and then went out with a pop and the smell of melting plastic. In the pitch dark, she froze, afraid to move, unable to judge the distance to the wall or kitchen counter. She ruthlessly crushed the thought that someone could be standing right next to her, and she would never know it. All she could do was wait.

Lightning crackled across the sky. It illuminated the empty kitchen just enough for her to lunge for the nearest counter before the dark descended again. Where was Neal? The door to the turret stood open, but she didn't hear him moving over the sounds of the storm. As much as she hated lightning, a few extra bolts would be helpful right now. She edged her way to the turret door. "Neal?" She called even louder, "Can you come down? I'd like to talk to you. But the power's out, and I don't have a light." She strained for a reply. There was no way she was going through that door.

Above the sounds of the storm, she heard a muffled cry. "Neal?" she yelled.

No answer.

She gritted her teeth and shuffled forward. She felt along the grit and cobwebs of the hallway until she reached the window. "Neal, are you alright? Come on, this isn't funny."

What kind of game was he playing? There was no hint of light other than the occasional flashes of lightning that flickered in the windows above. Something was wrong. Neal might stay silent and ignore her, but he wouldn't sit in a dark turret to do it.

Behind her, the kitchen was as dark as where she now stood, flattened against the turret wall and barely breathing. Where were the others? Going back wasn't an option. It would take too long without a light, and Neal might need help. She clutched at the iron banister with both hands and climbed, one deliberate step at a time. Her bare feet felt the worn pattern of all the lighthouse keepers that had come before her in the aged stone.

Turn after turn, she climbed steadily higher, the rough metal bumping under her hands. She sensed it was important to be quiet. She must be almost at the top, she thought, then pitched forward hard on the stair edge. Stone bit into her shins, and she gasped in pain. She slid against the wall until she was seated and fought the nausea that gripped her. Where had all this water come from? The stairs were so slick with it, she could feel it soaking into her shorts. She pulled heavily on the railing and hauled herself upright. Hand over hand, she edged toward the landing. A few more steps and the railing ended, her foot sliding out onto the level floor.

She got down on her knees and crawled forward, feeling for the anchored wooden ladder in the center of the room. She slid her hands forward into more water, then bumped against something solid. She snatched her hands back. "Neal?" she whispered in panic. Reaching out tentatively, she felt a leg and worked her way up, patting him for injuries. "Neal, come on. Say something." If only she could see. No arms or legs twisted away from his body at odd angles, so maybe he hadn't broken anything. She gingerly skimmed his shoulders and face. He must have fallen and knocked himself out. She had to get help. He was warm but lying in water. "Dan," she shouted. "Neal's hurt!"

Just then lightning splintered the sky, shards of black electrically lined with white. It flooded the small landing and burned the scene into her mind before blackness fell again. Blood, not water. So much blood— on her hands, her knees, and seeping out from the back of Neal's head. His eyes were fixed and lifeless, and her bloody handprints were all over his face.

Screaming. Someone was screaming. It echoed around the small turret and seemed to come from everywhere, from someone else, but it was her. When Sophie realized, she clapped her hand to her mouth. She scuttled back against the wall, unable to turn away from the horror just feet away. It was etched in her mind: Neal dead, the staring eyes, and the blood that dripped down the stairs.

Where were Dan and Chelle? Had something happened to them too? The wall at her back vibrated with the force of recurring thunder. It was as though the storm had stalled over The Point, raining down rage and sorrow on the lighthouse. With the next flash of lightning, she crawled to the staircase and grabbed the rail, but a pounding of feet on the stairs had her scuttling back against the wall.

The pounding rose steadily toward her, and a bobbing light beam slashed the darkness, illuminating disjointed angles of the turret. It hit the ceiling, window, stair, and all that blood, before stopping on Neal's feet and going no further. She stifled the urge to whimper by biting her lip. Come on, just a bit farther, she pleaded silently, and I can get by. The beam of light rose steadily with each last step but didn't waver from Neal's lower limbs, until the bearer reached the landing. The light moved slowly up Neal's body and stopped briefly on his face before swinging sharply away. "Good Lord," Dan murmured. Another flash illuminated the room, and he saw her, cowering against the wall. "Sophie! Are you hurt?" He crouched down beside her. "What happened?"

"I don't know." She struggled for air. "I called him. When he didn't answer, I came to see. I thought there was water everywhere, and then I fell, and it got on me. But it was blood," she whispered. "He was dead. Still warm, but dead . . . ."

"Shh," Dan soothed as sobs racked her. "We've got to go down and call the Sheriff. Sophie, I don't want Chelle seeing him like this." When she didn't appear to hear him, he repeated deliberately. "Hey, there's nothing we can do here."

She kept her eyes fixed on him as she struggled for control. She took a large gulp of air, and then another, holding the sobs in and silently shuddering. She let her breath leak out in bits, then nodded when she was ready. Dan murmured in approval and led the way down the slick stairs, her hand tightly held in his.

At the base of the turret, they met Chelle carrying an ancient oil lamp. "What happened?" Chelle cried, when she saw her covered in blood. "Where's Neal?"

"There was an accident." Dan blocked his sister's move for the stairs. "It's too late, Chelle. He's gone."

"What happened?" Chelle demanded, turning to Sophie.

Sophie drew back at the accusation in Chelle's eyes. "I don't know. We argued and he left to check the turret. When I went to apologize, I found him at the base of the ladder. He was already dead." She held out her hand in appeal, but Chelle recoiled at the blood on it.

"He was just here." Chelle trembled in disbelief. "How?"

"I don't know." A break in Dan's voice betrayed his calmness. "But it looks like he could have fallen."

"We have to call Matt," Chelle said distantly. Dan pried the lamp from her grasp and passed it to Sophie.

"Can you get her to your room, while I call the sheriff?"

Sophie nodded. Although she was still shaky herself, she recognized Chelle was worse. She partially supported Chelle with her free arm and urged her along. She was afraid Chelle would collapse before she could get her upstairs. As they passed the office and began to climb the stairs, the women heard Dan promise not to move the body until the sheriff arrived. With the weight of his words, Chelle crumpled and began to cry in earnest. Sophie staggered forward, half-dragging Chelle up the remaining stairs.

Because hers was the only room with a bed, she settled Chelle there with a warm quilt and lit a second oil lamp, leaving the other on the dresser. "I'll shower and come back to check on you." Sophie hefted the extra lamp and heard the oil slosh inside. "Is there anything you need right now?"

Chelle turned away from Sophie without a word and curled into a ball, dragging the quilt over her shoulders.

Sophie tucked her sweatpants and shirt under her arm. "I'll be right back." She didn't want to leave her alone, but she couldn't stay covered in blood.

When she got to the bathroom, she stripped down to her underwear and jammed her shorts and shirt into the tiny trash can under the sink. Even if she could get the blood out, there was no way she'd ever wear them again.

The idea of Neal's blood running down her body made her ill, so she began at the sink instead of the shower. She twisted on the faucets with bloody fingers and avoided looking in the mirror. As she scrubbed her hands and forearms vigorously, the stains thinned and followed the water around the drain in a slow crimson arc before gurgling down the pipe. She kept her lips clamped shut, lowered her head, then rubbed her cheeks and mouth. When the water finally ran clear, she braced her hands against the sides of the sink. She let the faucet run, as if turning it off would allow the tainted water to bubble back up.

How fragile they were. There had been nothing wrong with Neal, but now he was gone. He was broken like her parents, Abigail's father and baby, and Abigail herself. What an incredible, tragic waste. Loss and bitterness burned in her throat. When the water gurgled in the drain, she realized it had been running for a while and turned off the faucet with a flick of her wrist. She lifted her head to look into the mirror. Shadowed eyes, hollowed by grief, stared back at her.

Something wavered in the mirror, catching her attention. It was a small movement just over her shoulder.

Abigail. She stood in the doorway and watched Sophie with sorrow in her eyes.

Sophie turned carefully from the mirror and took a step forward. "Why?" she asked in a trembling voice, then took another step.

This apparition of Abigail seemed to exist in the present. No gray swirls surrounded her. She simply stood with an emotional connection Sophie felt.

"Do you know?" she pressed, impatient with this silent ghost who pleaded for help but offered no direction. "You must know *something*. You've been dead long enough. Haven't you learned *anything*?" she half-cried, half-shouted at the silent girl.

For a moment Abigail stood immobile, then faded, leaving the entry vacant and dark.

Sophie sank onto the side of the tub and crossed her arms on her thighs. Her breath rattled in her chest and her mind scrambled. Why would Abigail appear now? Was she still asking for help? After Neal's accident, it was unlikely they would be allowed to stay. She wasn't sure she even wanted to.

She stiffened at more movement in the doorway, but this time it was Dan. He looked impossibly weary. "I found Chelle wandering around downstairs."

"I'm sorry." She pushed the hair from her face with both hands, then let them fall back onto her lap. "When I left her, she was lying down." She reached for a towel from the floor in a half-hearted attempt to cover up.

"She was on her way up to the turret." He rubbed his forehead. "I got her back to bed by promising to stay with Neal and giving her a sedative. It may be the worst thing to do with someone in shock, but I didn't know what else to do."

Sophie wasn't all that sure it had been the wisest thing to do either, but it was too late now. "She'll be okay," she said because she felt she should. When she thought of the cold vigil he had promised to keep, she shuddered. "You don't need to stay with him all night, you know. I mean, she would never know if you didn't."

"But I would," Dan said simply.

Sophie felt shame wash over her. "I'll stay with Chelle tonight and listen for the sheriff when he comes. You won't hear him from the turret."

He nodded. "Thanks. I don't know when he'll come. It might be as late as tomorrow morning. It'll depend on the storm." He appeared to focus on her clearly for the first time. "Are you okay?"

"I'm . . . " She waved a vague hand and let it drop. With all that had happened tonight, how could she know? Focus on the facts, she told herself. "Abigail was just standing where you are."

Dan didn't flick an eyelid. "I'm not surprised. Did she say anything?"

"No. She just stood there and watched me. She looked unbearably sad."

With a shake of his head, Dan turned for the stairs. "Who isn't? I'd better get back to the turret."

She listened to him descend the stairs and make his way through the house, the storm absorbing the sound of his steps. She stripped off her underwear, turned on the frigid shower, and climbed inside. She scrubbed off the remaining blood as hard and as fast as she could. By the time she was finished, she was shivering. She quickly dressed and padded softly back to her room where Chelle lay asleep. Dan said he'd found her heading toward the turret, but Chelle didn't look like she'd moved at all since Sophie had left to shower.

While the storm lashed rain against the windows, Sophie sat on the floor, holding her own vigil and thinking of Neal. When daybreak finally brought an easing of the winds, she drifted into an uneasy sleep.

She knew she was dreaming but couldn't wake herself. This had already happened, she thought, but it didn't matter. She was back on the beach, the storm raging, watching Nehemiah drop the baby into the churning waves below. "No!" she screamed. She scrambled over the barnacle-covered rocks, slicing her hands in the hurry to reach the baby. Just out of reach, the infant's thick black hair waved like seaweed in the water. She got down on her belly and stretched out her hand to grab a hold of him. "Come on," she begged, "please." She grasped a handful of hair, tugged him close, and turned him over. But it was not the sweet face of the infant she had seen only once before. It was Neal with his staring eyes and the blood that oozed around him in the darkening water. She screamed as a shadow loomed above her and collapsed, its watery weight dragging her and Neal in a tangle of arms and legs under the sea.

11

The Sheriff

Sophie broke to the surface of the dream with a gasp, her legs twisted in the blanket she'd dragged off the bed. She eased onto one elbow and blinked at the sun streaming through the window. The storm had not only passed but had left a cloudless sky and bright sun behind. It was as though the night's fury had never existed. But she knew the ravaged trees and debris covering the sand would tell a different story. And then, there was Neal. She closed her eyes and shook her head. Don't go there. You can't deal with it right now, she told herself.

A knock at the door downstairs had her hastily wiping her eyes on the sleeve of her shirt. She scrambled off the floor and saw that Chelle still lay in a drug-induced sleep. How much of the stuff had he given her? As much as she feared pills, there was a point last night when the image of Neal's lifeless face had surfaced so often, she'd considered taking some herself. She quelled the image and hurried to the front door. She found a solidly built man in a khaki sheriff's uniform standing patiently outside.

"Matt Thomson." The man touched the brim of his hat. "You must be Sophie Tyler." When she continued to block the door, he added gently, "Can I come in?"

She fought an irrational urge to shut the door in the man's face. "Of course. Dan's in the turret with . . . with Neal." She stepped back and led him to the kitchen. "Through there."

He moved with the easy vigilance of a cop who missed nothing. "Thank you." He paused in the hall. "I'll need to ask you some questions, Ms. Tyler. Stick around for a bit, would you?"

"Of course." She wasn't fooled by the casual tone. He was a man used to people listening, and he expected to find her waiting when he was done. "I'll just get ready for class."

"No need, if the school's in the area." Thomson stopped her before Sophie could turn from the kitchen. "The power's out all over the Cape."

"Oh, I hadn't considered. I mean . . . ." She rubbed her arms against a sudden chill. "We lost power here, but I supposed it was because we were so isolated."

"Craziest storm I've ever seen." He whistled softly. "It charged to shore as if someone had invited it in for a visit."

Sophie froze. It was the second time someone had suggested that the storm had been called.

Thompson looked at her curiously. "Is something wrong?"

"No," she said, and flinched at how untrue that was. There was so much that was wrong. Where would she start? "It's . . . I can't believe he's gone."

He nodded. "It's a bad business; that's for sure." Then he cleared his throat and quickly excused himself.

Sophie waited until she heard him climbing the stairs, then went to the living room and stood by the window. She ran her fingers over the sill while she looked for damage the storm had left. Leaves and broken branches littered the lawn, and some bushes had been uprooted. Nothing appeared to have been ripped off the house, but Dan would only be able to tell if there was damage when he got up there. Like all big storms, this one would leave scars visible in the shredded branches of trees and the gouged coastline below.

A short time later, the sound of voices reached her before the men did. "You're going to have to clear out of here," the sheriff said. Dan's response was terse and profane.

When they entered the living room, faces grim, Sophie felt a wave of alarm. "What?" she asked, looking from one to the other.

Thomson cut Dan off before he could answer. "We'll get to that in a minute. Could you tell me about last night?" He pulled out a notebook and a stubby pencil from his back pocket. "Start with when the storm broke."

She glanced at Dan, whose jaw worked as if he would erupt at any moment. What was going on?

"Ms. Tyler?" Thomson prompted, pencil poised.

"Right, sorry," she said and began with the picnic, the breaking storm, and their scramble up the bluff. She paused and watched the pencil scratch across the page. She avoided Dan's eyes and skipped the parts involving Nehemiah and the vacant Abigail.

When he finished writing, the sheriff glanced up. "Did you notice anything unusual?"

"Unusual?" she echoed, and then slid a look at Dan. What had he told him?

He counted them off on his fingers. "Something out of place, an open door that should have been closed, a person where they shouldn't have been?"

"No. It was just the four of us. We stayed together until we split up to dry off and grab supplies for the storm." She thought of the shadow she had imagined in the trees, then shrugged. "No one was out last night."

Thomson didn't miss the pause. "It seemed like you hesitated there. Anything you remember might help."

Sophie cast another quick glance at Dan and found him watching her too. "When I went to make tea," she said, "I thought I saw something move in the trees." The men exchanged glances, communicating silently. She spread her hands, exasperated. "Listen, it was nothing. I went to the door to check, then lightning flashed and there was nothing there." She didn't understand the point of the questions but knew that while they sat here talking about the storm and shadows, Neal was dead upstairs. "What does this have to do with Neal?"

"It doesn't appear to have been an accident." Thomson tapped the pencil against the pad.

"What?" She dropped heavily onto the windowsill behind her. "But I saw him. He'd fallen."

"He did fall," Dan said, "but because somebody had messed with the ladder."

"Would you shut up!" Thomson snapped.

Dan ignored him. "The joint of a top step had been loosened to tilt when someone stood on it."

"What is the matter with you?" Thomson demanded, tossing his notebook onto the counter in disgust.

"She doesn't have the muscle or the know-how to rig that stair, and you know it," Dan bit out.

Sophie felt the numbness of disbelief descend over her. "You think I killed Neal? That's ridiculous," she said, looking from one to the other.

"Why? How could I have known he'd be the one to climb the ladder? It could have been meant for . . . " she gestured vaguely, trying to think.

"Someone else?" Thomson finished. "That's what I told him." The sheriff jerked a thumb in Dan's direction. "But he's as pig-headed as the day he was born."

Sophie was surprised when Dan agreed with a grunt, adding, "It doesn't mean I'm wrong, though."

A creak on the stairs revealed Chelle finally awake and dressed. She had the old journal clutched in her hands. To Sophie, she seemed too pale, but at least she was upright.

"It wasn't an accident?" Chelle asked in a hushed tone. Before Thomson could answer, she turned abruptly and rushed up the stairs.

Sophie motioned for the men to stay put and hurried after her. As she climbed steadily, she heard quick rustling coming from the office Chelle had used as a bedroom. She found her at the desk, jamming random items into her worn backpack. Silk shirt, sweatpants, and sneakers were stuffed into the pack haphazardly.

She knew there was nothing she could say to fix any of this, but she could be useful. "I can drive you home."

Chelle grabbed a fistful of socks and shoved them into the pack. "No, but thanks."

"I really don't mind." She put a light hand on Chelle's arm.

Chelle escaped her touch and strode to the window. She threw it open with enough force to rattle the panes. "There's no air in here."

Sophie had to agree, but she hadn't noticed until Chelle had shoved the window open, letting salt air and the smell of crushed leaves swirl into the room. The sun winked in the remaining water drops on the panes behind her, and it seemed too beautiful a sight for the loss she was feeling. "What are you doing with the journal?" She nodded to where it lay beside Chelle's backpack.

Chelle lifted a shoulder and turned from the window. "Neal mentioned yesterday it was starting to get interesting."

Sophie tried to place the conversation. "I didn't hear him say that."

"He told me when we were collecting firewood." Chelle scanned the room to see what she'd missed. "You were talking to Dan."

"What'd he say?"

"Something about Will Morgan and his shadowing the Aldens. I just felt . . . " Chelle's voice trailed off, and she needed to start again. "I just felt I should finish where Neal couldn't. Find out what happened to

Abigail, finish the restoration, you know?" She crossed over to the desk and gathered the things she'd left strewn across its surface. Lip balm, bug spray, and a tube of lotion got crammed into the backpack on top of everything else. "I just can't do it living here."

Sophie could relate to finishing what others had left undone. Hadn't she finished building the storage chest her father had started and planted the roses her mother had always wanted after the accident? She'd been young with limited skills but pushed on with splinters and bruises because it wasn't only for her but for them as well. Every measurement and cut, every spade full of dirt, had been a tribute of sorts. "I don't know if we'll be able to stay here anyways. The lighthouse will be closed as a crime scene, at least for now. Who knows what Philip Bishop is going to decide to do with it afterward."

Chelle visibly wilted. "I hadn't thought of that."

She appeared so defeated—Sophie could have kicked herself. She mentally scrambled for something encouraging to say when the crunch of gravel drew them to the window. Frank Morgan descended the stairs of the lighthouse and walked over to meet the approaching Medical Examiner's van.

"What's Frank doing here?" she asked, glancing at Chelle before returning her attention to the scene below. The last thing she wanted to do today was to deal with Frank and his sly talk.

"He must have heard the sheriff call it in and came to help," Chelle said, shrugging.

"Help? More like snoop." She shifted self-consciously when Chelle looked at her in surprise. "Sorry. A lot of people 'stopped by' when my parents died. Most of them were sincere, but some of them just enjoyed the drama."

"People?" Chelle echoed, looking blank then panicked. "I can't deal with more villagers today. I've got to get out of here." She shoved a final sweater into her bulging backpack, tucked the journal under her arm, and bolted out of the house.

Sophie charged after her. She faintly registered Dan and Sheriff Thomson's surprise, as she dashed past them. She dodged Frank, who was helping the medical examiner roll a collapsible gurney, and caught up with Chelle as she was buckling herself into the Mini. "Please let me drive you, Chelle," she begged. "You're too upset to drive. I'll just drop you off. I won't even come in."

"I'm fine." Chelle reached out the open window and clasped Sophie's arm. "I just need to be alone." Turning, Chelle picked up the journal from the front seat and shoved it at Sophie. "Here, you take it."

Chelle's quick change of mind didn't surprise her in the least. Sophie had been impossible when her parents had died. It was one of the reasons she and Jacqueline had fought so much. Good grief, she thought, Jacqueline. What was she going to tell her? Would she tell her? Like most of the things she didn't have the answers to lately, she put them off and reassured Chelle.

"I'll hang on to it for you, and we'll figure it out together, okay?" When Chelle nodded and started the car, Sophie stepped back. She had driven with Chelle before and wasn't taking any chances of getting run over. As she expected, the Mini shot down the hill toward the woods, spraying gravel against the shrubs as Chelle powered through the curve. With anyone else she'd think they were being deliberately reckless, but Chelle always drove hell-bent for leather.

Sophie sighed and walked back toward the lighthouse. She paused by her own car, turning the worn journal over in her hands as she debated. It might be considered evidence and confiscated, sitting for months or years in lock-up and then where would they be? She opened the passenger door of her car and tucked the journal under the seat, before she could fully weigh the meaning of the phrase "obstruction of justice" and change her mind.

She didn't know how long she stood there justifying hiding the journal, when the front door opened. The medical examiner, assisted by Frank, rammed the plastic draped gurney over the threshold and guided it down the stairs. Her stomach lurched when she recognized the shape of Neal's body wrapped inside the thick plastic. The men guided the gurney into the waiting black van that looked like a squat beetle to her—all shiny and hard with its dark tinted windows. She walked slowly to the porch and mounted the stairs, forcing herself to breathe deliberately until the nausea passed.

She was still queasy some time afterwards when Dan exited the lighthouse carrying an overnight bag and keys. "I've got to get home and check on Chelle. That is where she was headed, wasn't it?"

"I think so, yeah." It hadn't even occurred to her to ask. Sophie imagined that Chelle would head for somewhere safe. Home was where she would have headed if she'd had one. Who knew where she would end up sleeping tonight?

Dan twisted the ring of his keys without looking up. "Thomson's closing the lighthouse until the investigation is over."

"I figured as much." It came as no surprise. She'd seen enough crime shows to have expected it.

He lifted his hands and let them drop to his sides. "I was getting used to having Neal around."

She bit her lip, then nodded. "I know. It seemed like you were getting along better."

"We were burying the past . . . I just can't get my head around it," Dan said, looking blindly towards the woods.

"I don't know what to think either." She lifted her shoulders in a helpless gesture. "It feels like the world has gone crazy."

He turned back to her and nodded. "There is no way to make sense of any this, at least not now." Taking a deep breath, Dan steadied himself. "I have to go check on Chelle. I was thinking you could stay with us out at the house, but it would make your commute to work much longer."

She lifted a shoulder. It wasn't important. She'd find another place to stay in town.

He sorted through his keys and worked a shiny brass key off the ring. "But there is the loft above the White Horse if you want it. It's still under construction, but it has a cot and a full bath. It would be closer to your work too."

As simple as that, he'd solved her housing problem. Sophie felt a weight shift and the loss settle more firmly. "I'd appreciate it, thanks."

He placed the key in her palm. "I never got around to having Frank make another copy, so be careful with it." He gestured toward the stairs. "I can wait, if you want to go pack a bag."

Sophie nodded and hurried to her room. If he was willing to wait, she didn't want to keep him longer than was necessary.

Despite her best intentions, it took a good twenty minutes before she finished packing her clothes, bedding, and school materials. She was lugging it all downstairs, when Thomson came hurrying from the kitchen. He had a roll of yellow crime tape tucked under his arm and a police radio held to his ear. He said in a clipped voice, "No, he's still here. I'll tell him."

Whatever it was, it had to be serious. "What is it?" she asked, dreading the answer.

"Chelle was in an accident," Thomson answered without breaking his stride and ushered her to the door. "Missed the corner near the

Douglas place and crashed into the marsh. She's being transported to the hospital." He opened the door and waved her through. "Out. Now."

Sophie scrambled outside, dumping her things into a pile on the porch. Thomson closed the door and secured a yellow tape across the entry. She never should have let Chelle drive herself. Her palms began to sweat, and she paced. Dan would never forgive her, and she wouldn't blame him. She watched Dan walk toward her. But the sheriff swung him around and marched him back to the cruiser, explaining about the accident as they went.

After the cruiser tore down the dirt lane, she found herself alone with the medical examiner and Frank. "There was an accident," she felt forced to explain, her voice unsteady. "Chelle missed a turn and crashed her car. She's on her way to the hospital now."

The medical examiner, a serious young man in blue coveralls, nodded. "Try not to worry too much. It can't be that serious if the sheriff left without the sirens on." He climbed into the van and gave Frank a wave. "Thanks for the help."

Frank responded with a curt salute and watched the burdened van turn a tight circle and lumber back toward town. "It was just a matter of time before she crashed that car." He pursed his lips and angled her a look. "Where'd he say it happened?"

"Somewhere off a curve near the Douglas place." She bent to collect her belongings, not eager to spend more time with Frank than needed.

"A lot of water there, a good five feet, at least." He made a grimace that to Sophie's mind lacked sincere concern. "She was lucky, but the car and everything in it is a total loss, guaranteed. Saltwater's hell on metal and electronics."

"I'm sure it's the least of her worries right now." Sophie walked to her car with Frank trailing behind. He always cornered her when she was least prepared and couldn't get away from him fast enough. She pried open the passenger's door with the tips of her fingers, dumped her armload onto the floor, and slammed the door shut.

"Where you headed?" He dogged her steps as she circled to the rear of the car and popped the trunk, tossing her bedding inside.

She closed the trunk and headed for the driver's door. "To The White Horse, until I hear news about Chelle, then maybe the hospital." Her voice was clipped. Couldn't this guy just leave her alone?

"How 'bout a lift back to town?" he asked, shuffling behind her, closer than she was comfortable with.

Sophie jerked open the driver's door and turned to face him. She squinted against the sun and asked, "How did you get here, anyways?"

"I took a path through the woods, but I did something to my knee helping load Neal into the van." He made a big show of rubbing the joint and twisting his face in pain.

She railed at the fact that fate seemed to be out to get her. "Get in," she gestured impatiently. "But watch your feet, I've got papers all over the floor."

"That's very generous of you." Frank scurried around the car and hopped in with more speed than someone with a bum knee should have.

Sophie waited while he settled, then looked pointedly at his supposedly injured knee. "It looks like the pain comes and goes."

Frank flushed and returned to rubbing his knee. "Something like that," he said, and turned to look out his window.

She started the car with an annoyed twist of her wrist and put the car in drive. As she headed for the woods that separated The Point from the road, she clenched the wheel and held her breath. She'd lived here for months now, but she had never shaken the feeling that there was something dark and watchful in those trees, something twisted that stalked unseen.

As the car shot onto the main road, she sat back and forced herself to loosen her grip on the wheel. She was surprised and relieved that Frank hadn't already started on Nehemiah or Neal. She glanced over to find him staring at her.

"What?" she demanded and turned her eyes back to the road. The last thing she needed was to crash on the way to town.

Frank leaned close, his eyes sharp. "The woods," he waited a beat, "They bother you, don't they?"

Sophie flushed and tried to think of a plausible excuse. "I think they're too damp, too thick."

He nodded as if confirming what he already knew. "I could tell you were all tense-like when we passed. Lots of folks don't like them."

"Why? Are they supposed to be haunted?" It came out sarcastically, but he was getting to her. It was most likely what he'd intended all along the old goat.

He gripped her arm and leaned toward her. "Something waits there."

Despite herself, hair rose on the nape of her neck. "What do you mean, Something?" She darted her eyes from the road to Frank.

"Don't know." His tongue wet his lips, and his fingers tightened on her arm. "But people feel it, feel watched."

"If that's true, why do you go?" She tried shaking him off, but his grip was surprisingly strong.

He finally released her arm and shifted back to the sweeping views of the marsh. "It's not waiting for me."

She felt a spurt of fear. She'd felt that something watched and waited there. But what did it want?

"I wouldn't let it worry you none." Frank plucked at his blue work pants absently. "It only watches the lighthouse."

She had no idea what he was talking about. "Frank, if you have something to say, spit it out."

He crossed his arms as she guided the car inland toward the village and remained stubbornly silent. People were out gathering fallen branches and righting overturned yard furniture. Bits of torn leaves stuck to windows and houses like green confetti, making the air smell sweet and humid like a bag of lawn clippings.

"What waits in the woods?" Sophie demanded, and came to a sharp stop in front of *The White Horse*. The jumbled pile on the floor slid against Frank's feet and buried his ankles in schoolbooks and folders.

He nudged the pile aside with his foot. "Not quite sure," he muttered so softly she had to lean in to hear. "I've only seen it from the back."

She couldn't understand how anyone in their right mind would track something or someone they didn't know through those woods. "You followed it?"

"More like came up on it a few times." Frank lifted a shoulder. "It was watching the lighthouse, has done for as long as I know of. I've only seen it, myself, a few times." He bent to tidy some of the books and uncovered the hidden journal that had slid out from under the seat. His hand rested briefly on it before he stacked more books on top. "And only at night when the lighthouse was burning."

"You saw an apparition." She couldn't believe it. "You saw someone watching the lighthouse when it burned—the same night Abigail disappeared."

"It must have been. It's only burned once." He seemed to regret telling her and fumbled with the car door. "I've got to go."

She hit the door lock. She wasn't about to let him leave until she got some answers. "Did you see Abigail?"

He glared and rattled the handle. "Let me out."

"Did. You. See. Her." Sophie leaned toward him. She was close enough to see a small vein pulse above his left eye and feel his breath across her cheek. She forced herself to remain still, despite the smell of old man sweat. She waited and willed him to speak.

"No, I didn't," he snapped and turned to the window like a moody child. "It doesn't happen that often, and when it does, I only see the house burning and someone watching."

"A man?"

"Yeah, but it's not something you should be playing at. Alden created a mess up there, and it belongs in the past." Frank scowled. "Nothing good comes from poking at old wounds." He rattled the door handle once again. "Now, let me go."

She released the lock, and he lost no time scrambling out. It just figured. Usually, she couldn't get away from him fast enough and today when she had something she really wanted to know, he'd all but run from her.

Sophie knew from experience that the back entrance to The White Horse loft offered its own built-in security. The parking lot was always full of arriving or departing customers, it was well-lit by streetlights, and a spotlight beamed down on the second-floor landing. Although she would never be able to sneak in or out, no one would be able to sneak up on her either. And given the circumstances surrounding Neal's death, this wasn't a bad thing. The inside, however, was exactly as Dan had described: a space in the finishing stages of construction. Sand gritted underfoot, and the space was lit by a bare bulb in the center of the ceiling. And although the walls had been repaired from the rain damage earlier in the summer, the sheetrock joints and screw holes taped and sealed, it was still unpainted. It made the room look like someone had jotted down Morse code in plaster.

She dumped her clothes and books by the cot and peered out the only window in the loft. There wasn't much street traffic, but people were about, leaning on rakes and talking over fences. Most of the town had taken the day off, or been forced to stay home, because of the power outages. No one seemed particularly rushed to clean up. Either it would get done or it wouldn't. There was always tomorrow.

Except for Neal, he was out of tomorrows, and who knew what tomorrow held for Chelle. Sophie had resisted going straight to the emergency room to give Dan time to see how seriously Chelle was injured. If he didn't call later, she'd go camp out at the hospital until someone gave her news or demanded that she leave.

She dropped down onto the squeaking cot. At least Chelle had Dan with her and wasn't alone. Was Neal? she wondered. The image of his stripped body on a cold, stainless steel table waiting for the medical examiner took shape in her mind. If there was any mercy in this world or the next, his spirit wasn't lingering at the base of that ladder or hovering above his corpse, crying for help as Abigail had been. Maybe he had passed straight on to wherever the dead went. She fervently prayed he had. She curled onto her side and folded her arm under her head. The mattress fabric was scratchy, but she didn't have the energy to dig out her bedding. The most she wanted to do right now was watch the shadows lengthen across the gray patched wall.

When Sophie woke, she didn't remember for a moment where she was. She brought her watch closer to her eyes and squinted. Three o'clock. She couldn't believe she'd slept for four hours and straight through the lunch rush at The White Horse. Chelle. She leaned over the side of the bed and dug for the cell phone in her bag. She had missed two messages, both from Dan. While she willed the message to play faster, she stood and paced until she heard him say that Chelle had been admitted to the hospital with serious injuries, but that the doctors were optimistic. Relief coursed through her. The second message was also from Dan saying that Chelle was stable and that he would check in with Sophie later. "Thank God!" Sophie murmured.

Her stomach growled, reminding her she hadn't eaten at all today. Food. She should eat. Before heading downstairs for something quick, she grabbed her toothbrush and found the bathroom. It was tucked under an eave with a tacked bed sheet for a door. She had just put toothpaste on the bristles when the phone rang. She tossed the brush onto the side of the sink and scrambled for the phone.

"Where have you been?" Dan demanded from the other end. "Are you okay?"

"Sorry. I'm fine." She bit her lip and shifted. It wasn't as if he didn't have enough to worry about without her adding to it. "How's Chelle?" She moved to the window, glancing out over the street and the parking lot that was visible from the loft. Traffic was beginning to pick up.

"A bit groggy still, but okay."

She nervously picked at the chipping paint on the sill. It was the kind of thing people said when they didn't want to talk about it or didn't know what to say. "How badly is she hurt?"

"A few broken ribs and a concussion that she says makes her head feel like it's going to split in half." Dan exhaled a frustrated breath. "She was lucky she had her seatbelt on and that Kyle Douglas was home from work. He fished her out of the water and called the ambulance."

"I'm so sorry. I never should have let her drive." Down the street, Sophie saw Babs, backpack slung over her shoulder, exit the library and walk toward *The White Horse*.

Dan gave a humorless laugh. "Come on. We both know that short of tying her up there was no way to keep her from doing what she got in her head."

"But she was so upset . . . ." To Sophie's mind, there was nothing worse than not acting as you should and it leading to disastrous results.

"There may be more to it than that." Dan sounded grim.

She froze. She didn't know what he was talking about, but that knot in the pit of her stomach was back. "What do you mean?"

"Chelle claims that when she went to brake for the corner, the pedal went straight to the floor . . . the brakes were gone."

"But it's a new car. That doesn't make any sense." Sophie lifted her gaze from the paint chips she had scraped into a pile and watched Babs stop to talk to Tom Reed. The two of them appeared to be waiting for someone.

Dan grunted in agreement. "That's why I'm having Sean, over at the garage, take a look at the brakes after he hauls it out of the marsh."

She swiped the flaked paint onto the floor and wiped her hands on her pants. "You think it was sabotage?"

"Like you said, it's a new car. The brakes shouldn't have failed. And yeah, Chelle drives fast, but she's never careless. After what happened to Neal, I think it'd be stupid not to look into it."

Outside the window, Frank joined Tom and Babs, and the trio made their way to the tavern. He was most likely filling them in on the tragedy up at the lighthouse. Neal's death, Chelle's accident—the whole thing was surreal. "It's unbelievable," she said.

"You'd think so, but . . . ." Dan paused so long she feared they might have been disconnected. "Listen, do me a favor and be careful, alright? Don't let anyone in and stay away from the lighthouse. Someone's out there picking us off, one-by-one."

"Of course," she said, suddenly short of breath. "But don't you think we could be overreacting?"

She heard a bang, clatter, and muffled cursing as though he had dropped something. "No." He sounded sure. "Someone poisons Aesop, forces you off the bridge, tampers with the ladder, and possibly sabotages Chelle's brakes? That's not just a string of bad luck."

As fantastic as it seemed, she knew he was right. "Have you told the sheriff?"

"I did. He's going to investigate but keep this quiet."

"Of course." After assuring him she'd be careful, she hung up and leaned against the window. The village seemed so harmless; it was a quiet town with individuals and families going about their business. People were carrying packages and walking dogs. But someone out there, someone who knew their habits, was a killer. Sorrow for Neal was joined by the fear that they were not safe.

Sophie dropped onto the mattress, suddenly not hungry. She reached for a stack of student papers and forced herself to grade. She pushed through the first few before her mind circled back to the attacks. There was no other word for them. Why did somebody want them gone badly enough to kill? Were the separate accidents tied to the lighthouse renovations, or could it have something to do with Abigail? She dug through the pile, pulling the journal from under a stack of papers. Neal had said it had been getting interesting. Maybe he'd found an entry that would tell them where to look for Abigail and her baby.

The worn journal crackled when she opened to the first page. Black cramped letters slanted across its surface: *Property of Captain Stephen Parker, Pocasset, Massachusetts 1717.* The journal had been started the year before Abigail had disappeared, she noted and flipped through the pages. Unfortunately, it was the only date in the journal. Parker had not dated his entries but simply had separated them by a space. It also appeared that they were not daily writings but events and information the captain had found interesting. She sighed. There was no way around it. She'd have to start at the beginning and wade through the pages until she found some mention of the Aldens or about Abigail's disappearance.

She tilted the journal toward the harsh light of the hanging bulb and began to read. Captain Parker, at the age of seventy-two, had kept the curiosity of youth while doing away with the sleep needed by the other members of the village. Because he had found his waking hours rather dull, he seemed to have split his time between the tavern and roaming the lanes of the village. So, the "tattle" he collected and recorded were oftentimes the result of personal intelligence gathering. He'd *seen* Roger Beckett, the drunken sot, try to stack barrels to reach the second-floor window when his wife had locked him out. He'd *seen* the thievery of neighbor against neighbor: eggs and fruit and sometimes a pail of milk disappearing in the small hours of the night. And so, he felt, if it were from someone's lips and he'd seen some evidence with his own eyes, it was more than "tattles." It was fact.

Sophie huffed out an incredulous breath. The old busy body had been a menace. The only redeeming quality he'd had was that he'd never shared his findings with the village. She got the sense that the villagers had been fond of him, perhaps despite themselves, and they had taken care to maintain a cordial relationship with him. But when all was said and done, he'd been a colonial blackmailer. She rolled onto her side and propped her head up with her fist. He'd recorded that he'd seen a "cloaked woman's figure stealthily exit the cobbler's home." Two entries later he wrote of his deep appreciation for the new coat Mistress Livingston had charitably given him as well as the new pair of boots the cobbler had donated. Baked goods and savory stews had regularly made their way to his table, and kind services were offered without recompense. He always thanked God for generous Christian good will at the end of every entry. She noted that these various "bounties" and "good deeds" often followed a few days after he had observed some villager's nocturnal activities. The captain had held a gun he'd never needed to fire—it was enough that he'd seen and known.

In entry after entry, she read about the villagers, their petty crimes and infidelities, until her lids began to droop. Despite the bare bulb glaring light in a tight circle over the mattress, she fell asleep.

Shards of glass crackled underfoot as he worked the lock outside her door. Because the sound was slight and the shadows deep, he didn't fear being discovered. When people did pass, he crouched low against the door, ear pressed to the cold metal, and became a shadow himself. "Pick the lock. Pick the lock," he whispered once they'd passed. He scratched at the keyhole, harder and harder the longer it denied him.

12

Founders' Cemetery

Sophie let the hot spray beat on her bent head. Worry over Chelle and the sense of being hunted had given her the mother of all headaches. She'd choked down aspirin in the early hours of the morning with little result and was hoping the shower would lessen the steady tattoo of pain. The shower was just starting to ease the misery when she heard the urgent beating of a fist on the door.

"Sophie!" Dan shouted, and pounded again, "Open up."

She screwed her eyes shut against the pain. "For pity's sake, stop shouting," she whimpered. She twisted the water valves off and wrapped a towel around her. "I'm coming. I'm coming." She flipped the latch and yanked the door open.

"Why didn't you answer?" He pushed past her and searched the loft as if expecting someone else to be there.

"I didn't hear you." She dragged dripping hair out of her eyes. "What are you looking for?"

He strode back to the door and pointed to the lock and the shattered bulb. "Someone tried to get in here, and when you didn't answer . . . ."

"Where?" she demanded, pushing past him to squint at the door. Deep angry scrapes scored the surface of the lock and the doorframe where the latch clicked home. Her scalp tingled. Someone had tried to break in while she slept, and she hadn't heard a thing. There was fear simmering under her skin but also anger.

"You can't stay here," Dan said flatly, and turned her by the shoulders to face him. "Pack your stuff."

"I don't have anywhere else to go and I'm not being forced out . . . again." She broke free and stomped over to the bed. She pulled a pair of slacks and a blouse out of her bag, smoothing the creases against the mattress. Her students would just have to tolerate her wrinkled. She drew her brows together against the throb behind her eyes.

"Whoever it was didn't get in this time, but they're going to try again." Dan was beyond reason. "Come stay in Chelle's room until she's out of the hospital. Maybe by then Thomson will let us back into the lighthouse. It's not safe here." He threw his hands up when she remained silent. "Can't you see that?"

"Look, can we talk about this later?" Sophie squinted toward him but only saw the shape of him outlined by blinding sunlight. "I've got a mammoth headache, and I'm late for class."

"The school's closed. Will be for about a week." At her hiss of disbelief, Dan sighed and explained with exaggerated patience. "There was water and electrical damage from last night's storm." He tugged her work clothes away from her and pulled jeans from her bag. "Put these on instead. I'll wait outside."

"Wait for what?" Of all the pushy demands he'd made in the past this one was a beauty. "I'm not going anywhere," she said slowly as if he were hard of hearing and needed to lip read.

"What are you going to do—sit here all day?" he asked. "I'm going to the garage to find out what Sean has to say about Chelle's car. Come with me."

As much as she wanted to be defiant, she wanted to hear what the mechanic had to say in person. He had her where he wanted her. "Alright, I'll go to the garage with you, but I'm not staying at your house."

"Fair enough." Dan stepped outside and closed the door after him with a snap.

Sophie frowned. That was too easy. She was sure he was up to something. Her suspicions weren't eased any when she opened the door a few minutes later and found him with a cup of coffee, a brown bakery bag, and a travel-sized bottle of ibuprofen.

"I figured we'd walk." Dan gave her the cup and tapped two tablets into her palm.

She wasted no time taking the medicine and washing it down with the coffee. She hoped the ibuprofen would be more effective than the aspirin she'd taken earlier. So far, all she'd been able to manage was to hold herself upright and squint. The pounding behind her eyes remained. "Thanks."

He nodded and handed over the brown bag. "Thomson called to tell me they found a cousin of Neal's to claim the body. After the coroner is done, they'll release him for burial."

"That's good. I was afraid he might not have any family left." At least he had someone. Everyone should have someone, she thought. "Any confirmation yet about how he died?" she asked as she dug a breakfast sandwich out of the bag and took a bite. She still wasn't particularly hungry, but maybe eating would help ease her headache.

Dan tucked his thumbs into the loops of his jeans and shrugged. "So far, it's what we suspected. It looks like Neal died from the fall not a direct attack."

She was not sure what she believed anymore. "The whole thing is strange."

"Tell me about it."

As they made their way down the sidewalk shaded by arching trees, the shops stood shoulder to shoulder like spectators watching their progress. Most of them were closed, but the clerks were moving about inside, getting ready for the day. Normally, she liked walking the storefronts, but today all she felt was exposed. A target.

Pinard's Garage shared parking with the hardware store on Locke Street and bordered the woods. The garage appeared as if it had been built around the same time as the Model T, but the double bays were equipped with hydraulic lifts, compressed air tools, and diagnostic equipment. Chelle's crumpled Mini was suspended in the air on one of the lifts and a battered pick-up truck was on the other. A stocky man in a visor used an acetylene torch to cut a piece of metal off the truck, sending orange sparks flying everywhere. He lowered the torch to the ground, hefted a mallet, and pounded at the offending pipe. The blows clanged in rhythm to the music blaring over the radio.

"Sean!" Dan yelled. "Sean!" When he didn't answer, Dan stooped under the truck and tapped him on the shoulder.

Sean tipped back the visor, revealing a likeable face liberally covered in rust flakes. "Didn't hear you." Sean nodded toward the muffler. "The damn thing's rusted solid," he said, then flushed when he saw Sophie standing just behind Dan. "Sorry, ma'am, I didn't see you."

Dan appeared to enjoy the mechanic's discomfort. "Sophie Tyler, Sean Pinard," he introduced them. "Sean keeps most of the village on the road."

"That's a pretty tall order." She smiled, hoping to put him at ease.

"Most of the time it's alright. Today not so much." He tossed the visor onto a crowded workbench covered with tools and grabbed a rag to wipe his hands.

"Did you get a chance to check on Chelle's brakes?" Dan asked, getting straight to the point.

"Yeah, I did. Brake pads and cylinders were in great shape—almost new, in fact." He grabbed a black length of tubing slightly bigger than a pencil off the bench and gave it to Dan. "It's the brake line that's the problem."

Dan tilted it toward the light and bent it back and forth. "It's got a hole."

"Holes," Sean corrected. He leaned forward to point to the other areas. "Break lines can tear or puncture during an accident, but the holes that happen are irregular. These are round and evenly spaced. This was no accident."

Dan cursed. He paced from the bench to the door and back again. "Nothing else could have caused this?"

The mechanic grimaced. "No."

Sophie didn't want to believe someone wanted Chelle dead. "How could they know she would be taking a corner when the brakes failed?"

"They didn't, but it really wouldn't matter." Sean shrugged. "They made enough holes, so that every time she stepped on the brakes, fluid would leak out. There's only about a pint and a half of fluid in the brake system. With the number of curves there are in the roads around here, ..." He spread his hands as if that said it all.

"And knowing how Chelle drives," Dan added. He shook his head. "It was a pretty safe bet that she'd crash."

Sean lifted an eyebrow at Dan. "You want me to let the sheriff know?"

"I'll call him." Dan gave back the break line. "He'll want to collect this tubing as evidence," he said, and wiped his hands on his pants. "Thanks, and keep this quiet, will you?"

"You bet." Sean nodded and headed back to work under the pickup truck.

Dan and Sophie made their way back to The White Horse lost in thought. They walked in silence past the villagers still cleaning from yesterday's storm. Finally giving up on her racing thoughts, she asked, "Now what?"

He looked at her directly for the first time since they'd left the garage. "I'm picking up my truck and heading over to the hospital to check on Chelle. Want to come?"

"Of course," she answered. The sight of the wreck had shaken her, and she needed the reassurance of seeing Chelle in person. It was hard to believe anyone could have walked away from that accident. "I'd like to grab something from upstairs before we go."

"Fine, but I'm going with you and you're going to pack it all." He didn't wait for her to answer and went up the stairs ahead of her.

He didn't sound like he would take "No" for an answer, and there wasn't any real sense in arguing. They were better off together than alone. While she could be stubborn, she hoped she wasn't stupid.

Sophie eased past him into the loft. She grabbed her clothes and the journal, filling a bag before he could pack for her. She left the school stuff where it sprawled across the floor. She could always come back for it later. The campus would be closed for at least a week, anyways. She stowed her things in the bed of Dan's truck and climbed aboard. It took no time to make their way to the large county hospital. Fifteen minutes later, they were walking into Chelle's room. The pale green walls were unadorned except for a clock that kept audible time like a metronome.

Chelle lay back against the pillows with her eyes closed, bruises blooming on her chest and face. She appeared as if she'd been hit by a baseball bat. "Geez," Sophie breathed. "She looks awful."

Chelle's eyes fluttered open. "Hey," she said weakly.

"Weren't you wearing your seatbelt?" Sophie asked, moving to stand beside Chelle's bed and adjusting her pillow when Chelle sat up.

"I was." She tugged aside her gown to show a vicious vertical bruise across her chest. "It was the air bag that did my face in."

"It makes you wonder if they are worth it," Sophie said and gave her the small ivy she'd bought in the gift shop downstairs.

"It could've been a lot worse without them." Dan sat at the end of Chelle's bed and gave her foot a pat. "We'll live with the bruises."

Chelle gave a feeble nod of agreement. She fingered the leaves of the ivy, and said, "Thanks for the plant."

"I hoped it might cheer you up." Sophie sat in the chair by the bed. She wondered how much Dan would tell her about the Mini and didn't have to wait long. He broke the news that the car was totaled but stopped short of sharing the information about the brakes, until Chelle pushed.

"Someone punctured the brake line. It was just a matter of time before they gave out."

"Why?" Chelle's voice was tinged with panic. "Who's doing this?"

"We'll find out." Dan placed a comforting hand on her leg. "I promise. Sophie's agreed to stay at our house, and we'll see what we can find out together."

A nurse came bustling in with a paper cup and two yellow pills. "Sorry folks, time for meds and vitals."

"I'll be back later, Chelle." He rose to give her a peck on the cheek and moved aside so that Sophie could say goodbye. "Get some rest."

Sophie bent to give her a careful hug. "I'll be back too, and I promise to keep him out of trouble."

"Be careful, both of you." Chelle grabbed Sophie's hand and hung on. "Whoever is after us has been very good at getting us alone."

"We'll be careful." She gave Chelle's hand a careful squeeze and forced a reassuring smile on her face.

Sliding past the nurse, Sophie joined Dan in the hall. As they made their way through the halls of the hospital, the polished floor squeaking underfoot, they saw patients sitting by windows and others in bed watching television. Despite the restful colors, she found the place oppressive. The lack of windows that opened, and the lingering smell of disinfectant, made her feel like there wasn't enough air to go around. Then there were all these people just waiting: waiting for doctors, nurses, medication, and visitors. Some were waiting to go home, even though some of them never would.

"I hate hospitals," Dan said, echoing her own feelings.

She murmured an agreement. She felt a pang for Chelle who was stuck here for a good while, if she had to guess. "When Chelle starts to feel a bit better, she'll be climbing the walls for sure. How will you manage when she's released?" When he didn't answer, she continued. "If you need someone to stay with her, I'd be happy to help out."

"Thanks, there's no way I could leave her alone. Injuries aside, it's too dangerous until we know what's going on." He stepped inside the elevator and held the door for her.

"Where to now?" she asked.

"I guess we can swing by The White Horse, pick up your car, and then I can show you the house."

It might be awkward staying in The Robbins' house just the two of them. But what other choice was there? The lighthouse was out, and although the loft had proven secure, who wanted to stay alone in a place where someone had tried to break in? She would trade the awkwardness for the added security any day.

"Sure," she said finally, and pressed the button for the lobby. "That'd be fine."

Sophie drove behind Dan along the winding back roads of Pocasset, stands of mature trees lining the road. She didn't need help seeing where Chelle had crashed. There were no skid marks in the curve, but the mashed reeds and marks of heavy machinery used to drag the Mini up the bank were clearly visible. She flinched. Fixing her eyes on the taillights of Dan's truck, she didn't move them until he slowed before his house. The Robbins' house sat at the bottom of a hill in the belly of a curve. A small Cape in colonial green, it invited passers-by to pull into the driveway for a visit. Soaring cedars flanked the tidy home and added to the peacefulness of the place.

She shifted the car into park and shut off the engine. Dan opened her passenger door and ducked his head in. "Come on. I'll show you around, then I have to go check on a few jobs." She climbed out quickly but only caught up as he was ramming a key into the lock.

The door opened onto a rustic kitchen in soothing earth tones. He ducked his head under the low doorway, waving her before him, "Kitchen, living room, and bath are on the first floor. The two bedrooms are upstairs."

She relaxed for the first time in weeks. "This is lovely." She breathed in the scent of lingering wood smoke. "How did you give this up to sleep on the floor of the lighthouse?"

He considered, then shrugged. "I guess it's because it has always been here, and I knew I could come back anytime I wanted."

She took a moment to sink her fingers into the loops of a moss-colored afghan tossed over the back of a chair. They hadn't passed a single car on their way here and none had passed the house since they'd arrived. "How far away are your neighbors?"

"Quarter mile or so in either direction." Dan smiled at her surprise. "It doesn't take long to get into the country around here. We used to live in the village but moved here a while back."

She came back to the question that had featured in almost every conversation since Neal had died. "Is it safe?"

He sighed and shrugged. "I don't know. There's an alarm and at least you won't be alone."

She took a breath and let it out slowly. Sometimes she wished he was a little less honest. She forced a smile and backed away. "Right. I'd better get my stuff."

"I'll get it. Why don't you take a look around and see if you need anything. I can pick up whatever's missing while I'm out."

She nodded and made her way through the small house. All the interior walls were painted the color of baked scones, joining the rooms seamlessly. The simple color made the house feel open, but cozy. On-site laundry, computer room, a bathroom with soaking tub, and a recently renovated kitchen made it a perfect fit. It had been a long time since she had lived in a real home. There had been many studios and one-bedroom apartments, but their walls had been covered in paint that looked like old china and the floors smothered in gray carpet. They had been neutral, sterile almost, to appeal to tenants who lived there for short stretches of time.

Only one bedroom on the second floor didn't follow the woodland feel of the other spaces. It was decorated in restful Caribbean blues and greens. It had to be Chelle's. If the feminine touches hadn't given it away, the racks and stands of empty plant holders would have. She'd get the sheriff to let her into the lighthouse and rescue those plants. It was a small thing to do, and it might bring Chelle peace knowing her plants would be well-tended.

She heard the front door open and hurried downstairs to find Dan lowering her things by the cast iron stove. "I won't need a thing," she said in perfect honesty.

"Good." He pulled keys out of his pocket and jingled them. "I'll show you how to set the alarm, then I've got to get going."

The house was lovely, but it would be odd to be left here alone. She quickly planned her afternoon and said, "I'll leave with you. I have some errands to run, and I want to pick up some groceries."

Dan nodded and strode to the door. "I'll see you later."

"The alarm," she reminded him, fearing she would never figure it out on her own. Thankfully, it turned out that this alarm system was user-friendly. A few pushed buttons and the house was secure.

Dan tore down the road for work, but Sophie took her time. Pine and the sweet smell of maple leaves swept through the open window as the car hugged one back road after another. Eventually, when enough time had passed and she still hadn't seen the road to the village, she realized she must have missed her turn. Brilliant, Sophie, you're lost. Well, it's not as though there was any place she really needed to be. She turned left and followed a road that seemed more traveled, hoping it would lead to the village center. After passing several fields and skirting a pond, she found herself outside the Pocasset Founders cemetery and, for a reason she couldn't explain, pulled through the wrought iron arch.

Normally, she wouldn't have visited here on a good day. Yet here she was, two days after Neal's death, sitting in a cemetery. She glanced around uneasily, but it all seemed perfectly benign. Sun slanted through the trees, bleaching the headstones white, and small birds flitted among the bittersweet. The path was barely wide enough for a car to pass and forced visitors to the rough stone chapel in the center of the cemetery.

Sophie released the brake and let the car glide downhill to the chapel. There was no obvious monument with ALDEN carved on it, and she wondered where Nehemiah was buried. Gravel crunched under the wheels as she swung into a makeshift parking spot near the chapel. She turned off the car, climbed out, and scanned the front of the small structure. Sometimes old village cemeteries had directories of the family plots that visitors could consult. She had no such luck here. She resigned herself to a careful search and set off through the neat rows, scanning the names of colonial families as she passed.

Despite her awareness that life had been harder and life spans much shorter, she was still moved by how young most of them had died. A headstone for a child named Rebecca particularly touched her. Someone must have loved her very much to have carved tiny rosebuds around her name, building her an eternal garden in which to rest. The child had been only nine years old. Alden, on the contrary, had lived to a remarkably old age, despite cheating, stealing, and ruining lives. She was sure his fellow villagers had believed his divine punishment was slow in coming. She certainly did.

She made her way up and down the well-tended rows seeking Nehemiah's grave, but row after row of careful searching didn't produce his grave. In the end, she found it completely by accident. When she finished the final row, she glanced across the cemetery and saw two large cedars growing side by side, away from the rest. Her mother had always told her that, "Nature grows as it wants to, Sophie, not in two by two's." Although nothing was visible from where she stood, she trekked over to investigate.

She crouched low and shifted aside the thick cedar branches. In the heart of the growth, she found a lichen-covered headstone engraved with the name ALDEN. So here he was—as marginalized as possible. By the looks of it, no one had wanted to be buried by him, and no one had ever tended to the grave. The cedars must certainly have been planted by the groundskeeper when Nehemiah had died. Otherwise, she imagined, things had remained as they'd been since his burial.

Sophie scraped away dirt at the bottom of the headstone. She saw that under Nehemiah's name Abigail's showed her birth date and, surprisingly, a date for her death. Her death was listed as October 15, 1718—the night of the fire and the date she had disappeared. Three nights from today, she noted with a shiver, almost three hundred years ago. The entire town still swore that Nehemiah was responsible for Abigail's disappearance. Had Alden engraved her name in stone as a last effort to tie her to him? Or had one of the villagers done so as an ultimate judgement on a man so many of them hated? She would have to ask Babs if Alden's Last Will and Testament had included burial instructions.

She carved out Abigail's name with a small cedar cone and removed the remaining dirt. According to Frank, the loss of Abigail had broken William Morgan. Had Will been Abigail's lover? Had he been satisfied trailing behind the Aldens, never confronting Nehemiah, never learning from Abigail why she couldn't wait for him? Not William Morgan. She was sure of it. The man she had seen in her dream returning to Abigail on the bluff would have gone to her as soon as his ship had docked. She wondered what Nehemiah had thought about that, another man marching through *his woods to claim his wife* . . . .

Through the numbness that surrounded her like ocean mist, Abigail saw the shrubs on the edge of the woods shift. A man stepped into the clearing before the cottage where she waited. Most days she wandered from door to window, pressing her palm to the glass to connect with something beyond. But no one ever came, not any longer. The man who had stepped from the trees was a confusing presence in the static oaks and tall bluff grasses which usually met her eyes.

He walked to the house sure of his welcome, a kind of tense anticipation creasing his face. Despite the unruly hair and ill-fitting clothes, she felt no alarm. She moved to the door to send him away, as she had been schooled to tell all the others. She repeated the words to herself lest she forget.

"All business is to be undertaken in the village where you will find my husband," she said carefully, and stopped the stranger with her words. "There is nothing for you here."

"Abigail," he said with distress. "They told me in the village, but I couldn't credit it. Even believing me lost, could you not have waited a bit longer?" He stepped forward to take her hands.

A vague alarm penetrated the numbness she felt. She did not fear this man but the other, always the other. She attempted to twist out of his grasp and nervously scanned the bluff behind him for the other's return. "All business is to be undertaken in the village . . . ."

"Why?" he interrupted. "How did he convince you?" When she didn't respond but continued to struggle in his hold, he dropped her hands in disgust. "So, 'tis true, then."

She smoothed the folds of her skirt and replied in careful, measured tones, "All business is to be undertaken . . . ."

He peered into her face. "What's he done to you?" When Abigail began to tremble, he cursed. "Marriage or no, I'll not leave you like this." He reached out to draw her forward but was shoved from behind.

"You've no business here, William Morgan." Nehemiah pushed himself between them, attempting to block Abigail from view. "And if you trouble my wife further, I'll see you brought up on charges."

"Your wife?" Will said bitterly. "She's not fit to agree to anything, let alone marriage." He glanced at Abigail, who shrunk away from them both. "I'll go to the church and have the marriage annulled, or I'll petition the magistrate. She'll not stay here at your mercy."

The wind rose, tumbling leaves against the doorway. Nehemiah tilted his face to the darkening sky and smiled slowly. "But that will take time, will it not? Who knows what may befall one by then." He hitched up his wife by the arm so that her feet barely brushed the floor, dragged her inside, and shoved the door closed.

Will heard the bolt ram home. "Abigail!" He shouted, then pounded on the door. He heard her sobbing the only words she'd managed to say since he'd arrived, as though the chorus would stop what she feared was to come. He scrambled to the window and pressed his face to the glass. He saw two

shadows moving away, the erect figure of a man who commanded all he
wished and the cowering girl he dragged along besides him.

Sophie scrambled back onto her haunches. "What did you do?" she whispered, shaken but relieved to be back in the present. "Wasn't it enough to break her?" She tossed the small cedar cone aside and backed away. She put some distance between her and the grave. "I know you're still accounting for what you did while alive, you evil man."

The cemetery became utterly still, unnaturally quiet. She searched overhead for the sun, but the sky had grayed, blocking out its warmth. The birds no longer sang, and the squirrels had disappeared. She knew something was coming. She could feel it. It was evil, unharnessed evil. She sensed it in her gut, and the certainty drained the blood from her face.

Wind whipped out from deep within the woods. She heard it snapping branches and flattening the greenery as it swept into the cemetery clearing. It stung her with small stones and forced her back toward the chapel. *"Who dares?"* it hissed as she scrambled for the car. A desperate sob escaped her when she tripped over a marker and battered her knees.

The wind made it impossible to breathe. Every time she gasped, her mouth filled with sand and shredded undergrowth. And the smell, sour like rancid meat. What had she done? Whimpering, she crawled to the car door and yanked, but it wouldn't open. She used the handle as a grip and hauled herself through the open window. She collapsed on the seat in a heap. "Leave me alone," she screamed, jabbing at the window button. When the switch refused to work, she lunged for the ignition. The wind whipped the contents of the car against her face. She slammed the car into reverse and stomped on the gas. Yanking the wheel hard right, she swung the nose uphill. She fumbled with the gear shifter until the car lurched into drive and shot up the lane. The wind chased and taunted, *"Who dares?"* until it echoed in her ears.

13

Fire

When Sophie finally braked on the side of the road, the cemetery was no longer visible, and her teeth were chattering. "Stupid! Stupid!" She beat her fists against the steering wheel. "What were you thinking?" Breathing hard, she gave the window button a sharp jab and it now moved easily. "Damn!" She slammed her fist against the door. She held her arms out and saw they were hatched by scratches. She was sure her face was no better. With shaking hands, she threaded her fingers through her hair, pulling twigs, grass, and even gravel from the tangled strands. The wind had blasted her with everything small enough to lift.

What had Carol said? "*The past was in the past and only images remained.*"

Bull. If evil could materialize into something tangible, Alden had been there. She was willing to bet her life on it. She glanced into the mirror and saw a thin line that sliced across her forehead. Her hair had shielded her from the worst, but she was filthy.

A strange leveling occurred as she sat there. Surer than anything she had felt in the past, she knew she would find Abigail. "I'll find her, you sorry excuse for a man!" she yelled out the window, turning her head so that her voice carried in several directions. "I'll find her, and when I do, I'll tell everyone." Bearing witness is what Carol had called it, and she would do exactly that.

Sophie used the car mirror to tidy her hair as best she could, then used tissues to remove most of the dirt. Her makeshift clean-up wasn't nearly enough to make her presentable. She still looked like a mess and caused eyebrows to raise at the grocery store, although people were too polite to mention it.

At the library, she located Babs at the reference desk and found the librarian didn't have the other villagers' restraint.

"What in the world happened to you?"

Sophie self-consciously smoothed her hair. "Wind squall."

"Hmm." Babs seemed skeptical but didn't push. "What can I help you with? You look like you're on a mission."

Sophie tidied a stack of bookmarks on the counter and chose her words carefully. "I happened by the cemetery today and stumbled across Nehemiah Alden's grave." It wasn't a good lie, but the essence of it was true. "I'm a bit confused. Why is Abigail's name on his marker? I thought they never found her body."

"They didn't." Babs held up one finger as the phone rang and turned to answer it. "Pocasset Village Library," she said, sliding over a pad of paper and grabbing a pen.

While she waited, Sophie mused. If there was no body, why would a death date have been inscribed and who would have done it? For someone with as much pride as Alden reportedly had, Abigail's desertion would have been enough for him to disown her, not have her name carved in stone. She rocked her head from side to side as she considered, then pursed her lips. It couldn't have been William Morgan. Her research showed that Will had died before Nehemiah, so it wasn't him. Another villager, maybe? The whole thing was odd.

Babs hung up the phone and gave her a rueful smile. "Sorry, a parent found out this morning that her daughter's project on the Witch Trials is due in two days." Babs jotted down a few resources from the computer screen and slid the notepad and pen aside. "I'll pull these for her later."

She felt a pang of sympathy. Teacher or not, she had been on the opposite end of looming deadlines and couldn't help but feel for the girl. "It sounds like she's got her work cut out for her."

"She sure does. Her mom will skin her alive for putting it off for so long, but Emily will get it done. She's a smart girl. She just doesn't see what all the rush is about." She folded her hands on the desk and leaned forward. "Back to your question, Abigail's body was never found to my knowledge."

"Then why the inscription?" Sophie asked with a frown.

Babs threw her hands up. "One of the mysteries of Pocasset. No one knows. It didn't appear until a long time after Nehemiah had died."

"How long are we talking about here?"

"As far as I can make out, about a hundred and thirty years. There wasn't a formal request to have her name added, if that's what you wanted to know." Babs shrugged. "One day it was just there, and the town was outraged."

"There couldn't have been many stonemasons that would have done that job in the area," Sophie said, tapping her fingers on the counter.

"True, but from what I could tell from the village records, none of the monument companies had been hired to complete the work. To be honest I'd be surprised to know if they agreed to do it at all, even in secret. They hated Alden too much."

Sophie was silent for a moment. "So, it's a mystery."

"One among many." Babs' phone rang again, and she rolled her eyes. "Pocasset Village Library." *Sorry*, she mouthed as she listened. "I'm sure we have the most recent edition. Let me see if it's in."

Sophie took advantage of the call to slip away. She had enough of her own questions without trying to answer Babs'. She'd exhausted all the resources she could find. The oral tradition was strong and colorful, but it was tainted by the hate the villagers still held for Alden. The only useful journal she had was written by an old sailor with a knack for collecting gossip for profit. Although she didn't put too much faith in the truthfulness of the journal, it was a more reliable source to explore. And to be honest, it was her only one. She headed back to the Robbins' house for another session with Captain Parker's journal.

In the living room, buried under the moss green afghan, Sophie gave a sigh of pure bliss. She'd removed layers of dirt and grit from crevices she didn't remember she'd had and settled down with the journal. She opened to where she had left off. What had it been like to live in a small village where everyone knew everyone else's business? The discord in families, intrigue among villagers, even business ventures in their infancy would have been common knowledge in that tightly knit community. Surely someone should have known what had happened to Abigail. She settled back, toying with the afghan's soft loops as she thought. As much as she wished someone had helped Abigail escape, all the evidence pointed to the fact that she'd never left the lighthouse. With a sigh, she turned the page and caught up with life as it had been in 1718 Pocasset.

Hours later, darkness slowly settled around the snug little house and made it difficult to see the page's cramped writing. Sophie rose to turn on the light and stretch her back. When she saw Dan's truck pull into the driveway, she went to open the door for him.

"That was pretty quick service," he said, then scowled when he saw the alarm panel completely dark. "Why wasn't the alarm on?"

She shrugged, a bit embarrassed. "I forgot, but all the doors are locked."

"It takes less than a minute to break a window and open a lock," he snapped. He tossed his keys onto the kitchen table in disgust. "The alarm instantly contacts the monitoring service and the police. Use your head."

He was right, but it had been an honest mistake. "Why are you in such a foul mood?" she demanded. When he didn't answer, she said stiffly, "It won't happen again, I promise."

She turned to march past him, but he stuck out his arm to stop her. "Wait," he said.

"You've got two seconds to let me pass."

"I'm sorry." He held up his hands in surrender and let them fall limply to his sides. "I had a lousy afternoon, and I took it out on you."

"Ditto here," she said, "but I didn't take it out on you."

"Again, sorry." He scrubbed his hands over his face. "The job sites were a mess, and when I stopped by to see Chelle, she wasn't doing well. I've been looking for something to kick all day. You happened to be in the way."

Sophie felt a spurt of fear. "Is she okay?"

"I don't know." He shrugged and rubbed the back of his neck. "I hope so."

"Come on, tell me what happened." She pulled him to the sofa and forced him to sit beside her.

Dan let his head fall back against the cushion and stared at the ceiling. "She had a severe headache come on this afternoon and the doctors are running some tests. They think she might have developed some bleeding, or a blood clot, that's putting pressure on her brain."

She felt an icy fist clutch her heart. "Is it life-threatening?"

"They're not saying until they have more information." He lifted his head and turned to her, his eyes tired and bleak. "What am I going to tell my parents? I told them she'd had an accident, but that she was alright."

Because she'd often received her sister's tightly controlled information, she normally would have encouraged him to tell them the whole truth. But with the Robbins' distance and the lack of details, all he would do is alarm them. "Why don't you wait until you have something concrete to tell them?" she said. "Things could be fine, and you might worry them unnecessarily."

He was quiet for a bit. "I think you might be right," he sighed, then nodded.

"I understand, more than you realize." Sophie shifted self-consciously and began to pluck at the sofa. "My sister used to keep stuff from me all the time. It drove me crazy, but I understand why she did it."

He placed his hand over hers to stop her nervous picking. "You know, you've changed a lot. Before, the fight we just had would've sent you running for cover."

"I don't run from problems," she said tightly, pulling free and standing. The man was impossible.

"You're leaving now, though." he pointed out with a smile.

"Exactly," she snapped. "It's called leaving before I say something I regret." She turned and stomped up the stairs. At the top, she pressed her hands to her cheeks. She rarely lost her temper, but she'd done so twice now in a matter of minutes. And as much as she hated to admit it, he was right. Not too long ago she would have avoided a fight instead of pushing back, as he claimed. That's what happens when your nerves are frayed from living in a haunted lighthouse and you lose friends before their time—you get angry.

She heard footsteps on the stairs and saw that Dan had followed. "Look," she said, turning to face him. "I've had an eventful day myself. So, if you don't mind?" She raised her eyebrows, silently inviting him to shove off.

He was suddenly alert. "What happened?"

"Another unwelcomed trip to the past, courtesy of Founders Cemetery and Alden."

"Damn it, Sophie!" He scowled. "You know better. What happened this time?"

She decided an exact account would end with another lecture on safety, so she gave him strictly the highlights of the encounter between the Aldens and William Morgan.

"So Frank was right. Morgan was involved with Abigail, and Alden did his most to keep them apart." He frowned. "It worries me that this vision happened outside of The Point, though. You didn't do anything to call it up, did you?" he asked, narrowing his eyes at her.

"Of course not." She mentally crossed her fingers at the white lie. "I just kind of slid into it as if I were watching a play, and then it was over." Another lie, but he had enough worries about Chelle without burdening him with Alden's temper tantrum. "I'm pretty sure Carol would say that the apparitions are getting stronger if they are happening away from the lighthouse."

He agreed with a somber nod and turned toward his own room. "Try not to do anything reckless. We're stretched thin with the living taking potshots at us without encouraging the dead."

"Right," she said in surprise to the door he'd just closed in her face. Marching into her own room, she slammed the door and flopped onto the bed. She hoped this evening was not a sample of what living with him would be like. Otherwise, it would feel like an eternity until Chelle came home. Maybe if all the stars lined up and she was lucky, that would be sooner rather than later.

Sophie's fears about living with Dan were unfounded. Because he worked long hours, she rarely saw any sign of him except for the scrawled notes he'd leave. By Friday, most of the repairs to the storm-damaged buildings had been completed. Her college was due to reopen at the beginning of the following week. Until then, she was left with plenty of free time. She'd read almost the entire journal and had come to know the long-ago villagers well, warts and all. Although, nothing had been helpful in her search for Abigail. Captain Parker rarely mentioned the Aldens directly. From what she could tell, the other villagers seemed to have had little to do with either of them, though many expressed pity for Abigail. It was a conspiracy of silence. She did read more about Will Morgan's increasingly odd behavior, the muttering and outbursts worsened by drink. She hoped that the journal would give her more clues before she finished reading.

Like her slow progress with the journals, Chelle remained in the hospital. Her severe headache had been caused by some bleeding that had stopped as spontaneously as it had started. Her doctors were monitoring her closely, hoping to avoid invasive surgery. It was a slow process of healing by degree. Her bruises had not yet started to shift from black to purple, but the headache had lessened. Chelle became more outspoken about her release, but the doctors still refused to discharge her. Sophie tried to break up the monotony by dropping by the hospital once a day to bring Chelle simple treats like a new magazine or news about the village.

Sophie was exiting the hospital one day when she ran into Babs and Frank. They were on their way to visit Chelle.

Babs lifted a bouquet of mixed flowers. "We hoped we could cheer up our girl a bit. She must be antsy by now. She could never sit still for long, even injured."

Frank stuck his hands in his pockets. "Drives too darn fast," he complained.

Babs silenced him with a look and turned to Sophie. "I wanted to ask you how you made out with those journals."

"They give an interesting view of the village at the time," she said, avoiding eye contact with Frank. The way Captain Parker had described Frank's ancestor was less than flattering and not something she wanted to discuss. The last thing she needed was to stir the old man up and listen to another lecture on how rotten Alden had been.

"Will Morgan must be in there." Frank glared at her, as if daring her to deny it.

"He is, and it seems he had a hard time of it," she said. "It wasn't fair what happened to him."

"Fair?" He pulled his hands out of his pockets and planted them on his hips. "Immoral is what it was. Alden poisoned everything he touched. He didn't want Will Morgan around and did a good job of destroying him."

Babs edged inside the door and tugged Frank's arm. "Come on, you know we agree with you. There's nothing you can do about it now."

Yanking free, he straightened his jacket. "That's what everyone has always said, and it's how he got away with it to begin with." He turned on his heel and stalked toward the parking lot.

"I didn't mean to upset him." Sophie said. "I couldn't lie. He would have found out the truth eventually."

Babs raised her eyebrows and sighed. "He already knows the truth about Will Morgan. Everyone does. I think that's the problem." She lifted the flowers. "I'd better get these upstairs. Don't worry about Frank. He's hot-headed and obsessed with the past, but he's loyal to his friends." She moved past Sophie into the lobby. "See you later."

"Right, 'bye." she said, and headed to her car. A short time ago, she would have laughed at the idea of the past controlling so many people. But she had seen the poisonous ripples still echoing out from the destruction Alden had wrought centuries ago. Maybe the last few pages of the journal would hold the clue to what had happened so many years before.

Sophie swung by *The White Horse*, picked up the remainder of her schoolwork and headed for the Robbins' house. By early evening, the papers that had sprawled across the kitchen table had been graded, recorded, and stacked in neat piles. She dropped her head onto the tabletop in relief and closed her eyes. She dreaded correcting. She was always torn between the hope of seeing her students succeed and the fear that they had botched the assignment altogether. This set of papers had held no true surprises. The students she expected to do well had done so. The others, struggling or submitting slip-shod work since the beginning of the semester, had remained true to form. She wanted them all to succeed, but that never happened, no matter how much she tried.

She rose and stretched her back on the way into the living room. Good grief, she felt ancient. She flopped onto the sofa and reached for the journal she had abandoned the night before. Since her run-in with Frank, she'd had a feeling she was running out of time. "Tell me something useful," she murmured. She thumbed through the journal and found where she had left Captain Parker. He was settled at his customary table in the back of the tavern, complaining of the ache in his bones and the price of ale.

Years on rolling decks have hollowed my limbs so that the bones grind one upon the other. 'Tis worse on nights such as this when a storm churns off the coast, and they ache with the damp. Ale and a roaring fire dull the pain, but the cost of ale is beyond my means. So, I huddle in my corner near the fire and wait for company and a generous soul with deep pockets. Tonight, however, most men of sense are home bracing against the storm. Only Will Morgan and the barkeep are about, both of whom are unlikely to purchase a tankard for a man in need.

Morgan appears to be the worst for drink already. Pale and trembling, he holds his head with both hands and whispers to himself. Neither the barkeep nor I have gotten a clear response from him. To any question he answers, "She's done it. She's done it, herself," and moans while rocking. Poor pitiful soul to be so bewitched by a woman belonging to another . . . ."

Sophie placed the journal open on the table in front of her and turned the phrase over in her mouth, feeling the weight of it. "*She's done it. She's done it, herself.*" What had he meant? She gazed up at the ceiling and summoned the images of Abigail: the lonesome girl on the beach, the one who cringed in fear in the dirt of the cache, and the one so ravaged by sickness and sorrow that she had lost herself.

The pieces that had always been there shifted, and suddenly she knew. She grabbed the phone and called Dan. "Come on, come on. Pick up," she willed him. When the call went to voicemail, she grabbed her keys and rushed to her car.

It was horrible and surprising, but she had no proof. All she really had was an awful intuition. She needed to get to the lighthouse. Now. Tonight was the anniversary of the fire and Abigail's disappearance. If it were possible to force an apparition, she wanted to be there. The conditions would never be more perfect.

As the road swayed toward The Point, she glanced at the dark phone on the passenger's seat beside her. Would Dan be at the hospital or a job site? She should leave him a message, but it was growing dark and the twisting road made distraction dangerous. It would have to wait until she got to The Point. Tonight, even the familiar played tricks with her eyes. The trees that lined the road seemed to swoop toward the car, reaching out gnarled limbs to snag her.

It was the most foolish thing she'd ever done, but she felt some comfort that no one expected her at the lighthouse. And if she was right, it was someone living, not dead, who was the greatest threat to her safety. She'd hide the car in the shrubs lining the lane and sneak up through the woods. No one would see her. She'd have a clear view of the lighthouse and, hopefully, an answer to what had become of Abigail.

Shadows bent with the rising moon as she eased the car onto the sandy shoulder, angling it between two clumps of shrubs. She nudged the door open a crack and stepped out; the fern she crushed under her feet released a fresh, earthy scent. The soft ground cover muffled the sound of her footsteps, but she would still need to tread carefully. She fixed where the lighthouse lay through the darkness and picked her way around rocks and bushes.

Farther as she snuck through the trees, the sense of something waiting weighed on her. She crouched instinctively to make herself smaller and crept on all fours, pine needles and leaves digging into her palms, until the lighthouse came into view. The wind carried the sound of waves as they hit home, punishing the rocks at the base of the moonlit bluff.

She hunkered down, scanning the trees for movement. Time stretched out and it seemed even the woods waited in anticipation. Not a thing stirred. The leaves hung limp, and the animals remained hidden. She crouched on the damp forest floor, not daring to move until a cramp seized her thigh. She shifted to knead the stiff muscle and saw gray wisps slink out from beneath nearby leaves and twist from trees like snakes. They coursed over the forest floor so that it boiled around her and stretched out toward the lighthouse like a living thing.

She knew she was in trouble. She patted her pockets frantically for her phone, but it wasn't there. She'd left it in the car.

Ahead at the edge of the trees, a shadow separated from a trunk and stepped into the field. Breath froze in her lungs as she recognized the figure from her dream in stark detail. A man was draped in a dark cape, his riotous hair caught back in a strip of cloth. She crept forward slowly, determined to see his face. Not Nehemiah, she realized, but William Morgan. Alden had been fair while Morgan was dark-haired and slighter, the arrogance that characterized Alden missing from his face. Will may have been younger, but there was a weariness about him that broke her heart.

She followed his tense gaze and blinked in disbelief as the building she knew faded. The lighthouse and porches were replaced by a rustic cottage surrounded by moonlit flowers. Gray tendrils threaded along the foundation and through the garden like fingers, tracing edges and splaying stalks. She shivered, knowing she'd seen this cottage before in her dream. This was the night of the fire, the night Abigail had disappeared.

Wary of giving herself away, she inched ahead for a better look. She kept behind Will in case he should turn, using the trunks of trees as shields. He was eerily still and would have been mistaken for a statue, except for the flapping of his cape in the rising wind. Beyond his silhouette, she saw the second floor of the cottage suddenly glow strangely in the October sky. Then there was fire, licking up the curtains and dancing before the panes, engulfing the entire second floor in flames. Will Morgan remained motionless.

Small sparks dropped onto the first floor, creating light where there had been none. Sophie caught her breath as a shadow passed before a window. A woman carrying a candle, lighting her way through a house set afire.

As Will ran forward toward the house, shouting, *"Abigail!"* Sophie bolted after him. She searched the windows as she ran and heard the flames draw air through the house like a rattle. When the windows began to shatter from the heat, she covered her head and ducked away.

"Abigail!" Will charged in through the side door but reappeared almost immediately, choking on the smoke.

Sophie ran around the corner, straining for a glimpse of Abigail. The heat drove her back, arms raised, until she stood on the bluff looking helplessly at the cottage. The front door gaped open, but Abigail was nowhere in sight. "Where are you?" Sophie shouted. She saw only Will Morgan on his knees, coughing in a pale ribbon of moonlight, the gray tendrils twisting past him to the edge of the bluff. And there, in a soot-streaked nightgown, stood Abigail facing the ocean.

"*No!*" echoed out over the bluff as Will rushed toward her. Before he could reach her, Abigail slowly fell forward to the violent waves below. "*No!*" He collapsed at the bluff's edge, crying into the wind.

"Will," Sophie whispered, moving toward the man sobbing on the ground. "I'm so sorry," she said, tears running down her cheeks. "She was so lost. Abigail loved that baby, and she loved you too." Sophie reached out to touch him and passed straight through cool air. "I know she never meant to hurt you." Sophie choked back a sob. "She was broken herself."

He struggled upright and stared into her eyes for a moment. The horror and devastation she saw there brought her to her knees. She grieved for them all—Will, Abigail, the baby, and even Alden, the damaged child that had grown into a man who had hurt so many. As she cried, William Morgan turned and walked for the tree line, disappearing back into the woods from where he'd come.

14

Fallout at the Point

Sophie remained kneeling as the gray mist receded. At first, the movement was almost unnoticeable, but gradually the mist thinned to tattered wisps, slinking back into the forest until the field lay clear.

The air in front of her suddenly shimmered with movement until Abigail appeared before her. Sophie had never seen her like this. Her hair was neatly plaited in a long braid that hung over her shoulder, and she was dressed as though for travel. But what was most remarkable was her serenity; it soaked into Sophie's bones like an embrace. The encounter lasted only moments and ended when Abigail gently faded. Sophie felt a kiss as soft as a butterfly's wing brush her temple, and she took her first easy breath in hours. She noted with relief that her sense of urgency had vanished. She'd beaten the clock and found out what had happened to Abigail, the poor lost girl.

"You should've left well enough alone," said a voice behind her.

She whirled around, her heart pounding against her ribs. "Honestly, Frank," she said, struggling to her feet. "You'll be the death of me."

"So, you've finally come 'round to the truth of it, have you?" He spoke as though they had just met on the street and not on a bluff's edge in the dark.

She eyed him warily. "Did you see what happened?" she asked. "Abigail fell from the bluff, and Will Morgan saw the whole thing. Alden didn't have anything to do with it at all."

He shifted an object from one hand to the other, but she couldn't make out what it was. "I've known for a long time," he said. "I've got Will's letters."

"You've known?" What was the matter with him? People had been wondering for centuries what had happened to Abigail, and he'd kept silent? "Why didn't you say something?"

Frank's lips peeled back in a feral smile. "Will didn't want anyone to know what had happened. He wanted Alden to take the blame, to get what was coming to him." He snapped, "Alden killed her, and eventually Will, as sure as I'm standing here."

She couldn't argue with him. "That may be true, but don't you think it's time people knew what happened?

"No!" His voice caused her to take a step backward in alarm. He raised his arm. A gun was grasped comfortably in his hand. "Not any further."

Sophie froze where she stood.

"Alden stole from him, from me. The Point would have been mine if Will and Abigail had married, but because of him I have nothing. I work at a convenience store and do odd jobs, instead of running this village as I should."

He was stark raving mad. "The Point has never belonged to you," she said evenly.

"Thieves. All of them." Frank's mouth worked angrily, and she could see the shine of spittle in the corners. "But that's going to end too." He gestured toward the edge of the bluff. "One more accident, and they'll be forced to stop the renovations."

Sophie felt a rush of panic and smothered it. He was beyond reason, but she had to try. She'd never survive a fall from the bluff and her chances were only slightly better with the gun. "Why me?" she asked, her voice shaking. "I have no control over what happens at The Point. I'm just a glorified house-sitter."

"Because you and that dog were always in the way." The gun quivered in his grasp. "Because you wouldn't leave Abigail alone."

So many things suddenly made sense. "*You* killed Neal trying to get to me." She felt bile rise in her throat. "And what about Chelle? What did she have to do with it?"

"I heard her talking about finishing the journal." He swiped his hand across his lips. "I had to stop her. No one could find out what happened to Abigail. I never could have gotten into the Robbins' house like I did here." He smiled grimly. "I came and went as I wanted. I trashed the kitchen, listened at windows, and walked through the house while you slept. But then you ended up with the journal anyways. It was all your fault." His lips thinned. "It was always your fault, stirring things up where you should've left them alone." He stabbed the gun toward her, punctuating the air. "I poisoned your dog. I warned you, but you never listened."

"You killed Aesop?" Sophie forgot the gun in her anger and stepped toward him. "Over a secret no one cares about anymore?" she shouted. She was almost within arm's reach.

"That's far enough." Frank pointed the gun at her head. "I tried to break you with the dog and running you off the bridge, but you just wouldn't leave it alone."

"I won't jump." It tumbled out of her and hung in the air between them. It wasn't brave. Shot, shoved, or forced to jump, she knew she wasn't leaving this bluff alive, but she wouldn't go like Abigail. She wouldn't just disappear. She eyed him unsteadily and braced for the impact of the bullet, waiting for the report of the gun that would mean the tearing of tissue and the shattering of bone.

Calm again, Frank shrugged. "It'll be harder to explain, but I'm not worried." He pulled the hammer back smoothly and stared down the length of the barrel. "Goodbye, Sophie."

Before he could squeeze the trigger, an unearthly howl rose up over the bluff. It thundered out from the ocean like a tidal wave, building and rising with a sound so strong it rocked them both. Now, she thought, and threw herself at him, grappling for the gun. The howl circled as they struggled, arms twisted. She fought with teeth and nails, clawing at his skin. There'd never be another chance. She jammed her hip into his and forced him back until he staggered. The loose gravel shifted under their feet. She shoved with all her strength and saw him teeter on the edge. His mouth formed a surprised "O" before he fell backward, dragging her with him. She hit the edge of the bluff with force, knocking the breath from her and wrenching his grasp from her wrist. His long thin scream fell with the howl of the ocean and ended with the sickening crack of his body on the rocks below.

The silence was absolute. A wheezing sob escaped, and then another, until she was racked by them. She was battered but alive.

"Sophie!" Dan charged into the clearing and fell to his knees beside her. "Are you alright?" His eyes darted over her, searching for injuries. "That was too close."

She struggled upright. "I called you, but you didn't answer. Frank . . . " she gestured to the edge of the bluff. "He must be . . . the height, the rocks." She sucked in uneven gulps of air. "Can you see if he's alive?"

Dan nodded grimly and walked to the edge of the bluff. He took one look and turned away quickly, needing several moments before he could return. He crouched down next to her and said simply, "There's nothing we can do for him."

She nodded just once and started to rock back and forth. Think of something else, anything else, she commanded. "How'd you know where to find me?"

He wrapped his arm around her to stop her from rocking. "I found the journal open at the house and came to the same conclusion as you. I figured you'd come here to see if you could force an apparition." He murmured about people who had no sense, then helped her to her feet. "What possessed you to try it?"

She shook her head mutely and struggled to her feet.

Together they made it to the stone wall where they both sat. While they recovered, he said, "I hadn't even made it out the door, when I saw what Will Morgan witnessed the night Abigail disappeared." Both sorrow and empathy were clear on Dan's face. "The poor guy."

"Unbelievable, isn't it?" she whispered. The truth about Abigail was shocking, but what played mercilessly in her mind was that final shove. The surprise on Frank's face before he toppled over the bluff was something that would haunt her for years.

Dan let out a gust of breath. "By the time I got here, the woods were filled with that gray stuff, and I couldn't get to you. I could hear Frank talking, but no matter which way I went I always ended up where I started. When I finally made it to the tree line, you were struggling on the bluff."

"I didn't mean to push him," she said with a break in her voice.

"Yeah, you did, but you didn't have a choice," Dan said. "It'll be okay. I promise."

He checked his watch. "I called Matt Thomson on the way over when I suspected where you'd gone. He's going to wonder what's going on when he finds out Frank's dead." As if summoned, car lights swung up the lane and a cruiser parked near the lighthouse. "I'll take care of it," he said, and hurried off to meet the sheriff and to tell him what happened.

Sophie was relieved to let Dan handle the police. She watched the men walk to the bluff's edge. They took a quick glance, before turning and continuing their conversation. Shortly, more deputies arrived and combed the area. She wondered what they hoped to find. A second gun? Evidence that showed she was lying? Systematically spread out under the lighthouse spotlights, they formed a grid and swept the clearing between the woods and the edge of the bluff. The search was painstakingly slow. While they inched their way forward, they kept the medical examiner and the recovery team waiting. When the search produced no evidence, officers with headlamps on their caps made their way single file down the steep path to retrieve Frank's body.

Hours later, the bobbing of lights cresting the bluff announced the arrival of Frank on a narrow stretcher. She wrenched her eyes from his twisted limbs to the sky and watched the stars shift. While she waited for the questions that would come, she imagined the darkened lighthouse and Abigail watching along with her, finally at peace.

That night, weeks ago now, had stretched on forever. Matt Thomson had insisted on bringing them both in for questioning. When Dan had tried to postpone it and get her home, Thomson lost what little patience he'd had to begin with. "I just brought a body up that bluff and want answers. Now."

He'd interviewed them alone and together. Not believing a word about the Aldens, Will Morgan, or the apparitions, he had sent a deputy to rip apart Frank's house for the letters. When the officer returned hours later with not only the Morgan letters but also Frank's rantings on paper, the sheriff finally let them go with orders not to leave the area. A few days later, Sophie was officially cleared when they found the gun at the base of the bluff, bearing only Frank's fingerprints.

The scrawled rantings had also shown Frank responsible for tampering with the ladder that had caused Neal's death. Neal had finally been released to his family for burial beside his mother in Pocasset's larger cemetery overlooking the ocean. Sophie was relieved that he had not joined Nehemiah in the colonial Founders Cemetery. She couldn't think of a more uncomfortable resting place than with Alden as a neighbor. She took comfort from the beauty of Neal's site. The irony of breathtaking views for the dead were not lost on her. But if she'd learned anything in the last few months, she knew that the dead were certainly among us. It soothed her to know that Neal was buried with his mother in a place where ocean breezes ruffled the grass and whispered through the trees. Most of the town had turned out for Neal's burial, even though he had led a very private life.

It had been strange to return to everyday life at The Point. There really had never been any normal daily activity to take up again. Things had been off-center for months. But now the restoration was back on track, and Chelle had been released from the hospital. Chelle had tolerated Sophie's hovering at her parents' house. But when Dan had begun calling every few hours to check on her too, Chelle had drawn the line and moved back into the lighthouse.

The town had been stunned by Frank's death. They could relate to his obsession with Alden, but they couldn't understand the lengths to which he'd gone to keep his secret. The Morgan papers had eventually explained how Abigail's name had ended up on Alden's headstone. A Morgan relative had hired a stoneworker from Boston to engrave her name under the cover of darkness. The relative had hoped to bring Abigail peace and honor Will's wish to punish Alden.

Sophie sensed the townspeople didn't blame her for Frank's death, but it didn't make her feel any less awkward around them, especially Babs and Tom. It was a relief when the Thanksgiving holiday gave her an excuse to leave.

Outside the lighthouse, Chelle leaned against Sophie's car and watched as Sophie arranged piles of clothes and books in the trunk. "You will be back, won't you?" Chelle held out her gift of apple bread, tightly wrapped in brown wax paper.

Sophie shot a quick look over her shoulder and took the bread that Chelle offered. "Maybe, I'll have to see. I could finish out the rest of the semester online." She tucked the still warm bread against the wheel well and smelled a hint of spiced apple. "Jacqueline offered me a place to stay while I figure out what's next. It might give us a chance to work out what's wrong between us." She straightened out of the trunk. "I don't have much family left, so I think I need to make the effort. Life's too short as it is."

"But you'll at least be back by the beginning of next semester, right?" Chelle brushed off her hands and turned up the collar of her jacket against the settling coastal mist.

"Of course." In the weeks since Abigail had been freed, Sophie continued to feel drawn to The Point. The tranquility of the bluff and the roll of the waves soothed as no other place could. It was the one place she felt closest to Aesop. She had found the perfect stretch of beach to scatter his ashes. There were times, if she looked quickly, she saw him racing down the hard-packed sand after gulls or napping in a patch of late autumn sun.

The one person she hadn't seen much lately was Dan. In a way, that was just as well. Although their shared experience had brought her closer to Chelle, it had left her relationship with Dan a bit awkward. Maybe there was too much confusion caused by the Nehemiah-Abigail-Will apparitions to make their own situation clear.

As if Chelle had read her mind, she said, "Dan said he didn't see the point in sending you off because you'd be back in the way before long, anyways."

Sophie had to smile. "He's probably right." She gave Chelle a quick hug and climbed in before she could embarrass herself by crying.

As she started to pull away, Chelle stuck her hand through the open window and gave her a folded piece of paper. "He did ask me to give you this, though."

She gave a tight nod and tossed it onto the passenger seat, swallowing the lump in her throat. She turned the car in a tight circle, pointed it down the lane, and slowly headed for the main road. When the rearview mirror showed Chelle entering the lighthouse, she pulled to one side of the lane. This letting go was harder than she'd imagined it would be. She had lost so much with Aesop, and then Neal, that there was still a pang under her heart whenever she thought of them. To leave Dan and Chelle added another layer of sadness.

She picked up the folded note, the paper crackling as she smoothed it against the steering wheel. There in Dan's characteristic bold scrawl was one short line: "*Write Sophie, Sophie write, write and do not waste time.*" That tore what little control she had, and she started to cry in earnest. He'd remembered the Michelangelo quote she'd copied down months ago, adapting it for her. He'd remembered her wish to write and the fear that she would never be good enough. She wiped her cheeks with the backs of her hands and sniffed resolutely. She would go home and write . . . perhaps Abigail's story. She had to go home, but she'd be back, like he said she would. Then they'd see.

She slid the car into drive and let it glide downhill through the woods. Stripped of leaves, the trees stretched out limbs to each other, some touching, others reaching out and missing. The branches were all clear and distinct against the gray autumn sky. Soon the forest floor would be blanketed in snow and tucked in like a child until spring. This stretch of trees no longer disturbed her; the panic she had felt when crossing them had vanished when Abigail had been freed. Sophie gave one last glance in the mirror before she turned the corner. She thought she saw the form of a man in the mist, cradling an infant, a slight woman pressed to his side. Then the wind dispersed them, sweeping the last traces out over the water, free at last from the shadow of Alden Light.